Brother's Keeper

ELIZABETH FINN

⌘⌘⌘⌘

DEDICATION

For those Logan-cloud dwellers who just needed this man in print!
I hear you.

CONTENTS

ELIZABETH FINN

A NOTE FROM THE AUTHOR

This book has been edited from its original version. The changes made are not substantial and do not change the readability of the story. If you fell in love with Rowan and Logan in e-format, I promise you'll feel just the same about them after experiencing them on paper. ☺

CHAPTER ONE

Rowan

When I was ten years old, my life shattered in the blink of an eye. Escaping unscathed from a horrific car accident that claimed the lives of three people during rush hour traffic on I-35 north of Kansas City should almost be a cause for celebration. But when one of the unfortunate three victims is lying dead beside you in your mangled car, and she happens to be the most important person in your life, relief fast turns to devastation. I wanted to be dead too. They call it survivor's guilt. But the funny thing is I never felt guilty—just sad.

To add insult to injury, after my mother passed away, I ended up moving in with my father; he was long divorced from my mother, and I'd never had a relationship with him. Six months after her passing, he moved us to Allendale, a small community not far from Grand Rapids, Michigan. Allendale was a part farming, part urban sprawl community. It was a college town and a private university at that. Not that it mattered to my ten-year-old self what academia was offered in the local over-priced university. At least it kept the population young, and the businesses flourished. Most of the residents of this safe and quiet community worked in nearby Grand Rapids.

My father was raised in Michigan and apparently had fond memories of growing up in this place—though it's hard to imagine him having fond memories of anything at all, except perhaps his well-worn bar stool at the local tap, which is where he spent most of

1

his free time. He'd always been a temperamental man; it was the undeniable reason my mother had left him. Being forced to take on the unwanted responsibility of being a parent only seemed to worsen his violent streak. He was a mean drunk, and from my recollection, always had been. And with the drinking came the violence.

Though life dealt me a blow when my mother passed, it also gave me a gift. I met my best friend, Sara Harrington, on my nightmare of a first day at Allendale Elementary School. And thank God for her. She was a savior, nothing like my innate shy demeanor. Sara was the center of attention in any room she entered. She was pretty, smart, and outgoing. She was overt at times and ruffled a few feathers on occasion, but she was kind and fair to the point of being passionate in her judgment. Why she had befriended me is beyond my understanding even to this day. But from the moment we met, we were instant friends. Sara's family matched her kindness and openness to this shy new girl in town. No doubt they felt sorry for me, given my always less than appealing dress and tangled, dirty, unkempt hair—the hallmark sign of a girl without a mother—never mind my all but existent excuse for a father.

When my father was in a rare sober and somewhat gracious mood, he'd agreed to allow me to take dance lessons with Sara every Saturday. Of course, he couldn't be bothered to take me to class. That would be one of many small favors Sara's family ended up taking on—the second of which would be paying for my lessons after my father's check bounced. But they did so, happy to help their daughter's underprivileged friend. They were the type of family everyone wanted to associate with: popular, beautiful, accomplished, and wealthy—the postcard family. They became the only family I had, or at least the only family I wanted to claim. They were gracious enough to have me over for holiday dinners when my own father was sleeping away his hangover, even buying me Christmas presents—which I never received from my father.

The Harringtons were good people. You were lucky to be a part of a family like that, but not at all lucky because they would never deny their gracious good nature to anyone. Sara's mother, Ronnie, had made a good home for her family. She could talk a mile a minute, was a friend to anyone in need, and just like her daughter, had more beauty than any one person could need. She was an art teacher in the elementary school and was almost always covered in some remnant of her classroom, be it paint, clay, charcoal, or paper mache. She was excitable and fun—the polar opposite of her husband, Marcus.

Marcus had a successful small town law firm, and while he wasn't the next Jimmy Smits from *L.A. Law*, he paid the bills and then some. For the most part, this consisted of giving legal advice on contracts and the occasional divorce settlement. He was a kind and generous man but without the boisterous chatty personality of his wife and daughter. He was contemplative and almost stoic at times but with a genuine heart. He was tall with a full head of dark hair and handsome—even in middle age.

Sara's older brother, Logan, took after his father in looks and nature. He was seven years older than Sara and me, and he was mature even in his younger years. He was handsome in a very non-pretentious way and had the most intense dark eyes I've ever seen, also inherited from his father. On the occasion I was lucky enough to be caught in his gaze, it was quite mesmerizing. When his eyes were on me, I felt like a puppy ready to pee on the floor. Yeah, he was easy to have a crush on, even at ten. He was popular in school but not because he cared to be. The one thing that always struck me about Logan was how comfortable he seemed to be in his own skin, and for a young high school boy in an atmosphere that bred insecurity, this was quite a feat. People radiated toward him, attracted to his good nature as much as his good looks.

It was impossible to dislike any one of the Harringtons in their own right, and it was many years after my induction into this perfect family that I found myself being somehow inducted into another home.

⌘⌘⌘⌘

By the time Sara and I reached seventeen, I'd far surpassed the rest of our dance class. I had fast become the known talent of ballet, and during the summers of my sixteenth and seventeenth years, I spent a month in Chicago studying in the Joffrey Ballet Summer Program. Those were the perks of being the recipient of the Harringtons' benefactions. And this was to be my foot in the door as it was. Sara was, of course, proud of her best friend and happy to take a back seat to me, something she was not often required to do.

When Sara found the posting for the Performing Arts Scholarship on the University of Michigan's website, I was as reluctant as I could be. In fact, I was so convinced they were looking for someone far more talented than me that I refused to even consider the possibility for the better part of two weeks before Sara convinced me there was no harm in trying. I assumed it would be a long and, quite frankly, impossible shot. But Sara, persistent as always, had the application complete before I could convince her just how resolute I was in this matter. So, I buckled and gave into her wishes. Of course, I'll be required to thank her for the rest of my life for the part she played in my future, now far more promising than it had been before the blessed application.

She knew full well I had no intention of moving beyond an Associate's degree from Allendale's junior college, lest I be saddled with a small fortune in college loan debt for the rest of my life. When I received the notification letter I'd been awarded a scholarship, I was ecstatic beyond all measure, not to mention shocked. It was, after all, the only real way I could ever afford to put myself through school without ending up destitute on the flip side. Sara and I will both be attending the University of Michigan in Ann Arbor. Go Wolverines. And I owe it all to the illustrious and ever passionate, borderline obstinate, best friend. Without a doubt, I'll never live it down, and I will forever be thanking her for believing in me far more than I ever manage to believe in myself.

The scholarship is for the University's School of Music, Theatre and Dance—"*dance*" being the operative word in my case. And it's all subject to my achieving high academic marks during my senior year of high school. Sara naturally refuses to own any interest whatsoever in a possible career path of her own, destined to worry her parents into an early grave. But were they paying attention, they might find it just a bit too convenient that the University of Michigan has a strong medical program, and they happen to have a daughter more than capable of going down that path. When it comes to Sara, there is never any way to know for sure. She's determined to pave her own road, and I have no doubt she will pave it in gold; like I said, it's just her style.

I still think of myself as a plain Jane to Sara's radiant personality. And while the continuity and comfort of her friendship have allowed my once introverted personality to emerge into what has become a more outgoing sarcastic persona, she is perhaps the only person in the world who sees me as anything other than the same shy and plain girl of seven years prior—the sarcasm and wit saved for our ramblings alone. At least I dress in clean and somewhat fashionable clothes now.

My father is still knee-deep in the love of his life—drink. But at least he is bestowed with the honor of town drunk to show for it. And with his prestigious title come the drones of wannabe inebriates. This means when he comes home drunk and mean, he often doesn't come home alone. He brings home the drunkest and meanest soul mates he can muster in this small little town of ours. And it's times such as these when the ever-present pseudo-family becomes my lifeline. I have taken to spending many nights at Sara's house these days. The Harringtons know of my father's drinking habits—as does anyone within a fifty-mile radius of town—and they never mind my company, even when I don't get there until the late hours of the night.

Logan now lives on his own in an apartment building his parents own in downtown Allendale—one of many real estate investments they're part of. He commutes to Cooley Law School in Grand Rapids, which is to be his *Alma mater*. He is, of course, still very crushable. He's chosen to walk in his father's footsteps and is now in his third year of law school after graduating *magna cum laude* in his undergraduate studies at Grand Valley State University. He is still top of his class in graduate school as all little Harringtons are, including his younger sister. And he is even interning with the DA's office in Grand Rapids. He is already receiving a great deal of interest from law firms across the country, but it's Brighton and Brinks in Denver, Colorado where he intends to plant his roots.

They extended an early offer and Logan didn't hesitate to accept. The contract has been signed, sealed, and delivered, and our little burg will have to suffer the loss of our most handsome resident little more than a week after he completes his graduate studies. He's always intended to move to Denver after he graduates, and the offer from Brighton was too good to pass up. They are a well-respected and prestigious firm; Logan will fit right in. He only knows how to succeed. He is driven in a way most people could never imagine. It would be easy for Logan to rely on his good looks and charm to get him through life, but he cares little for anything so trivial and focuses all his energy on his education and, moreover, his career. His focus is singular, and it will be the thing that elevates him quickly in life; of this, I have no doubt.

His girlfriend, on the other hand, is a different story. Amy. She is the anti-Christ and everything self-conscious young girls dread. She's blonde, blue-eyed, voluptuous, and curvy in all the right places. I may have the blue eyes, but nothing else about me comes close to her physical perfection. I'm boyishly built, undersized in all the wrong places and have the most boring, plain, reddish-brown hair. I keep it perfunctorily long to make it easy to pull back in a bun, but otherwise there is nothing impressive about it. Amy's personality is the complete opposite of Logan's. She's good at playing nice with people, but that's all it is, playing. She's selfish, and if I were guessing, she likes Logan more for the way he looks on her arm than who he is. She sees him as a ticket to the sweet life, somewhere bigger and better than she can achieve on her own. It's impossible to see why he likes her so much; well, actually, from his point of view, it's quite obvious what he sees in her. Sara can't stand the idea of having her as a sister-in-law one day and loves making snide comments behind her back, which I'm always more than happy to second.

Sara is also kept busy with school and helping her parents around their lake house at nearby Spring Lake. They are restoring the neglected property and pay Sara top dollar for her help. I occasionally go with her to help out but have a weekend waitressing job that limits the time I can spend there. And it's on an Indian summer weekend six weeks into our senior year of high school that I find what is to be my new sanctuary.

CHAPTER TWO

Rowan

W orking the weekend shift at the Little Tuscan Bistro is how this poor girl from the wrong side of the tracks keeps herself in decent, albeit generic, clothes. That being said, this is no ordinary bistro. There is nothing Tuscan, little, or bistro about this place. But as is the case in small town USA, a title can go a long way in convincing us we really do have the finer things in life.

On Friday nights, we usually finish up around ten or shortly thereafter, and this night is no exception. At ten fifteen, I duck out the back door and begin the short bicycle ride toward the mobile home park my father and I live in. Riding a bicycle isn't my first choice of transportation, but it's the only means I can afford. I try to convince myself I look like every other health-savvy suburbanite by choosing the green alternative over the oil-sucking monster that is the automobile, but quite frankly, I'd take a car any day over my old bent-spoke, sad-looking bicycle with its over-worn seat that threatens to impale my tush should I hit a pothole. But alas, I'm a bike dweller. And while I may be well on my way to owning my own car, thanks to good tip money, unfortunately, *"well on my way"* isn't the same thing as *"there."* On occasion, my father will allow me to take his car when he doesn't need it, but that is never on a weekend night. His old beat up car is reserved for his recreational drunk driving only on weekend nights. Fortunately, Sara has a car, and I'm not forced to show up for class on a bicycle too often. Though I must admit, I wear my best exercise costume on those days when I must to drive the point home; I'm not poor, people, just healthy, damn it!

When I arrive at our trailer, it's dark and empty. There is always a concern upon arriving home to our old, ugly trailer that my father will be there, spewing venom for words and ready to hate me for being alive. It's early, though, and often on the weekends, he feels the need to congregate with his folk until at least midnight. I'm tired and filthy from playing waitress for the night; after all, it's Friday and spaghetti à la tomato paste was on the menu. After showering and changing, I crawl into bed for what I hope will be a quiet, uneventful night.

I've become very adept at dodging my encounters with my father. He hasn't landed a blow for years, and while I'm sure many have suspected him of physical abuse, they'll be hard pressed to prove it by me, and I will be no help to them. I have no relatives, at least none who would claim my father, and I know full well that means a juvenile home for me if his little temper ever surfaces to meet the public eye. Not even Sara understands how truly violent he can be. She knows as much as I tell her, which is little. It's no secret he's a less than great man. Fortunately for him, cuts, bruises, and even the occasional concussion can easily be explained away—if he can just remember to pace himself. Social Services has a short memory, and active young girls have accidents all the time. Besides, he's a surprisingly good liar when it comes to talking with Social Services.

But those were the earlier years. Now, as I've mentioned, I've become the skilled escape artist, and in his drunken state, he forgets very quickly his daughter's room is empty and her ground floor window ever so slightly cracked. Sara's family knows I work late and never care when I come over. It's the perfect solution ... most of the time. But not on this night.

On this night, my normal vigilance is replaced with uncharacteristic exhaustion. Perhaps I've become lazy, or perhaps he's learned to tiptoe drunk. In any event, it comes as quite a surprise when my bedroom door is flung open and the meanest man I've ever met comes staggering in to pick a fight with a seventeen-year-old. That's alcoholism at its finest.

The first blow strikes the left side of my head—hard. That first blow to the left side of my temple sends my right temple smacking against the wall, and all I can register are the fireworks suddenly flashing in the back of my eyes from the impact. The next backhand lands nicely on the corner of my mouth, and soon blood is dripping down my chin from where I was struck. The instant pain that shoots through my jaw feels as though it's unhinging from the joint.

The nice thing about glancing back-handed blows is they tend to spin a drunk man like a top, and spinning drunk men aren't all that familiar with balance. Thus, I'm afforded my moment for escape. The window, my normal escape route, isn't an option as he's blocking my path directly to it. Which leaves the front door as the only alternative.

I grab my book bag sitting on the floor by the door as I skirt past him while he staggers to his feet. As I run through the house, I hear him stirring in my bedroom. He sounds like an angry bull whose matador has just done something very rude and unpleasant to him. But I'm quick. In a matter of moments, I'm out the door and bicycling fast for parts unknown.

Normally, I would have made my cursory call to Sara from the phone in my bedroom before he even had the chance to stumble his way down the hallway to my room, nothing more needed than a quick, "Hey, Dad's drunk and I don't feel like arguing. Can I come over?" followed by her ever happy to see me, "Of course." But this night is different.

Because of my slip, my heart is racing, my hands are shaking, I'm crying, and my head feels like it's exploding. I have no idea what time it is, and judging by how soundly I was sleeping, it could be well into the early morning hours. I will have no choice but to explain the bloody lip, which means lying to my best friend, and worse than that, no way of knowing just how bad it will look in the morning when we join her parents for breakfast.

I consider not calling her and just killing time until morning when I can go home, but I'm cold and tired and hurting. After two blocks, I come to the old Amoco station and decide it's either a cold, uncomfortable night on my own or a nice, warm bed and good company.

I stand at the pay phone with tears still streaming down my face and notice for the first time my feet are bare and bruised from the metal pedals of my bicycle and the hard chewed up asphalt of the old gas station's parking lot. I fish a handful of change from the side pocket of my backpack and dial Sara's cell number. I'm not looking forward to this conversation but eager to hear her familiar voice.

And that's when things changed.

9

I'm so busy trying to decide what to tell her I somehow miss the overtly masculine voice on the other end of the line. Instead, "Hello" in Logan's sleep-laden and somewhat annoyed voice is the first thing I register. In my over-adrenalized idiocy, I start to wonder how I've managed to dial his number before I realize I wouldn't know how to dial his number if I wanted to because I don't even have the number.

After a few confused, terrifying moments and several impatient "Hellos" from Logan, I finally find my voice—the stammering voice that is my alter ego of humiliation. "Uhhhhh … L-Logan? I-Is S-Sara home?"

"No, she's away at the lake house. She forgot her phone… Wait, Rowan…? What's wrong? You sound like you're crying. What happened?"

Shit! That isn't stammering, it's sobbing. This is not good. Regroup. Deep breath. Change of subject. "What are you doing answering Sara's phone?" Good, that will throw him off.

"I asked you why you're crying. What the hell is going on, Rowan?"

Okay, redirection didn't work. We'll just go with a lie instead. "I'm not crying. I've just been riding my bike." This can't get any worse. Not only am I trying to lie, I'm coming up with really stupid lies.

"Bullshit. Rowan, why the hell are you calling Sara from a payphone in the middle of the night in tears?"

Caller ID. Oops. What do all smart people do when they're caught in a lie? They keep lying. Adamant rebuttal is fool proof. "Logan, really, I've just been riding my bicycle… I forgot something at work and needed … uh … to talk to Sara… I… Why is she at the lake house this weekend? I thought … you know … uh … comp report… I mean, it's due Monday, and she was supposed to be home…"

"Okay, that's it. Where are you? I'm coming to get you. And don't even think of saying you're fine, and don't even think of telling me you're not crying. Just tell me where the hell you're at before I call the cops."

Well, that just didn't work at all. I think about hanging up, but the sound of Logan's voice is paralyzing. He's angry, not to mention confused. For all he knows something bad has happened to me, and well, he wouldn't be all that wrong. If Logan wanted to, I have no doubt he could have the cops out looking for me. It's a small town, and he's well known and respected. The last thing I want is the cops to be pounding on the door to the trailer where my drunken father is likely trying to pass out to some obscure early morning infomercial. That could be really bad.

"Logan? I need help." It's barely a whisper.

I don't recall ever saying those words to anyone in my life, especially in connection to my father's drunken behavior. Strangely, I immediately feel an odd sense of relief. I know there's nothing Logan can really do for me, but just saying the words out loud in some way is liberating. I'm tired. Secrets are draining, and this one's a doozy. And with this confession, a sense of the inevitable starts to slowly sink in.

"Can you please pick me up at the Amoco at Vine and Eighth Street?" I don't wait for a response. I hang up.

No one until now has known what life is like in the Rowan Avery household. But in a short time, someone will. I better just hope I'm prepared for the fallout.

CHAPTER THREE

Logan

She better have a damn good explanation. She must think I'm the world's biggest idiot. Riding bicycles in the middle of the night. What is she, five? Please. This is the thanks I get for dog-sitting—should have just taken the stupid dog with them like they usually do. But no, dog has an ear infection, and everyone knows dogs with ear infections can't possibly go to lake houses. Never mind the fact that Rufus doesn't exactly enjoy having his ears messed with. Rufus becomes Cujo real fast. And if that isn't enough, my bedroom's been turned into a damn hobby room. Who the hell is going to be using this hobby room? Not that I don't love sleeping on the couch in the den. It's better than Sara's room, clothes always strewn about and constantly oversaturated with the latest perfume all girls her age seem to bathe in. And now it's two thirty in the morning, and her phone starts ringing.

Her leg better have fallen off while she was riding that damn bike. She better need a tourniquet. *Shut up, Logan*, the decent part of my brain is saying. *You're just tired and crabby. You like Rowan, and if she's crying, then something must be wrong. She takes a lot in stride with no complaints. Stop obsessing.* But the dickhead part of me is floored.

Why tonight? I have to be at the office early tomorrow to help with discovery on the Gleason case, and now this. *Gee, sorry guys. You don't mind if I just curl up on the DA's desk for a quick snooze, do you?* She better be bleeding... Wait, she is bleeding.

My headlights sweep the parking lot of the Amoco and find her sitting against the wall of the station with her knees pulled to her chest, and as she looks up and meets my eyes, it's clear she really is hurt.

She's barefoot and wearing only pajama pants and a tank top. She looks tiny. She is tiny, but she looks even smaller than her normal petite self. It's the end of a long warm summer, and while the weather's been nice, the nights are chilly and tank tops and bare feet are no longer appropriate.

She's bleeding from the corner of her mouth. I've seen enough domestic violence cases to know a good backhand across the face will leave telltale signs. If I didn't know her better, I'd say a jealous, violent boyfriend had done this work. And then it occurs to me, perhaps a nasty, drunk father.

It's no secret Rowan's father is a drunk asshole. The few times I've crossed his path while picking Rowan up for one thing or another, I've gotten the distinct impression there is little in this world he cares about and that includes Rowan. Never mind the number of times he's been brought up on charges of disorderly conduct, or public intox, even an assault charge after one of the many bar room brawls he'd been involved in.

But surely he didn't do this to her. People would know, wouldn't they? There would be speculation and rumor, wouldn't there? But there had been years ago. He had even been investigated by Social Services at one time. Nothing had ever come of it, and the issue just seemed to disappear. Even Sara couldn't get her to admit he'd done anything wrong. But Sara would surely know if something was going on even if Rowan denied it, wouldn't she?

I park up along the side of the building, and as I approach Rowan, she lowers her head and begins to quietly cry. The look on her face isn't pain alone—it's humiliation and depression. I squat down beside her and touch her cheek, too close to her mouth, and she inadvertently flinches. I just stay there, looking at her as she cries, wanting to help but not sure where to begin.

"Row, look at me." She raises her head but can't quite bring herself to look me in the eye for longer than a second or two at a time. I have to know, and I ask. "Did your father do this?"

She just gives a slight nod.

I look at her for a moment longer before I have to lower my head to disguise the fury that's boiling up. I've known Rowan since she was a child—hell, since I was a child. How could I have not known this? I see things like this all the time. Abusive parents don't decide on the spur of the moment to become violent. He's always been violent, which means she's always been abused. My fury is as much for myself as it is him. I have to consciously force myself to focus on her and not on my building anger as it threatens to take over me. But one look at her face and I'm snapped back to this place—my fury put away in exchange for concern.

I take off my fleece pullover and help her put it on. She's shivering and so miserable it's hard to look at her. "Let's go." I'm not sure where to take her but want more than anything to get her away from this dirty old station with its oil-stained concrete and permanent petrol stench.

As I load her bike and backpack into the back of my Cherokee, she hobbles shoeless across the asphalt and in obvious pain to the passenger door. I decide to call my parents. But as I search the front console for my phone, I realize I've left it charging in the kitchen at their house. Shit. I have no choice then but to take her straight to the hospital and call my parents from there.

Rowan looks at me, and in the meekest voice pleads, "Please don't tell anyone."

She can't be serious! I give her a stupefied look, and her face instantly drops as the realization of my intentions clearly registers in her mind.

"Row, why wouldn't you—?" I start asking.

"Can I just get out, please?" she says quietly, her eyes suddenly wide and terrified.

Had the hit to the face broken her brain? I'm not letting her out! She's hurt and needs to see a doctor. I know she's been physically abused and assaulted, but what if there's more? The idea of that disgusting man laying his hands on her body is a sick, evil thought lurking in the back of my mind.

To my shock and horror, she begins to open the door of my moving car. What the hell is she thinking? Now I know the knock to her head has loosened some screws. I pull screeching to a stop in the middle of the deserted and quiet residential street just in time to see her manage the door open and take off barefoot down the street. I throw the car in park and go after her.

She doesn't make it far; the hard, uneven, pebbly road makes running difficult on her already painful feet. I catch her around the waist and hold her tight. She squirms and struggles for a few moments until she finally stops fighting. She calms as I pin her to me with her back to my chest, and she gives up with an exhausted whimper.

"Please. Please just let me go…" It's absolute desperation I hear in her voice. "Please."

"I can't do that," I respond quietly. "You know I can't. You're hurt and need to see a doctor. We *have* to call the police."

I turn her around to face me, and before I can say a word, her head collapses to my chest, and she buries her face there, sobbing quiet tears. I hold her for a long time not wanting to let her go.

She finally asks, "Can we just go home? I promise I'll give you an explanation, but please don't call the police. Not until you've given me a chance to explain."

"Row, you're hurt. He hit you and God knows what else. You *need* to see a doctor."

"I won't talk to the police. I'm sorry, but I won't. I'm fine. I promise it's not as bad as it looks. I swear. Please, just give me a chance to explain." She's begging, pleading, and quite frankly, telling me exactly what she is and is not willing to do, and as I stare at her while standing there in the street, I make my decision. Most would say the wrong one.

CHAPTER FOUR

Rowan

W e're silent the short ride back to his parent's house. I know I've asked him to go against everything his logical mind is telling him to do, and I hate myself for that. I stare blankly out the window, trying desperately to concentrate long enough to figure out a way to fix this mess, but I'm exhausted. His fleece pullover is warm and soft against my skin. It carries the amazing scent of his body, and all I want to do is drift away in the warmth of him.

When we pull up in his parents' driveway, he silently helps me from the car and leads me upstairs to the bathroom. He then helps me onto the counter, and with a warm washcloth gently and carefully cleans my face, studying and appraising every inch of my skin. He's surprisingly gentle for a man, or perhaps my experiences with my father have tainted my opinion of men in general. It's quite an emotional experience realizing how genuinely kind and compassionate a man can be. He takes his time, intent on sparing me any more pain, and as unexpected as his presence is on this night, I'm so thankful to have him here.

My mouth has stopped bleeding but is sore as hell. I feel numb everywhere else; even my brain seems to be running on autopilot, and I don't remember ever feeling so tired. I thoughtlessly run my tongue to the corner of my mouth as he brushes his thumb over the same tender spot. I can't help but glance at him in embarrassment before looking away again. He just looks at me steadily, his face showing none of the unease I feel having just touched him with my tongue.

He then pulls over a stool and sits in front of me. I'm sure he's going to start the interrogation, which is the least of what I deserve. But he doesn't. He gently lifts one foot and then the other, inspecting the soles for any sign of serious injury. Apparently satisfied that my feet aren't going to fall off, he washes the soles of both as I try unsuccessfully not to flinch from the pain. The skin is raw and scraped in areas where small pebbles have punctured the skin and larger rocks have bruised my soles.

When he's finished with my feet, he helps me gently down from the counter. He takes a deep breath, looking weary. "We can talk about this tomorrow. Get some sleep."

I quietly pull off his fleece, handing it to him before slipping away to Sara's warm bed, and I drift off quickly and dream. I can't recall the dream exactly, but I'm running away into the dark. Terror grips my heart as I'm pursued by something awful and unknown. Perhaps it's more a memory than a dream. I awaken in a start. I don't even realize I've screamed out until Logan bursts into the room ready to attack.

"I'm sorry," I whisper. "I just…" I'm panting as I recover from the terror. "Just a bad dream. I'm okay."

He watches me for a moment as he catches his own breath. He nods subtly, still holding his attention on me. But when he finally leaves, he doesn't stay gone for long. I wake him in another fit of nightmares, and again, he's in the room before I'm even fully awake. This time, he stays.

Without a word, he slips into bed next to me and pulls me into him. Pathetically, I've never laid this close to a man before, and even in my exhaustion, I have to admit it has its perks. He's warm, and I feel safe. His body is the most amazing replacement for his fleece pullover, and I'm held secure in his arms, breathing in the scent of his skin. I don't wake again until late morning. There's a note on the bedside table from Logan.

Row,

I had to go to the office this morning, but I'll be home shortly after noon. Try to rest while I'm away, but don't leave. I expect you to be there when I return so we can talk.

Logan

Apparently, he hasn't forgotten about my promise of explanation…

I take a long hot bath that feels painfully good on my scratched and bruised feet. Most of my facial damage is limited to the inside of my mouth but still shows lightly on the corner of my mouth. It could be worse. That's one small favor I suppose; I have to work this evening, and the last thing I want is to draw any attention to myself. I anxiously await Logan's arrival, still unsure what I'm going to tell him.

When I hear his car pull up in the drive, my heart starts racing. I'm in Sara's room making the bed, or perhaps just trying to look casual, when he comes in. He looks awful. Which is to say, he looks like some hysterical kid woke him in the middle of the night when he had to be up early the next morning. He watches me intensely, waiting. How does he do that? His eyes drill holes through me until I get so nervous I sit down. He stands, leaning against the nearby dresser, waiting patiently and adamantly for my response.

Redirection and distraction having worked so poorly for me the night before, I decide to give it another go. "Are you hungry?" I look up to his dark eyes furtively.

"Please stop, Rowan. I just want to know what happened."

I sit there contemplating for a very long moment before offering what I know is a terribly pathetic response. "I know, but I have to be at work at five. I really have to go home and change before then. I promise…"

"That's hours from now. Call in sick for all I care. I just want answers. Now. I've been waiting all day to find out why I broke the law for you."

I look at him, suddenly puzzled, until he elaborates, his irritation seeping around his words. "Oh, you weren't aware it's illegal for me to withhold this type of information? You just thought I was allowed to make these judgment calls on my own? So just because I'm not a lawyer yet, you think I can't destroy my career by breaking the law for you? Don't you get it? Believe it or not, there's a whole department solely charged with investigating child abuse that should be handling this by now. But wait, you already know that." The angry sarcasm is seething from his voice.

"I-I'm sorry—" I start.

"I'm not looking for an apology, Rowan. I want answers. Damn it! This may be nothing new to you, getting the shit beat out of you

18

in the middle of the night, but it's real fucking new to me!" To say he's angry is an understatement. "After all of this, you're just going to shut down and say nothing?"

I don't know what to do. I'm terrified to speak. Not the fear of physical violence I get at home, but the fear of utterly disappointing him. I can't bear the thought of him being upset at me, irritated at me, or worse yet, hating me. But that's exactly the situation I'm in. I open my mouth, trying to find the words, grappling at them helplessly, but nothing comes out. When I close my mouth again, he shakes his head and he turns and leaves the room, leaving me sitting there guilty and heartbroken. I start to cry. I know I have to talk to him. He deserves every last bit of the truth from me, but what will he think of me once he knows?

CHAPTER FIVE

Logan

I don't know why I got so angry with Rowan. The second I went into that room all I wanted was to be sleeping soundly next to her like the night before. But in daylight, I could see the slight swelling of her mouth, and the truth of what happened to her couldn't be ignored.

After leaving her staring stunned at me in Sara's room, I escaped to my parent's room, pulled off my shirt, and collapsed on the bed. My guilt eats into me as my weary body tries to sink into sleep, and I end up cursing myself for being so cruel to her. Her fear, her pain was so obvious on her delicate features as I railed against her, and I let my exhaustion and my selfish desire to invade her life control my actions. She doesn't deserve my anger. She deserves my support and my compassion. I was an asshole, plain and simple. And as I continue to drift in half-sleep, loathing my behavior, I feel the soft movement of the bed and my opportunity to fix what I've done.

Rowan is sitting on the side of the bed. Her back is to me, and her head is down. God, I'm such a shit. I sit up behind her and reach my hand to the nape of her neck. I want to apologize but don't know where to begin. Her hair is pulled back, and the skin of her neck is smooth and warm to the touch. It occurs to me that I'm too close to her. I have never touched Rowan in this way. I have never had any interest in Rowan other than the familial. She is, after all, just a kid and far too young for me. But my desire to comfort her feels strangely, almost arousingly, intimate.

Rowan isn't beautiful in the sultry curvaceous sense of the word, but she *is* beautiful. Her face is angelic and easy to look at. Her eyes are round and open, and every emotion she feels can be read there plainly. Her small size and slight feminine lines are nothing like what I'm used to, but the way she looks sitting on the side of the bed makes me want to touch her all the same.

Her head is down, and as she feels my touch she responds by tilting her face toward me. "I'm sorry." Her voice is so quiet and hesitant.

Apology not being my strong suit, I slowly and gently stroke the skin of her neck, wanting to assure her that everything's going to be all right. After a few moments, she begins to tell me a story. It's the story of a young girl who's gone from a loving home to losing a mother to gaining a monster. I've always known Rowan's story was a sad one, but I never dreamed it could be this overwhelming. Hearing her talk about the abuse she suffered from her father is agony.

As she relives the worst of it, I can't help but match up the lies she told my family and everyone else to the injuries she is now relating to me. She talks about the times Social Services were called. And I remember such an occasion. Sara was so worried and wanted desperately for Rowan to tell her it was all a big mistake. Rowan obliged. We bought into her lies so willingly, not wanting to believe the alternative. I understand now why she spent so many nights with Sara, to avoid confrontations with him. It worked, or so she said, but I'm looking into the eyes of a young woman who had blood running down her face just twelve hours ago. It hadn't worked at all. She had just been temporarily lucky. He was a monster, and there was no way he would stop using her as his own private punching bag.

Listening to her feels like being punched in the stomach. How could this have happened and nobody known? I want to kill her father. I could kill him. Without a doubt, I could kill him and think nothing of it. He deserves to die. He's supposed to care for her. He's supposed to protect her. She doesn't deserve this. But I hide these traces of violent imaginings as I continue to push her for more information.

And when she's finished speaking, I find my voice again and the question I really need answered, "Why didn't you want me to call the police last night?"

She turns to me, instantly finding my eyes. "No. I'm sorry, but I won't talk to the police."

"What do you mean? He can't get away with this. You don't deserve to live like this. Why would you want to protect him? You don't owe him anything, Rowan."

"It's not him. I hate him. He was nothing to me before my mother died, and he's nothing to me now."

"Then why? I don't understand…"

"Because I have nothing. Don't you understand? I don't have your family. I don't have your life. My mother was the only child of parents who passed away before I was even born. My father's family is non-existent. Or if they exist, I've never seen them. I don't get to go on with my life, my education, my dancing, my future… My life will be turned upside down. I could end up in a group home for the next couple months, and for what? Don't you see? I will be on my own next year. I can make it until then. It's so close. I've already received my scholarship letter. I can't screw that up. I work as much as I can, but I can't afford to be on my own right now. I'll be eighteen in less than two months. Sara and I will be in Ann Arbor by next fall. I will never have to go back to that life and his shitty trailer. But I have to get there first without destroying everything I've worked for."

She's fighting back tears and speaking so forcefully. It's obvious this isn't something she's considering for the first time. She has gone over and over and over this scenario many times before. But it isn't right. He can't get away with this. He's already gotten away with years of child abuse. Now that she's nearly grown, should he get away with this assault as well? There has to be some other way.

"My parents would let you…" I start thinking out loud.

"That's easy for you to say. You're their son. I can't do that. I'm sorry. I just can't. They've already paid my way through dance school for the better part of my life, and I feel guilty enough every time they foot the bill for me. You have to understand, this hasn't happened for years. There's just no point."

But I can't accept the conclusion she's trying to push me to. "Don't ask me to keep this a secret for you. You can't ask me to do that."

She's crying again. "I'm sorry. You were never supposed to know."

Her comment hits like a ton of bricks, and I'm suddenly struck by the sobering words she's saying. I might never have known had it not been for that one phone call. The idea this could have continued to go on without anyone ever finding out is terrifying. And now she wants me to make a decision that's not only unethical, but also dangerous. This isn't a decision I can make in an instant.

"Row, you have to give me time to think about this. I can't even think straight anymore, and I need to know I'm making the right decision."

At that, the conversation is over, and Rowan stands to leave the room. I watch her leave, wanting to call her back and keep her with me. She's suddenly the most vulnerable part of my life and that which I feel an undeniable need to protect. And with her gone from me, I start to drift asleep again, but my mind is racing. I know what I want to do, but I'm compelled to think about what will happen to her if I do. I can't force her to comply. Were I to call the police, what would she ultimately do? Refuse to speak with them? Refuse to acknowledge what he's done?

I've watched Rowan grow up, and I know to what degree she was neglected by that man. She has wanted all her life while Sara and I have wanted for nothing, ever. She is poor, desperately poor. She has no support system whatsoever. Should I be the one that pushes her away now? But as heartbreaking as it is, I can't overlook the fact that she's been wronged, and the man responsible has yet to be held accountable and never will if she has her way. He has to pay, but at what cost to Rowan?

CHAPTER SIX

Rowan

Logan is sleeping soundly, and I have to get home and change for work. I quietly grab a pair of Sara's shoes and find Logan's keys on the kitchen table. I unload my bike from his car before returning the keys and heading toward home. I change quickly, not wanting to spend any more time there than necessary.

Dad's watching TV in the living room, not the least bit interested in the world around him. Fortunately, his anger always fades with sobriety, and the post inebriation amnesia kicks in. The fact I escaped him the previous night evades his memory completely. I leave the house without saying a word and manage to make it to work with a few minutes to spare.

It's Saturday, and we will be busy. I spend most of the evening going through the motions. My mind is fixated on Logan. My future is in his hands, and I haven't forgotten it. I feel like I'm waiting for the doctor to tell me the inevitable bad news. On the one hand, if Logan can't come to terms with lying for me, not to mention setting his conscience aside, then my life as I know it is over. On the other hand, if Logan does keep my secret, I'm responsible for pushing him into a lie he shouldn't be a part of and that jeopardizes his reputation and possibly his career. So the diagnosis is detrimentally bad and detrimentally bad. And as I obsess about his decision, I'm driven insane by my worry. What must he be thinking? What will he decide?

And then I see him.

He's just strolled in with Amy. Have I mentioned I hate Amy?

She's gorgeous and everything every man in every world has ever wanted. She's a bitch, but she hides it well. She's the type of girl who would slit your throat to keep you down but talks sweet as pie. Logan's been seeing her for the better part of the past two years, and everyone thinks they're the perfect couple. It's sick. Sure, they look perfect together, but what he could possibly see in her is beyond me. He is nothing like her; he has none of her selfishness. Logan has always been caring in a way she would never understand. He is good, she is bad. It's as simple as that. I suppose she just puts on a good show for him. Never mind I hate her by virtue of the fact her boobs are three times the size of mine.

To my horror, they are seated in my section, but hey, at least I look good. Ha! What could be better than being seen in the obligatory uniform of black pants, white button up shirt, and a pathetic looking red ascot? Oh, and let's not forget the customary black beret. I hate being lame, and I especially hate looking lame in front of beautiful women. Just once, I'd like to be the beautiful one—not the one looking like a circus sideshow freak.

Logan watches me as I approach their table. My hands are shaking as I fill their water glasses, and by the uncomfortable look on Logan's face, he's well of aware of this fact. Amy is off in her own little world, looking around to see if anyone she knows is there. He says "Hi", and I manage a "Fancy to see you here," the fake casual tone of my voice a little too contrived and obvious.

Amy suddenly decides to join the rest of the world and finally acknowledges my existence. Not, of course, in any civilized manner. "Oh my God! What happened to your face? You look terrible." Her words are as fake as her blonde hair and pathetic personality.

My embarrassment is palpable as I look desperately around for any excuse to leave their table. I find nothing and abruptly give a bizarre nod of my head before turning heel and heading back to the kitchen. Sometimes I just can't act normal to save my life.

I realize, as I'm halfway down the corridor to the kitchen, Logan is behind me. I keep moving, suddenly sure I have some sort of food stuck to my butt and completely unsure what to do next. He makes that decision for me by catching up to me, taking me by the elbow, and pulling me into a small side hallway.

"She didn't mean anything by that, Row," he starts as he turns me to face him.

I open my mouth to object but then think better of the decision.

He's done a lot for me and insulting his girlfriend isn't the best way to make it up to him. Besides, disagreeing with him will only put him in a position to make a choice between us. He will either support the mega bitch or me. He doesn't owe me any allegiance, and why should I care anyway? It's not like he's my boyfriend. If he wants to be enamored with the blonde bombshell, so be it. Oh, who am I kidding? I do care, and I'm not at all sure I want to know how he would choose. I settle on the non-response, resorting to staring at the ground. I sense him staring at me, waiting patiently for my response.

"Why did you come here?" I ask quietly.

"I wanted to make sure you got here okay."

"Well, you can see I did." I finally look up to him. "Will you please leave now? The food here sucks and…"

"Why are you trying to get us to leave? We just got here, and I'm hungry."

"Because, it's … it's humiliating being seen in this stupid outfit and having to work around you." My eyes widen as I realize what I just blurted out, and I look away instantly.

Logan contemplates this as embarrassment burns through my cheeks. There are many long, awkward moments of silence where I know without looking at him that his eyes are trained on me.

"Well, I happen to like seeing you in this little getup, and having you serve me seems quite appropriate after the night you put me through."

I look back at him, my cheeks warming more by the second. He reaches his hand up to the front rim of my beret and flips it with his finger as he smirks. He's enjoying himself. I can't help but smile back at him. He's just so beautiful, and I wish again that I was one of the beautiful ones too. Just once.

But his smile falters as his focus moves to my mouth. He reaches for my face, running his thumb over the corner of my mouth as his fingers cup by jawline. His brow furrows as he studies my lips. His touch is gentle. "It doesn't look too bad," he comments reassuringly, but his voice is quiet.

I nod without saying anything else.

I manage to get them through dinner without dropping anything or humiliating myself further, though I can feel Logan's eyes on me as I move through the restaurant tending to other tables. I'm sure he's thinking, *This little girl is hardly worth my trouble.* And I can't help

26

but feel ashamed he knows so many awful things about me.

When they finally leave, I'm relieved to see them go. It's the first time my body hasn't stood at attention since catching sight of him. My shoulders instantly slump, I stop sticking my pathetic mosquito bites out trying to pretend I have breasts, and I let my body relax. How pathetic am I? The rest of the evening is a blur, and I'm glad when ten o'clock finally rolls around. We finish up quickly, and I head for the door.

As I enter the back parking lot through the employee entrance door, I immediately notice my bike is not leaned up against the dumpster where I left it. I then become aware of Logan's Cherokee parked by the other employees' cars. He's standing leaning against the hood of his Jeep, talking on his cell phone. When he looks up and sees me approaching, he wraps up his call.

"You ready to go?"

"Go where? I thought you were on a date." I suddenly have posture and boobs again by the time I reach him.

"I decided to make it an early night. Besides, I felt bad about what Amy said to you earlier. She doesn't always understand the meaning of tact, and you didn't deserve to be put on the spot that way. Get in."

"You didn't answer my question. Where are we going?"

"To get you an overnight bag from your house. You're not staying there tonight."

"Oh, I'm not? Logan, I don't understand what's going on."

"Look, I'll make you a deal. If you want my silence, then here's the way it's going to be. Any night, regardless of what night of the week it may be, that your father goes to the bar, you will stay at my apartment. The only exception is when you have plans to stay with Sara. No one except us will know about this, and that includes Sara. She can't keep her mouth shut, and the last thing I need is my parents finding out, or worse yet, the DA's office. I have a spare bedroom that will be yours, and you can leave anything you need there so you can come over anytime, even when you can't get home for your stuff."

He grabs my hand without taking his eyes from mine, unfolds my fingers gently with his own, and places a key in my outstretched palm. And while I'm stunned to the point of being shocked at what he's saying, I still note the shiver that runs through my body at his lingering touch on my skin.

"This is yours in case you are unable to get ahold of me and need to get into the apartment. Oh, and here." He hands me a cell phone. "It's a prepaid phone, and my home and cell numbers are already programmed in. I don't care who you give the number to, but I want you to use it anytime you need to reach me. No more payphones in the middle of the night. I'll take care of adding minutes when you need them."

I'm sure my mouth is gaping as he's speaking, but this is unreal, and more than that, unacceptable. As if it's not bad enough I've allowed myself to be supported by his parents, now I have Logan managing my life.

"Logan, I can't—" I start to protest.

"I'm sure you think this is open to negotiation, but I assure you it's not. I've been considering this since you left today, and I will accept nothing else. If I'm going to risk your safety and my ethical conscience by keeping your secret, you will give me the assurances I want." He pauses, staring at me for some seconds before continuing. "Do we have a deal?"

What reasonable choice do I have? I fumble and stutter to get the words out. "Yes. Yes ... But ... but I feel bad that you're doing so much. I can't..."

"Why don't you just say 'thanks' and leave it at that? Okay?" He smiles a gentle and reassuring smile at my concern.

"Thank you. I mean it, Logan. I really appreciate you doing this."

"I know you do. Of course, I have a contract you'll be required to sign." He raises a brow as he rounds the front of the Jeep to the driver's door. There, he stops and watches my slack-jawed expression with amusement before letting me off the hook. "Relax. I'm just kidding. Now get in. I'd like to be in and out of your house before he gets home."

We head toward the Elm Crest Trailer Park and my trailer. The house is dark when we arrive, and my father's car is missing. I'm embarrassed to let Logan see the inside of our old, dilapidated, ugly trailer.

"I can just run in. You don't need to..." I offer as I open the car door and step.

But as I look back toward him, it's just to see him climbing from the car and scoffing dismissively at me as he shakes his head. I turn back to the house, sighing as I start toward the front door. Awesome.

We enter and go straight to my room. I collect a couple pairs of pajamas, the ones that aren't too ugly and tattered for him to see, and clothes for the next day. He stands by looking around at the wood-paneled walls, disgusting dirty carpet, and outdated decor. I can tell he's not impressed with our decorating sense. We leave quickly, and it's silent on the drive to his place.

When we finally reach his apartment, it's late. His apartment is a renovated old brownstone in the downtown area of our little burg. When the Harringtons bought this complex five years before, it was in desperate need of renovation. Logan spent an entire summer helping his father fix up the apartment complex every evening after Marcus finished up at the law office. Even Sara and I helped with some of the work we could do. Marcus has a huge woodworking shop at their house and loves doing this type of work. The result: a beautifully restored building that has its original character blended with a contemporary style to create one of the most sought after buildings in town.

His apartment is neat and organized; not anal retentively, but enough so you know it looks this orderly at least ninety percent of the time. The smell is not overly masculine, like cologne, but clean and inviting. His furnishings are tasteful and simple. There are exposed bricks and tall ceilings throughout, and what walls aren't brick have been kept white. His furniture is contemporary and simple. A sectional sofa in a light-colored linen makes up his living room, with a beige rug sitting in front of the fireplace. He has natural mahogany furniture pieces his father made and black and white photography on the walls. The kitchen is contemporary but blends well with the original brick wall that runs along one side of the room. The spare room looks out over the front of the building and his room over the courtyard in back. Each of the two bedrooms has its own bathroom, and the common area has but a half bath for visiting company.

The spare room, like the rest of the apartment, is decorated simply and tastefully. The bed has clean sheets and a green quilt folded on top, but it is yet to be made. Logan helps me make the bed and then finishes giving me the tour of his apartment. His bedroom is larger than the spare and has more of his father's pieces. His bathroom is well organized, and I can't help but notice the extra toothbrush in the holder. A pang of jealousy hits, and I pathetically wish Amy wasn't in the picture—as though I could ever compete. I really hope I won't have any run-ins with the she-bitch.

Logan catches me staring at the toothbrush holder. "Don't worry about that. I'll take care of keeping her out of your way." Whatever the hell that means. Maybe he's alluding to dumping her... I'm daydreaming. Back to reality.

After showing me around and making sure my spare key works, Logan settles in to relax and watch a movie and asks me to join him. It's late, and I fall asleep halfway through the movie. Logan wakes me when the movie is over and walks me to my room. He follows me in and sits down on the bed. My heart is pounding—confused at why he followed me.

As is his custom, he watches me until I'm so nervous I start stammering. "Logan ... thank you again for..."

He smiles gently with a nearly amused expression on his face. "I didn't come in here because I wanted you to keep thanking me, Rowan." He pauses, his face becoming far more serious. "I know telling me about your past was really hard for you to do, but I'm glad you did. I just want you to be honest with me... I *need* you to be honest with me. We've known each other for a really long time, and I care about you. I just want to make sure you know that. You know if you need anything, you can come to me."

"I know." My voice is soft as my eyes flit away from him.

"I'm going to bed. If you need anything, just let me know."

"Okay."

As Logan stands to leave, we say good night, and I'm finally alone. I'm not sure I really want to be. I lie there, thinking about the past twenty-four hours and how many things have changed, and I can't help but wonder what else is in store for me.

CHAPTER SEVEN

Logan

It's unnerving knowing Rowan is sleeping in the next room. I should have left her there and gone back over to my parents' to keep Rufus company. But I let him out and gave him his medication just before picking Rowan up, and my parents are going to be home early the next morning to help with the church rummage sale. He'll be fine until then. Besides, I want to be here. I want to be with her. Hell, truth be told, I want her in my bed like last night. What am I saying? Rowan's not my girlfriend. She never has been and never will be. She's my sister's best friend and nothing more. She is only seventeen, after all. She's barely more than a child. *Please. Who am I kidding?*

When I was seventeen, I knew plenty of seventeen-year-old girls who were hardly naïve and innocent. What made me think she was? I wasn't a virgin at her age. What makes me think she is? But that thought is infuriating and brings on a sudden and intense wave of juvenile anger. The thought of some stupid kid touching her and fucking her is almost intolerable. Is it anger or jealousy I'm feeling? If I'm honest, I'd have to admit it's jealousy. Jealous of whom? Don't I have to be jealous of someone in order to be jealous? What the hell is wrong with me?

I have a beautiful girlfriend who can't seem to get enough of me. But I'm just so damn bored with her. She can be flaky, but she's easy, no pun intended—though the pun is just as accurate as my meaning. She lets me focus on my studies, on my future, and quite frankly, she makes it easy to set her aside when I need to. There's nothing much to her really. But everyone seems to think she's great for me.

She was furious when I ended our evening early. She almost always spends the night with me on Saturdays, but I had other things on my mind and was looking forward to seeing Rowan again. Had I actually chosen to spend time with Rowan over Amy? I obviously needed to speak with Rowan about our arrangement, but still, I was happy to see Amy go. I just need to stop letting myself get so close to Rowan. That's all.

I can't sleep. This is going to be a hell of a long night if I'm going to spend it thinking about Rowan instead of sleeping. I'm just so restless. When I finally start slipping away, it's long after I first lie down. I dream of Rowan. It's the type of dream where you can't remember exactly what happened, just the feeling. It was intimate and intense. I remember looking at her and her huge, beautiful eyes looking imploringly back at me, though I've no idea what the rest of my body was doing to her. Our eyes were locked on one another, but I don't know why. And when I wake suddenly, it's with a loud admonishment ringing through my mind. *Get a grip!*

Now I'm waking myself up dreaming of her. Wait... I heard something. As I come out of my dream world and the fog of my mind lifts, I remember hearing a noise that woke me. And then I hear it again. I get up and slowly move through my bedroom to the hall that adjoins the bedrooms to the living room. And as I enter the living room, I can see the sink light in the kitchen is on. Did I leave that on? I try to remember, but I can't.

Then I hear a voice. "Shit! What the hell... How effing tall is he?"

"*Effing?*" What the hell does that mean? It's Rowan's voice I hear, and she's obviously frustrated by something. I enter the kitchen to see her trying futilely to reach a glass on a high shelf in the cupboard.

"Can I help you?" I ask. My voice sounds a little too seductive and warm.

She jumps, clutching her hand to her chest and laughing nervously.

Again she's in pajama pants and a tank top—a different pair from the night before. The pants are baggy on her and the tank top tight. She's wearing her military, geek, chic reading glasses I've seen only a few times before. She is so small and delicate and truly fuckable, reading glasses and all. Or perhaps I'm just feeling the effects of my dream. I can't help but let my eyes slowly take in her entire body.

Her breasts are small but perfect and round, her nipples hard and tight beneath the white tank top. What I wouldn't give for those nipples to be in my mouth at this moment. The baggy pants leave much to the imagination, but I know her legs are lean and her bottom round and firm. I imagine running my hand down her flat stomach and under that waistband and below, touching her, fingering her clit, and then entering her tight warmth, making her come. I wonder what she would sound like coming for me. I'm instantly hard with arousal for her, and I thank God for my own baggy flannel pants. Though if she cared to glance, I'm sure she would know what I was thinking.

She startles me from my fantasy by speaking. "I'm sorry. Did I wake you?"

My breath hitches in my throat as I'm brought back reluctantly to reality. "No. I mean yes, but it's okay. Is the bed comfortable?" Please say no. Just give me any reason to get you in my bed.

"Yes, it's fine. Thank you. I just… I'm sorry I woke you. I just can't reach the glasses."

I walk over to where she's standing, and from behind her, I reach around and above her for a glass. Any closer and my cock would be up her damn shirt. It's on a rather tall shelf in an awkward corner, and I have my poor spatial planning to thank for this little temptation.

She uses the glass to get a drink of water while I continue to watch her. She seems uncomfortable with my eyes on her, but I have no intention of looking elsewhere. Finally finished unintentionally tormenting me, she excuses herself. And I watch her walk away, catching the fabric of the pants brush against the strong and round cheeks of her firm bottom.

I have got to get a hold of myself. This is going to be a very long year if I'm going to turn into a hormonal teen again every time she's around. Hormonal teen or not, I have to take care of this raging hard-on. And as I stand in my bathroom alone, I imagine her kneeling in front of me. My hand becomes her mouth, and I want so much to look down and see her eyes looking up at me as she sucks me deep into her mouth. I come quickly but with little sense of relief. I don't want it this way. I want her to make me come. But that's impossible.

As I collapse back in bed frustrated, I can't help but think this is just a passing whim. It's been a long and strange weekend, and I'm sure when I wake in the morning she'll just be Sara's young friend I've known since childhood again. I hope.

CHAPTER EIGHT

Rowan

He looked so gorgeous standing there in the kitchen with nothing except his flannel pants on. His chest and arms were well muscled and tight. I could feel my nipples tightening as he watched me and hoped he wasn't noticing my shaky hands. I lie here in bed after that encounter and feel more inept than ever before.

I have so little experience with men it's a joke. Aside from the two times I kissed a guy at some stupid party that Sara dragged me to, I'm worthless. I just wish I knew what it felt like. I don't think I even wanted to be with those guys. It just seemed like the thing to do. I wanted some experience to lean back on if and when it should ever become useful. But seeing Logan, I knew my body wanted it.

I could feel the wetness between my legs. He made me feel so soft and warm when he looked at me. All I wanted were his hands on me—everywhere. This is ridiculous. He has a beautiful girlfriend and would never want to be with someone like me. He thinks I'm just a kid, and men aren't interested in kids like me. I fall asleep depressed and loathing myself. This is not a new feeling for me.

When I wake the next morning, I'm more rested than I've been in a long time, and I roll over to see I've slept in way too long. It's nearly ten o'clock. I get up, brush my teeth, and shower. As I enter the living room, I see Logan sitting at the kitchen table working on his laptop.

He looks up. "Good morning."

"Hi. I didn't mean to sleep in so long." I smile at him.

"It's okay. I'm sure you were tired. It's been a long weekend."

"I better get going. Is there any way I can get my bike from the back of your Jeep?"

"Sure. I'll get it for you when I drop you off at your house."

"You don't have to do that. I can ride from here."

He looks up from his work, giving me his searing trademark expression of seriousness. "I said I'll drop you."

Ten minutes later, he's pulling up in front of my home sweet trailer.

"Thank you," I say as I take the handlebars of my bicycle that he's just finished unloading.

But his hands move to cover mine rather than releasing the bike. "Don't forget about our agreement," he reminds me.

I watch him for a moment before I nod.

"Rowan, I mean it. I will blow your little story if you don't play by my rules. Got it?" He's dead serious now.

"I understand."

His face relaxes measurably with my reassurance, and he smiles—finally releasing his grip on my hands.

I run inside my house just in time to catch the phone. It's Sara. She apologizes for not letting me know she was going to the lake house. Her parents had decided last minute that she should come too, and she'd tried to call me Friday night, but I'd already left for work and then, as I already know, she forgot her phone. She asks me to come over for Sunday dinner and work on our Composition papers that are due Monday morning. I'm nervous about seeing Logan with his family there but don't have much choice but to go. My report, or at least what I've done of it, is saved on their computer. I do all of my papers there because we don't have a computer.

Sara comes to pick me up a half hour later and talks the whole way back to her house. She had a boring weekend and is excited to finally have me to talk to. She asks how my weekend was, and I lie saying I just worked. Normally when something happens that is out of the ordinary, I want to share it with Sara. But even if Logan hadn't sworn me to secrecy, I'm not sure I'd have told her.

Sara and I help Ronnie in the kitchen with dinner. Logan hasn't arrived yet, and I find myself nervous as hell waiting for him to get there. When he finally does arrive very shortly before dinner, he seems surprised to see me there. He says hi to his family and me, but

36

when he gets to me, it seems strained and uncomfortable. I wonder if he wants me there at all. I sit across from Logan at dinner and keep catching him looking at me. I can't tell if he's irritated I'm there or not. He must be sick of me after this weekend and wanting a break, and that admission has me feeling that all too familiar stab of self-loathing guilt.

Sara and I hole up for a few hours in the office, working on our reports, and as I start typing, she starts speed talking. "So whadya do this weekend?" Seriously? She should know me well enough to know I never do anything interesting when she's gone, but wait… This weekend *was* interesting.

I lie. "Oh, the usual. Work, TV, work, sleep."

But the look on my face apparently isn't convincing. "Huh?" She's stroking her chin as I try to focus on typing and not on my building anxiety. She gives up her suspicion and finally, at seven o'clock, we both finish and decide to call it a night. As we come back downstairs, I see Logan sitting with his parents around the kitchen island deep in conversation. They look up as we come down the stairs, and I have this awful fear he's decided against helping me and has confessed all.

But my fears are calmed when Ronnie speaks. "Are you girls finally finished? These better be good papers as much time as the two of you have been working. I thought we agreed you guys would work on your procrastination issues this year." She's smiling.

"I'm going to run Row home. Be back in a bit." Sara comments as she grabs her keys from the kitchen counter.

"Uh… I'm leaving. Why don't I?" Logan looks at Sara, but he glances at me quickly before his eyes flash back to hers.

Sara shrugs. "Sure."

And then his intense eyes are on me again. We say our goodbyes for the night, and he holds the front door open for me as we leave.

Logan glances toward me as we head to his car. "You thought we were talking about you in the kitchen just now, didn't you?"

"I thought it was a possibility. How did you know?"

"The panicked look on your face gave it away. Those big eyes of yours were practically popping out of your head. Well, you can relax. Against my better judgment, I haven't changed my mind, and I didn't tell them anything."

As we drive in silence, I decide to ask the question that's been plaguing me. "Did you not want me to be there tonight? I mean…

You're probably sick of me being around, and I don't want to be in your way. I just don't want you to get sick of me."

"Rowan, I haven't gotten sick of you in the seven years I've known you, and I'm not sick of you now. Where's this coming from?"

"I don't... I just thought maybe..."

"You're being ridiculous. I didn't decide to do any of this out of some sense of obligation. I'm helping you and letting you stay with me because I want to. Don't ever think you're some burden to me. You're not, and you never will be. Okay?" At that, he reaches over and takes my hand in his, glancing at me before pulling his hand from mine and returning his eyes to the road.

I feel the same pang of guilt and embarrassment as I always do when his family pays for a dance lesson or supports me in some way I don't deserve. But I also feel the very unfamiliar feeling of security I've started getting used to this weekend. I nod my head.

He pulls up outside my house, and by the sudden drop of his face, it's clear my father's car in the driveway has not escaped his notice. I start to open the door when he stops me. "I don't like that he's here."

"Logan, if he's here he's not out getting drunk. He usually keeps it pretty low-key on Sunday nights because he has to work early on Mondays. Please don't worry about this. I have to see him."

"I just don't like it."

"It will be okay. I promise. I know how to get ahold of you, and I will call you if there is any problem."

"Damn it. If you were at my place, I wouldn't have to worry about this."

"Sara is picking me up tomorrow morning for class, and I need to be here. I've agreed to stay with you when I need to, but I can't just because he happens to be home. He lives here. I can't avoid him completely. You know that."

"Yeah, well I don't have to like it." He reaches up and puts a gentle hand on my cheek, running over the corner of my mouth with his fingers, his brow furrowing. "Row, just promise me. Just ... say it. Don't take any risks with him."

"I promise." I look at him a moment longer before hopping out of the car, and as I cut across the lot I can feel his eyes watching me; I know he's unhappy.

The rest of the evening passes without incident, and I take

advantage of the quiet to catch up on homework. At ten-fifteen, the cell phone Logan gave me starts to ring. I know it must be him because I've not given the number to anyone yet.

I answer, and I instantly recognize the worry in his voice. "Hi. I just wanted to make sure everything was all right."

"Everything is fine. I'm just getting ready to go to bed."

"Okay. Call if you need anything."

"I will. Good night."

"Good night."

I wish I was at his place in that nice, big, warm bed or better yet, his bed.

CHAPTER NINE

Rowan

The next weeks pass in quick succession. I begin looking forward to every minute I get to spend with Logan and find I all too desperately look forward to the nights when my father is off on a binge. When I'm with Logan at his apartment, it's comfortable yet intense. Logan loves to cook, and I've learned to love spending time with him in the kitchen, laughing, chatting, and debating anything and everything worth debating. Logan loves to challenge me at any chance he gets, perhaps a habit he's picked up from law school. And I never hesitate to rise to the challenge. He's smart, and the more I talk to him, the more intelligent I realize he is.

My birthday has come with the chill of winter, and like all others before it, it did not include even the utterance of a congratulations from my father. The Harringtons, on the other hand, bought me flowers and a very generous gift card to the mall—naturally, Sara commandeered the gift card and dragged my reluctant butt with her for her very most favorite activity in the world: shopping. And when I arrived at Logan's later that night after returning to a darkened trailer, signaling that my father was celebrating the blessed day at the bar with anyone but me, I arrived to the sweet smell of baking.

A cake was laid out on the table awaiting my arrival. Logan, with a slight sheepishness to his voice, admitted he'd seen my father's car parked at the bar on his way to the grocery store. Like everything else he cooks and, quite frankly, everything else he does, the cake was perfect. So, I guess I'm now an adult. Yet I feel just as naïve, immature, and helpless as I always have.

In addition to ushering in the celebration of my very insignificant entrance to the world, the change of the season has brought the arrival of winter. This north country town is beautiful this time of year, blanketed in thick snow that clings to the abundant trees, creating the most beautiful, peaceful world. Life has become peaceful in and of itself by virtue of my new place in it.

I've always known Logan to be a good person, but the more time I spend with him, the more I see what an amazing man he really is. I find myself more and more drawn to him as time goes on. Not just his looks, he's always been handsome, but his whole persona. He's confident, at times demanding, but kind and gentle all the same. I find myself loving his choice of music, his intelligence, his clothes, his smell. Every last thing about him arouses intimate thoughts. I could no more than hear a song on the radio I've heard while at his place than immediately be stuck with him in my head. I truly am a pathetic kid drooling after some popular, good-looking kid who is far out of my league.

I join the Harringtons on their final trip to the lake house to ready it for winter. Logan decides at the last minute to join us, and I fantasize it's me that beckons his presence. I know it's not, but what can I say; I'm a daydreamer by nature. Working around the lake house with his family is far more fun than I would have ever imagined physical labor could be.

I can't stop looking at Logan every time he's around me and somehow manage to fall off a step stool in the kitchen when he suddenly enters. I fall ridiculously to the floor. And as Logan pulls me to my feet, never taking his eyes off mine, I can't help but notice that his touch lingers just slightly too long, our bodies just marginally too close, and his eyes just a bit too intense. No one else is around, and the shared look between us is palpable to my perception.

As Ronnie suddenly appears, we both find ourselves startled, and while I struggle for composure and pray for the flush of my cheeks to cool, I think I catch the same look of discomfort on Logan's face. Ronnie, bright and carefree as usual, is caught off guard and appraises us for only a moment before she dismisses the situation and returns to her errand. She seems not to have noticed the tension in the room at all. I'm sure it was just in my head.

We return to the city on Sunday night, and as Logan drives me home, he casually and without looking at me asks, "Will you stay at my place tonight?"

Applying that same overly contrived casualty, I respond, "Sure." But my voice is quiet.

We say nothing as we hike up the flight of stairs to his apartment. And when inside, he throws in a CD, one of many I now solely associate with him and that seems to penetrate me and create my entire mood. I stand around uncomfortable for some time, still unsure why I'm here on this night. It's Sunday, and there's no good reason for me to have agreed to stay. For that matter, no good reason for Logan to have asked. He flops down on the couch, flipping through a magazine and obviously not nearly as off kilter as I. Naturally, I continue to meander about, unsure of myself.

But eventually I work up the nerve to speak. "Logan—"

"Given the fact you're pacing about, I'm going to hazard a guess you're wondering why I've asked you to stay. Am I right?" He gives me a knowing glance over the top of his magazine.

Of course, he's right. "Well, it's not that really, just that I ... um..." So much for playing it cool.

He gives me a quirky look as I attempt nonchalance. "I just wanted the company."

"Oh. I suppose Amy had plans tonight or..."

"I wouldn't know. I wanted *your* company."

At that, he continues reading his magazine without the slightest hint of distraction. I finally sit on the opposite end of the couch and grab a random magazine off the coffee table. I'm somewhat stunned by his statement and, more than that, confused by what it means. And as I attempt to immerse myself in a golf article about the appropriate address and backswing for your iron game, I realize I may have chosen unwisely from the magazine collection. Why couldn't there have been a *Cosmo* sitting on the table when I desperately needed something to help me play it cool? Unfortunately for me, Logan has noticed my error as well and starts chuckling in amusement. I give up trying to be casual and just give into my awkward idiocy. Thankfully, Logan doesn't allow my embarrassment to continue for too long before suggesting a card game instead.

We settle on poker, and for nearly two hours we spend our time staring one another down and trading our fortunes away. I end up winning the whole of Logan's student loan debt, and he somehow manages to walk away with an IOU for a quarter. We jokingly debate who came out on top—I argue in favor of my new fortune. It's late, and we finally say our good nights still laughing about our ridiculous gambling. I don't want the night to be over, but I know I'll have to get up early just to get home in time for Sara to pick me up.

CHAPTER TEN

Logan

Christmas is fast approaching, and the weeks seem to fall away. Rowan has spent little more than the necessary time at my apartment. I still enjoy every second of my time with her but have managed to keep things as platonic as I can manage. It's a constant struggle when she's around to keep my mind on this world and not my imaginary world where she and every part of her belong to me.

The problem is, I just can't seem to get enough of her. She's driving me crazy, and all I want is to be near her. My attraction to her is insane, not to mention inappropriate. I can't help but laugh at her silliness and shyness. She is so unsure of herself, yet she radiates intelligence and strength that are as much a turn on as her physical appearance is to me. I like seeing her in pajamas as much as I do in jeans or, better yet, the mandatory gondolier outfit she wears to work. And I'm constantly enticed by what is under her clothes. I can hardly sit in the same room with her without imaging myself pulling off her clothes and fucking her. I can't even think of Amy anymore with any interest. My thoughts just shift to Rowan.

I'm never sure when I will see her next, and it drives me insane with wonder. I spend long hours of the day, wondering and hoping today will be the day when her father graces the pub with his presence. I wish she was here every night, and I'm overcome by ridiculous jealousy at the thought of hormonal guys from her classes even looking at her.

I know I'm pushing the limits of decency with her but just can't seem to stop myself. I've always prided myself on my self-control, but it vanishes in an instant when it comes to Rowan. And it certainly hasn't escaped my attention that she's an adult now and more than capable of deciding who she chooses to fuck. But desire aside, I won't cross that line with her … not her. There is truly no point. I'm moving halfway across the country in little over half a year. And I won't take advantage of her, knowing I'll be walking away from her. Never mind the fact my family would kill me if I ever did anything to hurt Rowan. And I'm not entirely sure I could ever forgive myself either.

I try desperately to push the thoughts of her out of my mind, and I vow to get control of my feelings for her before it gets out of hand. I swear to myself, I won't allow myself to indulge in her company any more than is necessary. This decision, of course, sounds more like torture than decency, but I'm resolved.

Until the blizzard hits.

⌘⌘⌘⌘

The wind is blustery cold, and it rocks my jeep as I drive. There is little that could force me to be outside in this weather, but as I near an intersection, I can see that not everyone has my sense of self-preservation. But I know this coat, and I know the small body that's swathed in it. Her head is down, and her hood up, and she's staring at the sidewalk under her feet. There's little of the sidewalk to even see at this point with the snow falling and drifting faster than anyone's shovels can keep up with.

When I honk as I pull up beside Rowan, she whips her head up and around, losing her balance and starting to fall. But she manages to catch herself—not, however, before she ends up in a full and awkward squatting surfer position. She looks up to see me laughing at her, and she smirks in her best "eat shit" look.

Once she's gotten herself upright, she wades through the tall snow drifts to the passenger window as I lower it.

"That was pretty. What do you call that move?" I ask her.

She doesn't miss a beat. "That's just my asshole-honking-at-me move. It's usually followed up with my middle finger." She shakes her head, smiling shyly as she chuckles.

I wink at her. "Get in."

She opens the door and climbs in, rubbing her gloved hands together as she tries to warm herself up. "Do you always honk at young women on the street?"

"Do you always put on such a good show when you're honked at? Hell, if memory serves, it didn't even take a horn the last time you put on a show like that."

She instantly flushes with what can only be embarrassment. I'm reminding her of the step stool incident at the lake house only a month or so before. It had been an incredibly intense time being so close to her around my family. But that was my fault. I'd put myself in that position very intentionally so I could be near her.

"Damn you and your ever-quick comebacks," she mutters.

"Where are you going in this weather?"

"I have a dance lesson with Anthony."

"I see, and how is it Anthony's managed to stay open when the rest of the town is closed down?"

"He's technically closed, but I agreed to come in anyway. It's my weekly private lesson, and I didn't want to miss it."

"Huh. That's devotion, isn't it?" I pause for a moment, glancing at her quickly but returning my eyes to the road. "I'll take you. You shouldn't be out walking around, even in that adorable polar bear get-up you've got on." When I glance at her again, she's blushing.

We pull up to the studio within a few moments.

"Thanks for the ride, Logan." She starts opening the door.

I reach over, catching her arm gently. "How long will you be?" I don't bother looking at her when I ask. I feel a bit too needy at the moment to let her see.

She pauses with her hand on the handle. "About an hour."

"Why don't I stay and take you home after. I have some research material I need to look through, and I can start on it here. I don't want you walking home. It's supposed to keep snowing, and it'll get a lot colder when the sun goes down." *And I also just want to see more of you.* Of course, I can't say that.

"You don't have to do that. I'll be fine."

"You always say that, but you rarely are. You seem to enjoy making reckless decisions—like venturing out in this weather for one."

She smiles as she glances at me. "Fine, come in. There's a couch in the studio you can use."

I follow her into the building and into the studio where Anthony is waiting for her. I've known Anthony for years thanks to the fact that he's been Sara and Rowan's instructor since they were children, and after I toss him a quick hello, I make myself comfortable on the couch with a book. Rowan seems nervous that I'm there, and I'm not sure why, but it sends a trill of warmth and arousal through me knowing I have such an effect on her.

I beg my brain to concentrate on my book but can't seem to keep my eyes where they should be. I keep looking up and watching Rowan. She's pulling off her clothes, and I almost choke until I realize she has her dance clothes on underneath. She's sitting spread eagle on the floor, her back to me, lacing her toe shoes up her ankles. I can't take my gaze away from her. She looks up to the wall of mirrors in front of her and catches me watching her from behind. She smiles shyly, and I smile back. I sit with my book open on my lap for the entire hour but don't manage to make it past the first page.

I watch her as she stretches. I watch her as she goes through positions. She is beautiful—her lines so elegant. She may look small and unobtrusive at any other time, but when she's in her element, she radiates and takes over the room. Her face is confident and calm, seductive but not intentionally so. The way she moves is so effortless, and her body is so amazingly balanced as she easily forces herself into positions that would make the average person groan in pain. I almost burst out laughing as I remember the acrobatics she attempted just shortly ago outside on the sidewalk.

Watching her move is mesmerizing and does nothing for my vow to control my desire for her. Gay as Anthony most definitely is, I'm unrealistically jealous of the way he's allowed to touch her, pushing her legs into exactly the position he wants, turning and spreading her hips at his leisure, even sliding his hand around her firm buttocks to catch the back of her thigh and lift her leg at just the right angle. I catch myself holding my breath on more than one occasion, and by the time her hour is up, I'm her number one fan. I love ballet. She strolls over to me and sits down. She looks down before I even notice and sees just how far I've not made it in my book. I'm still on page one.

She smiles shyly before commenting. "Must be a boring book."

She has no idea…

"In comparison to other things, yeah, you could say that. Are you ready?"

We say our goodbyes to Anthony and head back out into the frigid Michigan weather. I don't want to take her home, and in a moment of weakness that has been building for weeks, I break my own rule. "Stay with me tonight."

The moment the words come out of my mouth, I know I've made a mistake, but I've denied myself with her for so long I can hardly bear it. I can see her looking at me from the passenger seat, and I resist the urge to look back, afraid she'll see the desperation in my eyes.

"Okay," she finally responds.

And we say nothing to one another on our way back to my place. I know full well I've broken the rules and have no good justification for doing so.

When we arrive at my apartment, we set about making dinner. I love being in the kitchen with her. Cooking is something I love to do, and I especially love her company when I'm doing it. We talk and laugh the whole time. She tries to help but can't even manage to cut a carrot without sending it sailing across the kitchen. She resorts to reading some of the research material I've brought home to work on out loud to me while I'm working. It's surprisingly helpful, and I absorb far more information than I thought I would. Besides, listening to her talk is a complete turn on, and I've given up stifling my desire for the night. I have no intention of acting on my urges, but I won't deny myself the pleasure of those feelings.

We sit at the kitchen table, eating and talking some more about the classes we're taking. I behave in a civilized manner and thank God she can't see what's going through my mind. I keep imagining her straddling me as I sit in my chair. She's riding me gently but taking all of me inside her. My hands are on those slender hips of hers that Anthony worked over so enticingly for me just a short while ago. I'm moving her back and forth to me. I imagine running my hands down her back and around her bottom, clutching her there and my finger stroking her anus. I imagine the initial shocked look on her face as my eyes lock on hers. I gently push my finger into her there. I'm gentle and go slow; even in my fantasy, I know she's not experienced, and I want to savor every moment of her pleasure. She accepts my intrusive touch and looks at me pleadingly. I slowly push deeper into her most secret entry, feeling my cock pumping her warm, wet pussy through the thin wall separating my finger from my dick. *Damn, I have an active imagination.*

The intimacy of my thoughts is intense, and by the time dinner is over, my body is more than ready for her. But I know my place.

Instead of in bed, we end up on the couch watching TV. The weather is continuing to get worse, and the snow keeps falling. She falls asleep with her head near me on the couch, and as she sleeps contentedly, I reach out and stroke her soft silken hair. It shines in the soft lamplight of the room, and it feels as silky as it looks. I shouldn't be crossing this boundary, but I can't help but steal this touch. At midnight, I decide I can't keep my eyes open any longer, and even though I'm not ready to say good night to her, I rouse her. She staggers off to bed, and I do the same. It will be another long, lonely night alone.

CHAPTER ELEVEN

Rowan

I feel so comfortable I could sleep forever, but I roll over and the alarm clock says six-thirty. I know I'll have to get up soon. I roll back over and close my eyes tight to try to squeeze in a few more delicious moments of sleep. When I wake next, it's because I feel the bed move. I roll over, and Logan is lounging on the pillows. He brushes a few strands of my hair caught in my eyelashes away from my eyes as I look up at him.

"Good morning," he says quietly.

"Hi." I stretch.

He leans down to my ear, and I tremble at the closeness. And then I feel his breath on my ear. "Snow day," he whispers.

My lips instantly pull up in a smile as I turn toward him, our mouths entirely too close together.

He pulls back quickly, clearing his throat nervously. "Everything's closed down. The university, schools, even all non-essential city jobs and most private companies as well."

It doesn't matter how old you are, when you hear the words "snow day," life just gets better. I get up as Logan continues to lounge on the bed, and I look out the window. There's at least a foot and a half of snow on the ground. My cell starts to ring, and I run over grabbing it from my bag. It's Sara calling me in case I haven't gotten the good news yet. She asks how I'll be spending my free day, and I lie that I'll likely just watch soap operas and binge eat. After chatting for a few more minutes, I let her go and join Logan on the bed.

"You're a shit liar, you know that, right?" He's smirking.

But it's an ugly reminder of what I've just done, and I can feel the discontentment showing on my face. "I know. I don't like lying to Sara."

His face softens. "I know you don't." He looks at me for long serious moments, understanding obvious in his expression. But he doesn't allow either of us to linger on this thought too long. "Come on. Let's make breakfast. Or why don't I make breakfast while you try not to injure yourself on any cooking utensils."

Now I'm smiling again. I love being with him.

We eat pancakes and lots of them. Afterward, I help with the dishes—the only thing he'll let me do in his kitchen at this point. As I wash, he dries, and I feel so comfortable that even this simple task is pleasurable. I watch as he stretches to place things on high shelves, and I'm struck when his shirt rises up, and I see his flat and tight stomach. It's not that I haven't seen his stomach before. But I'm caught off guard like the first night I spent here, and I gasp at the sight of him. He doesn't notice fortunately, and I do my best to act normal.

When we finish, we watch a movie that happens to have enough "strong sexual content" to make me blush, and I swear he senses it. We're sitting close on the couch, and I'm rigid with nerves.

He finally reveals his apparent psychic abilities when he speaks without ever even glancing at me. "Relax. You look like you're going to come unglued."

Yeah, right. I've never wanted to be touched more. I keep imagining his hands on my breasts and his mouth on my neck. I want that and more. I'm wet and wanting him to touch my wetness so much it aches, but he doesn't. To add insult to injury, Amy calls. They talk for a few minutes. Now that the roads are clear for the most part, she wants to come over, and of course, he has to refuse. He finally hangs up with her.

"You could take me home if you want."

"If I didn't want you here you wouldn't be here."

"If Amy wants to come over she should be able to. She is your…"

"I thought Amy came over if *I* wanted her to? Or am I wrong?"

He sounds annoyed with me, and I instantly fall silent. We're still sitting close on the couch, and after a few uncomfortable moments, he reaches over and takes my hand and offers a quiet apology. We finish watching the movie, but he doesn't immediately take his hand away from mine when the movie ends, and I find my body is pulsing with excitement at his touch. But eventually he moves away from me, and I'm left missing the warmth of his hand on my skin, the gentle caress of his palm, and his apparent comfort at being so close to me.

It's a wonderful lazy afternoon. He disappears to his room to fold laundry and hollers after me to grab him a water. As I enter his room, I'm nervous to invade his space, but he starts an easy conversation, and before long we're both sitting comfortably on his bed talking about nothing in particular. When I next look out his bedroom window at the winter sky beyond, I note with a stab of disappointment that the snow has stopped and it's getting dark. It will be time to go soon.

CHAPTER TWELVE

Rowan

With Christmas come the memories of my past. I can't help but be depressed every time I remember the holidays of my childhood. Memories definitely fade over the years, but not those cherished memories of Christmas trees, music, gifts, and most of all, my mother. We were never wealthy by any stretch of the imagination, but I always had more than I could want under the tree. Our family gathering had only consisted of the two of us, but it was festive regardless. Since my arrival in Allendale, Sara's family has always been good at involving me in their family gathering, knowing well that my own poor excuse of a family would be celebrating with a beer in some dark beer hall.

I usually spend the night with Sara on Christmas Eve and join them for Christmas Eve church service. Then I wake with the family the next morning to celebrate the day. I struggle every year to be cheerful at the Harringtons', and I know it doesn't escape their attention. They are, of course, gracious enough not to ask me about my quiet, distant behavior, understanding my reasons. I'm always thankful to be there, knowing full well the alternative is just too depressing to bear. Still, my emotions always seem to betray me, and I feel guilty for bringing my sadness to them.

So it comes as something of a surprise when mid-afternoon of Christmas Eve rolls around, and my father peers in my room. I'm just starting to get my things together to head over to the Harringtons' and can't hide my surprise to see him. He's sober and speaks nervously without the benefit of alcohol pulling the strings of his personality. I'm naturally shocked as my father usually only speaks to me when he's drunk and pissed off. He otherwise ignores me.

Awkwardly, he begins. "I want to have a dinner today… Like a Christmas thing. I've never cared much for all that holiday bullshit in the past, but you'll be gone next year, and I just … well … thought we should at least do that. You know?"

I manage a weak, "Yeah."

But the gaping-mouthed look on my face seems to make him think better of his plan, and he suddenly stammers on. "I mean, it's no big deal. I don't care if you don't want to…"

"No! I think that's a good idea. We can do that." I'm not by any means convinced my father actually wants to spend time with me, but I can't help but hope that maybe some part of him is trying to reach out to me.

He continues. "Well, I'm going out to the grocery store to get the food and maybe you could just put out the plates and whatever. Do you like fried chicken and stuff? I think they'll have that in the buffet."

"Sure. Um, that's … that's fine with me." I'm still struggling to keep the incredulity from my voice.

He suddenly turns heel and heads for the door. I sit on the side of my bed stupefied for at least ten minutes before heeding his advice and setting the table. I know he won't care what dishes are set out or if they're even made of something other than paper, but I decide, given the occasion, to use the real plates; nothing fancy or even pretty mind you, but if you dropped one on the floor, it would break, and that has to count for something. I set the table as neatly as I would at the restaurant and wait anxiously for his return.

CHAPTER THIRTEEN

Logan

W hy the hell isn't she answering her damn cell? She told Sara she'd call when she was ready to be picked up. And when five o'clock rolled around without hearing from her, Sara started trying to reach her. It's now nearly five-thirty, and the Christmas Eve service is going to be starting at six. With no word from Rowan, everyone starts to get concerned. My family knows she's always in a delicate state this time of year, but it's so uncharacteristic of her to simply not call like this. Their anxiety can't even compare to the angst I'm feeling, having firsthand knowledge of the powder keg she's living in.

I finally decide to go over to her house and skip the church service. Sara, naturally, wants to join me, but I'm happy when my parents, sensing a ploy to get out of church, tell her she will be joining them. The last thing I want is for Sara to witness my interaction with Rowan. I don't know what to expect when I reach her place, but I'm both furious at her for making me worry and terrified I might have reason to worry.

The drive over is agonizing. I can't seem to stop speeding, and I'm shaking with fear. When I reach her place, I can see her bike through the garage window but the house is dark and quiet. As I try the front door, I find it unlocked. As I enter, I can see into the dining room, and the lights are out but candles are lit and burned down low in their candlesticks. The table is spread neatly as though awaiting a feast to arrive. It looks like the perfect family dinner in preparation, waiting only for the guests to appear. Except this is no perfect family—so far from it that the sight of that table is almost disturbing.

I move toward the hall and quickly make my way back to Rowan's room. As I enter, I see her sitting on the edge of her bed, not moving, just staring down at her lap. She doesn't look up, and I'm struck with a wave of anger as I see her cell phone sitting on the chest of drawers. Before I can start grilling her on why she chose to bail on my family, she speaks. "Please don't be upset with me."

There is so much sadness in her voice my anger melts away just as quickly as it came. I want answers, but I know to tread slowly. I take my place beside her on the bed. She's strangely calm and distant. I reach down and take her hand in mine, lacing her fingers with my own. She turns toward me but doesn't make eye contact. She almost seems embarrassed, but I can't imagine why. I implore her for an explanation. She shakes her head concededly. "I'm just so stupid."

"Row, tell me what happened. Did he hurt you?"

She shakes her head. It takes her a few moments before she starts to speak, her voice rough with choked-back tears. "This afternoon my dad said he wanted to have a Christmas dinner today. I mean, we've never done anything even remotely like this. He's never even mentioned wanting to spend time with me. But he was sober, and I couldn't help but agree. He asked me to get the plates out and ready. I actually believed him. I thought, even if it was just for today, and if he never wanted me to be his daughter ever again, it was okay. It was enough just to have one real day. I really thought he'd come back. I believed him. I believed he wanted to be here."

She starts shaking her head again in incredulity. I finally understand. I sweep the hair from the side of her face so that I can see her eyes, and she looks over at me, making eye contact for the first time. She looks humiliated as her eyebrows twitch with restrained tears. I want to assure her she shouldn't feel that way with me, but I know it wouldn't help. It's a humiliation I don't understand, and my heart hurts for her.

"So you set the table and waited for him?"

"Yep. What a waste. I waited for hours for him to show. I really believed at any moment he would come through the door and tell me he had car trouble or had to go to another store—just something. Some realistic excuse because he would never make plans like this and then miss Christmas Eve dinner with his daughter. I should have known better. Why would I ever fool myself into believing he could care?"

"Because, you don't let yourself stop believing there's good in him. Don't feel bad about that, Rowan, and don't regret it. Your optimism is what drives you every day. That's something I've always admired about you. You let life throw the worst it has at you, but you don't ever let go of wanting the most out of it."

"That's because I'm an idiot."

"No, it's because you're far more determined than most of us have the patience and strength to be."

We sit in silence holding hands for a long time. I want to take her out of this place, but she needs time. My cell phone suddenly rings, and I realize we've been sitting here for so long church is now over, and my parents are ready for answers. Rowan watches me, and I know she's not up for my family this night. I answer the phone, thinking quickly of what to say. I lie to them, saying she's in bed with a bad headache. She looks at me, appreciation showing in her eyes. I then lie again and say I'm tired and think I'll go home for the night. My parents are not happy to hear this, but I'm adamant.

Missing Christmas Eve dinner with my family is wrong, but I won't leave her alone tonight. Her father is no doubt out drinking his sorrow away, and she certainly won't be staying anywhere except with me. As we leave the house, I blow out the candles in the dining room, leaving the house pitch black. When he's sober tomorrow morning, let him see what she did for him. If guilt is an emotion he's capable of, I hope he has a good serving of it tomorrow.

When we get to my apartment, Rowan says good night and excuses herself to her bedroom. I hate that she's so depressed, and I miss her usual perky self. I finally go to bed at nine o'clock. I'm not tired, but being here when she's sad like this has put me in a depressed mood. I fall asleep miserable and helpless. But I wake in the middle of the night as she crawls into my bed.

It's been so long since I've gotten to be this close to her. I love it when she's in bed with me. There is no doubt my feelings for her tend to lean to the sexual, even erotic, but they also run quite intensely to the compassionate and caring. I love comforting her and holding her as much as I enjoy imagining fucking her.

She nestles in next to me and wraps her arms around me. I stroke her hair and rub her back as I feel her breath on my neck. And when my hand that has been caressing its way down her back finally reaches her waist, I can't help but slip it under her shirt to feel the skin of her lower back. It's smooth, and my fingers glides over the contour of her shape. My hand travels to her waist, and feeling my touch there makes her breath hitch. I can tell she's aroused and nervous. From my hold on her waist, I ease her hips toward mine, and the second her groin meets mine, I know I've made a mistake. I'm hard as hell and there is no way she can't feel every inch of my erection.

My brain is screaming at me to stop, but the rest of me is refusing to listen to reason. She mindlessly shifts her top leg over mine and allows herself to get closer to me. I can feel the warmth between her legs against my rigid cock, separated only by a couple of thin layers of material. She pushes her hips toward me, trying to make the material disappear. I push forward, wanting her to feel my hard arousal. She does, and her body shudders when I press against the spot where I know her most sensitive bud lies hidden. I imagine we're unclothed and continue to slowly thrust against her. I can feel the cleft of her lips through the fabric, and my cock finds its place there. We move together, our arousal mounting, our breathing ragged and quick. I've never enjoyed having my clothes on so much with a woman before.

I want to make her come; hell, I want to come with her. But my brain is still screaming, chastising me and full out berating me for my stupidity. And at long last, after giving in for far too many minutes, my brain finally gets my body's attention, and I'm stopped by a mere thread of impropriety. This is wrong. I know this is wrong, and I have to stop before we go too far. With agonizing willpower, I slow our movements. I sense her confusion and can offer her little explanation without hurting her.

"Why did you stop?" she whispers.

There is no way of softening the blow. "You know we can't."

She rolls away from me, sitting up to leave. I wrap my arms around her waist, pulling myself up to straddle her from behind— my brain still screaming at me to stop touching her.

I whisper into her ear, "Don't go. I don't want you to leave."

"I'm embarrassed. Please, just let me go."

And making one of the few right decisions since her first touch, I do, and I'm suddenly left alone with my guilt in the darkness of my room. I want desperately to reassure her of how much I want her, to take away the rejection she feels right now, but admitting it to her would serve no purpose except to further complicate and confuse our relationship. The last thing I want is for her to confuse my compassion for her with the sexual intimacy I've allowed to happen. I'm too old for her, and she doesn't need a lover or even the idea of a lover. She needs me to be her friend. She needs to be able to trust me, and I'm destroying that trust every time I touch her. I'm ashamed of the way I've allowed my desire to cloud my judgment, and I have to make this right. She's been hurt so much already today. The last thing I want is to hurt her more, but I know, before even saying the words, I will. But they're words she needs to hear.

I enter her bedroom and can see her silhouette in the bed. She's facing away from the door and me. I sit down. "Row, I've made a mistake. We can't... It's not right for me to be so close to you. I've been inappropriate with you, and I can't do it anymore." I pause, expecting her to respond, but she's silent. "I love spending time with you, and I love talking with you, and I know I'm hurting you right now, and I'm sorry. But I don't want to make any mistakes with you. I care too much for you to violate our friendship. I'm sorry. Please forgive me." I sit for a moment longer, hoping for a response. I get none and silently stand and leave the room. I hate myself. I've hurt her, and all I want to do is run back in there and hold her.

As I lie alone in my dark room, I start to understand how different things will be tomorrow, and I'm depressed just thinking about how our relationship will change. The idea of being with her and not being close to her or being able to touch her is almost painful. But it's the right thing to do, and I renew the vow I should have kept long ago.

CHAPTER FOURTEEN

Rowan

I'm humiliated. I'm heartbroken. I'm pissed as hell. I really thought he wanted me. I wanted him so much. I would have done anything at that moment. I would have given myself to him in a heartbeat. What was all that bullshit about caring about me, violating our relationship? I just needed to be with him so much. I want to be in his arms, and according to him, that's wrong and won't happen ever again. He rejected me, and it hurts. He didn't want me, or he didn't want me enough. If he had, he wouldn't have pushed me away and made excuses. I can't stand feeling this way, and the tightness in my chest is painful. It screams at me to run, flee as far from him as possible as though the grip on my heart won't release until I've put a safe distance between us. I have to get away from him.

I wait for some time to pass until getting up quietly and dressing in the dark. I sneak out to the living room, tiptoeing by his bedroom door. But not quietly enough… I make it only halfway across the living room before he emerges from the hall and snaps on the light. I freeze and lower my head. Busted. I turn slowly to look at him but can hardly meet his eyes.

He speaks, or rather, he seethes. He knows my intention, and he's angry. "Where are you going?" His words are snarled in his fury.

"I want to go home."

"That's not the deal."

"Fuck your deal!" I'm angry too.

I turn on my heel and head out the door with him trailing behind me. He catches up to me in the small vestibule, and as I pull the door open, he reaches around me and slams it shut. He leans down and between gritted teeth commands, "Get upstairs … now."

I try pulling the door handle again, but his hand is still holding the door shut. It's no use. I spin toward him, push past him, and go back upstairs. He's right behind me, and he's fuming.

He immediately lays into me once the door is shut. "What the fuck were you thinking going out in the middle of night in the dead of winter? Does hypothermia sound like a good idea to you? You want to be pissed at me, fine. I'll deal with that, but don't ever think of breaking our agreement, because I don't care what I've done to piss you off; if the agreement is broken, your little secret will be anything but."

The whole time he's talking, I'm standing, facing him but unable to look at him—my own fury building to critical mass. And when I hit my limit, I finally explode. "Fuck you! I can't stand this. I'm not some little pet project. I don't need you treating me like some incompetent child. And right now, I'd rather be at home with him than you in a second. I've been taking care of myself for some time now and doing just fine."

"Really! I seem to recall a bloody lip not so far in your past. Is that your idea of doing fine? Please. You don't know what fine is. You may be good at getting by, but you don't know the first fucking thing about having a real life. You leech off the life of my family because you don't have one of your own. But unlike family and far more like an immature child, you run away the first time you don't get your way. It doesn't work that way. You want to take care of yourself, then learn to deal with this!"

Hurt is an understatement. I can barely breathe after hearing his comments, and I do the only thing I can do. I push past him and into my bedroom, slamming the door before breaking down in tears on the bed. Is it not enough that I think of myself as a leech already? Did he have to remind me of exactly how I'm seen by him and his family? I lie there most of the night, replaying the evening and not sleeping at all. I'm supposed to join his family for Christmas in the morning, and the thought of having to endure his company, let alone the company of his family, is gut-wrenching. I can't do it. I won't do it.

I'm determined to give escape one more try, and at five o'clock,

I rise again. I sneak from the apartment and am greeted by the cold, blustering, Michigan wind. I know it's stupid to walk home in this weather, but I have a good coat and would rather freeze than deal with seeing him this morning. It takes me an excruciating forty-five minutes to walk home, and that's jogging most of the way. I know he'll be furious with me; hell, I know there's a good chance he'll decide to follow through and call the cops, but at this moment I don't care. My pride has gotten the better of me, and I refuse to let him call the shots.

When I arrive home, it's barely starting to get light out, and when I enter the house, the dining room table is as I left it, and my father is passed out on the couch. Good. I'm tired from not sleeping and want nothing more than to crawl into bed for the rest of the day. Merry Christmas to me.

I know my phone will be ringing, and I'm prepared to tell Sara I'm sick again today. They will be leaving at first light tomorrow morning to catch an early flight out of Grand Rapids toward Denver. The Harringtons will be staying at their condo in Frisco, skiing for the next week and won't return until the day before New Year's Eve. In years past, I've gone on family trips with them, but this year I decided to work during the holiday to make extra money. I want Logan as far from me as possible, and I'm thankful I declined their offer to join them this year.

Like clockwork, my phone rings at ten o'clock, and I make my excuses. Sara says nothing of Logan, and I take that as a good sign he's keeping his mouth shut. I hibernate in my room for the entire day, only coming out for food and the bathroom. That night as I lie in bed, I'm depressed. I'm so angry at Logan but also heartbroken I haven't heard from him today. Tomorrow he'll be gone, and I won't see him for at least five days. I miss him already, but it's likely for the best.

⌘⌘⌘⌘

The next few days pass like a fog. I work a lot and make really good money with the holiday crowd in town. I need the money for a car, not to mention when Sara and I move to Ann Arbor next fall, and I'm again thankful I decided to stay home. I try not to think about Logan, but that is a near impossibility. I want to see him, but my anger is intense and unrelenting. I want to hurt him the way he's hurt me. He's probably not even thinking of me at all.

The first I hear from Sara is on the thirtieth when she calls me to say they've arrived back in town. She asks me to come over for dinner, but fortunately I have to work that night. I don't want to lie to her, but there is no way I'm going to go over there and risk seeing Logan. I don't ever want to see him, except, of course, that's a lie; I want to see him so much I'm miserable from it.

We make plans to go out the next night for New Year's. I don't know what Sara has in store for us, but she's made me promise not to back out. Sara's a socialite, and I often find myself in places I would never dream of going on my own. I'm shy in a crowd even if she's the center of attention. I'm sure she has some party lined up, and I'll probably end up getting drunk just to keep my cool.

The next night, Sara picks me up and we head out for the evening. After grabbing dinner in town, Sara lets me in on her plan. "Okay ... so ... we're going to a frat party, and before you sulk, just hear me out." I'm already sulking, and by the feigned look of warning and the chastising finger she wags in my face, she's going to tolerate none of it. "Jeremy is going to be there." And there's her lust-struck look.

Don't get me wrong, Sara is not promiscuous. Not in the least, but she gets attention. She always has. She's as beautiful as Logan, and guys drool over her. She falls into lust, they trail after her, she decides she's bored with them or they're too stupid, too intelligent, too bossy, too nice, too ... something, and then she's off to the next suitor.

"Who's Jeremy again?" Of course, I know who Jeremy is. She's been going on about him for the better part of two weeks. I smirk; it's hard given my piss-poor demeanor.

"Stop it. I *love* Jeremy." Her words are exaggerated and completely contrived, and I'm surprised to see she's not using her arm-across-the-forehead fainting move.

"You do not." Even though I fall into the familiar role of chastising her, her ridiculous dramatics have me smiling for the first time in over a week.

"Fine, but I might someday, and you wouldn't want to be the one to stand between me and the love of my life. Would you?" She's feigning desperation again. The drama this girl can throw down when she wants to get her way...

"I'm banking on this being just another guy you decide you hate in a week. I don't belong at a college party, Sara. You do. You fit in anywhere. I just look out of place."

"I won't desert you, I promise." And she never does, bless her heart, but it's terrifying nevertheless. This is her life, not mine. This is her fun, not mine. "I haven't seen you for a week. And quite frankly, you've been distant lately, and I don't like it." Enter the guilt trip. But she's right, and I *should* feel guilty.

"Fine, but I'm going to drink … a lot." And I do just that; I immediately start downing shots and chugging beer just to stave off the social anxiety that is crippling me, and before too long, life gets really interesting.

CHAPTER FIFTEEN

Logan

I met with Michael Brighton at Brighton and Brinks in Denver on my last day in Colorado. The contract has been complete for months now, so this was just a quick meet and greet while I was in town. But the moment I entered the posh downtown building that would soon be my professional home, a dark and confusing cloud settled over my mind.

I've known for a long time Colorado was where I wanted to be, but the plans I was once so certain of are suddenly cloudy. The contract is concrete, and lest I be required to fork over a year's salary for breaking it, there is little reason to believe I will be anywhere but Colorado in six months' time. I've sought out this life ferociously and planned it in painstaking detail. I've let no obstacle stand in my way, working tirelessly to achieve the highest marks in my education, but now… Every day seems to bring Rowan closer to the forefront of my mind, and it's clouding everything that was once so clear to me. And as much as I keep trying to tell myself the time away from her did me good, I know damn well it hasn't. I've been away from her for a week, spending a good portion of every day worrying about her and feeling guilty for being such an ass to her.

She didn't call yesterday once we had returned home, and she didn't come over last night. This party is something of an obligation to Amy that I feel like I can't get out of. I want nothing more than to see Rowan and make amends for all the awful things I said to her last week. And it's with Rowan consuming my every thought that I

ELIZABETH FINN

venture out on my date with Amy.

Amy is in her senior year at Grand Valley State University—the college where I spent my undergraduate years at before moving on to law school. And the party is at a frat house just off campus. I hate fraternities, and I was happy to say goodbye to them when I entered Cooley. But Amy lives for this shit. She's in a sorority, of course, and this is their brother house, whatever the hell that means.

As we enter the house, I can't help but think this is going to be a very long night. I wonder what Rowan is doing tonight. She is no doubt out with Sara somewhere. And with that unwelcome thought, jealousy hits like a sledgehammer to my brain as I imagine her hanging out with her classmates—specifically the ones with penises.

I follow Amy around the loud, obnoxious crowd, hating every second of our date and wanting to escape. And when I catch sight of Sara standing by some freshman with a glass of beer in her hand, I'm caught completely off guard. What the hell is she doing here? She looks drunk but seems to be behaving herself. If she's here, though, where the hell is Rowan?

I march over to Sara and take the beer from her hand. "Sara, what the hell are you doing here?"

To my surprise, she replies, "Rowan and I came, and we're doing the same damn thing you are. Having fun."

She's clearly missed the misery on my face. Then, like all good sisters do, she blows me off and starts flirting like a pro with the boy standing next to her.

However, at hearing Rowan's name, I'm suddenly her unwelcome new best friend. "You said Rowan came. So where the hell is she?" I'm fighting to keep the desperation from my voice.

"Jesus, Logan. What the hell do you care? She went upstairs with some very hot hottie. Leave her alone."

My jaw drops. What the hell had she just said? *Gone upstairs with?* That meant fucking around with or, worse yet, fucking. I climb the stairs two at a time ready to lose it. I start checking rooms, dreading what I'll find with each turn of a knob ... and then I hit the jackpot.

As I stumble into the dimly lit room, I can see two figures in an obvious state of sexual play. I turn on the lights afraid of who I'll see and am frozen in a state of shock and fury. Rowan is lying on the bed with a man nearly on top of her. Her shirt is off, and his mouth is on one of her small perfect breasts. Her head is back in an obvious state of ecstasy.

66

It takes her a moment to realize they're not alone, and when our eyes meet, she doesn't look away. Her eyes, usually so big and bright, have the laziness of alcohol. She's looking at me with no more shame than if she were fully dressed having tea with the queen of England. I want to scream. Instead, I storm over to the bed and grab the man by the collar of his shirt, yanking him from the bed. She lies there propped up on her elbows, watching with an almost amused look on her face.

"Get. Up," I order in a quiet, furious tone, but she doesn't budge.

The man is getting up off the floor, and for the first time, I realize who her counterpart is. He's a sophomore by the name of Benjamin Aaronson. I know him. Women apparently think he's *hot*, and I hate that his hands and his mouth were on her skin. He has a look of fury in his eyes until he sees it's me that has interrupted his little play time. He immediately starts apologizing to me but has no idea why he's sorry.

"Get the fuck out!" I yell.

He obeys, quickly slinking away.

Rowan is still propped up on her elbows seductively watching me. I've never seen her breasts and can't help but take them in. They're small like I knew they would be but perfectly shaped and round with beautiful, tight, pink nipples that are glistening from another man's mouth. She watches me staring at her, and when my eyes make their way back up to hers, she smirks.

"Get dressed now," I seethe.

She's obstinate. "Why should I?"

As I pick up her shirt and throw it at her, I can't help but bite back. "Because little girls don't get to play big girl games." Drunk as she is, that strikes a chord, and she has to fight back the hurt. It only takes as long as getting her shirt back on until the drunken obstinacy returns, and with that, the calm seductiveness that is starting to eat at me. "We're leaving ... now."

She knows it isn't a question, and she decides to let that one go without argument. She follows me back downstairs where we find Sara and Amy.

I tell Amy we're leaving, and naturally, she objects. "We just got here, Logan. Why do we have to leave so soon?"

"Why the hell do you think, Amy? In case you hadn't noticed, Sara and Rowan are drunk as hell, and Rowan was about ready to make some very bad choices upstairs with Benjamin Aaronson."

"Benjamin Aaronson? Why the hell would he want anything to do with Rowan? He could have any woman here he wants." Amy's laughing, and as angry as I am at Rowan, I want to kill Amy for insulting her.

As I start to snap at Amy to shut up, Sara, good friend that she is, comes to Rowan's rescue. "You know, Amy, some men appreciate a woman who doesn't throw herself out there like you do. Bleached hair and huge tits aren't the most important thing to everyone." This night can't get any worse.

"I said we're leaving." After more argument from Sara and Amy, I finally manage to get all three outside to my car.

I head toward my parents' house to drop Sara off. My blood is boiling, and I keep looking in the rear view mirror just to catch Rowan coolly looking right back at me. She's being coy and enjoying her drunken game far too much. I will absolutely have to punish her for that, but first, I have to get Sara home and ditch Amy. As we pull up outside my parents', to my surprise, both Sara and Rowan start to get out.

"Where the hell do you think you're going, Rowan?" I climb from the car, trying desperately to keep my intimate familiarity of her from touching my eyes as I speak with gritted teeth to her. I want to be away from Sara and Amy to yell at her, scream at her. My anger at her and my ridiculous jealousy have me crumbling. I'm not regarding her as a man who knows her casually but as a man obsessed with her, a scorned lover, a jilted boyfriend! I'm acting like a pathetic idiot, and it's a losing battle to disguise the inappropriate fury in my voice.

"She's spending the night with me, Logan," Sara quips in an annoyed tone.

"The fuck she is. Get in the car, Rowan," I snap back.

And while my fury and jealousy are right below the surface of my expression, Rowan watches me, still with her cool and calm glare. Eventually, she obliges, climbing back into my Jeep as Sara continues to argue. I finally grab Sara by the wrist and pull her up to the door. The lights are out and the house quiet, and once I start threatening to wake up Mom and Dad, she quiets right down. I then return to my car and head toward Amy's.

She lives on the other side of town, and I can feel Rowan's eyes on me in the rear view mirror the entire ride over. Every time I glance up, I see her looking back through long seductive lashes. The more I see those cool eyes looking at me, the more furious I get and the more aroused. I want to fuck every last bit of Benjamin Aaronson out of her mind and make her beg for her release.

When Amy realizes I'm heading for her house, she becomes furious. "Why are you taking me home, Logan? You promised we would spend the night alone. You can't be ditching me because the little whore back there decided to get herself fucked."

"Watch it Amy. I'm not going to argue with you tonight."

"Then tell me why? You're going to drop little Miss Trailer Trash off at her shitty ass trailer and then go home by yourself? That doesn't make any fucking sense, Logan. You either want to be with me or not."

My jaw is clenched to the point of pain as I struggle to maintain control. To my horror, she continues. "You never let me spend the night anymore, we hardly ever go out, I can't even remember the last time you fucked me."

At hearing the last part of this little tirade, my eyes snap up to see Rowan smirking. She's enjoying this far too much, and it's driving me crazy. Amy finally resorts to sulking when she doesn't get her answers, and we drive on in silence. After dropping Amy off and arguing with her for a few more minutes, Rowan and I are finally alone. She crawls over the console and into the front seat. She lounges against the passenger door while she continues to watch me.

"Your girlfriend's a real bitch, Logan. You know that?" She'll get no argument out of me on that one, and I ignore her. But she's incessant in her drunken state. "Are you taking me to my house, Logan?"

"You know I'm not."

"Then you're taking me back to your place, Logan?"

"You know I am."

"Why didn't you let me stay with Sara, Logan?"

"Shut up."

"Why did you drop Amy off, Logan?"

"Shut. Up."

"How much do you want to fuck me right now, Logan?"

I pull over, throw my car into park, and turn to her, leaning forward. "I will never fuck you, Rowan."

She also leans in, meeting me at the center console and replies, "But you want to, don't you, Logan?"

I do want to, so much my cock is stiff as hell and begging to impale her. Every sultry, seductive utterance of my name from her lips has me wanting her more. She's toying with me in her drunken confidence. Without moving her head, she shifts her eyes down to my crotch and back up to meet my eyes. She then reaches over and cups my crotch in her hand, gasping as she realizes just to what extent I want to fuck her. She smirks again. I grab her hand and shove it back to her, right myself, throw my car into drive, and take off. She again leans back into the door, and we drive in silence the rest of the way to my place. I'm angry as hell, horny as fuck, and I intend to make her suffer for her little game.

I march upstairs with Rowan staggering behind. We enter the apartment, and she collapses on the couch. I sit down next to her and take her shoes off. I turn on the TV and wait for her to start sobering up.

About two hours later, she starts to moan as she rouses from drunken sleep. I wait patiently. Soon, she pushes herself up and sits looking pale and very uncomfortable. And still, I wait patiently. A few minutes later, she starts to stand, looking dizzy and even more uncomfortable.

I smile at her in mock kindness. "Are you not feeling well?" I croon sweetly. "Someone should have told you alcohol can do that. Can I get you anything? Perhaps another beer would do the trick. Shot of whiskey perhaps?"

She's off heading for her bathroom. She tries to close the door in my face, but I stop it with it my hand. I enter, not exactly wanting to see her puke but definitely wanting to punish her for the evening. I sit on the side of the bathtub, studying her as she kneels. As she nervously looks over at me, it's my turn to smirk.

"Logan, please … just leave. I'm going to be sick. I don't want you here."

"That's too bad. I think I'll stay for the show." I'm emotionally torturing her, but while I'm hit with guilt and even sympathy for her, my anger pushes me further. I'll feel guilty later.

She whimpers as she keeps begging me to leave, until she can beg no longer, and empties her stomach. She reaches up quickly to flush the toilet, sparing me the view of her dinner. When her head comes up, her face is flushed and wet with tears, her nose is running, and she has slobber hanging from her mouth. This definitely isn't her best side. I continue to watch. She grabs some toilet paper to wipe her mouth and finally, shakily, finds her way to her feet. I think that should about cover punishment for now.

She flushes her face with cool water and starts to brush her teeth. I follow her to the sink and stand beside her, watching her. Her eyes find mine in the mirror as she feels me looking at her, and she glances away. She's hurt, angry, and humiliated. And while my anger is still very present, her embarrassment has finally softened my rage. And though I know I shouldn't, I place my hand under her shirt at the small of her back and start to massage her lower back. She meets my eyes again, and she starts to cry.

She finishes brushing her teeth, and I turn her to face me. She's still crying and so embarrassed she can't look me in the eye. I take her hand and help her to her bed. She lies down, and I help her out of her jeans. I crawl in with her and pull her back to me, and I find we're right back where we started little over a week ago. A lot can change in a week, and sometimes, you end up going full circle. We stay that way for the rest of the night, and I can't help but be glad she's lying next to me again. I'll finish being angry with her in the morning.

CHAPTER SIXTEEN

Rowan

As I wake, my head is splitting, and my mouth is so dry I can hardly swallow. I can't imagine what my father sees in this. Logan is sleeping behind me with his arm around me. I love the way it feels being in his arms, but I don't want to face him this morning. It's not a choice. He'll wake soon, and I might as well enjoy this while I can. I close my eyes for another half hour or so until I feel Logan stirring. I roll toward him, wanting to savor every last minute. I put my arm around him and feel his smooth muscled back with my hands. I lay my head against his chest and wait for him to wake.

When he comes to, I look up at him nervous of what mood he'll be in. He looks down at me. He isn't smiling, and he isn't frowning. He's just studying me. He finally trails his hand down my back to my bottom, rounds the cheek with his hand, and then cups it in his palm. He massages while I keep holding onto him, nearly holding my breath at his intimate touch. We lie there for many long minutes not speaking. He finally dips his head and kisses the small area where my shoulder meets my neck before pulling away from me to stand. He leaves without a word as I struggle to piece the events of the night together in my mind.

A few minutes later, he comes back in with a big glass of water and some Tylenol. He sits down on the bed as I sit up, and I take the Tylenol, washing it down with the water. "Logan, I—"

"I don't want to do this right now," he cuts me off.

"But I—"

"Rowan, I'm angry." He interrupts me again. "I'm not doing this right now. Get up and get dressed. I'm taking you home."

Logan leaves the room and I get up, dressing in my jeans that are lying at the foot of the bed. I hesitantly walk out to the living room, and Logan is already in his coat with his keys in his hand. He really is ready to get rid of me today, and I feel the same sting of rejection I felt a week ago. We make our way silently down to the car and say nothing to one another on the way to my house. When he pulls up, he doesn't look at me or say anything at all. I sit for a moment, expecting him to say something before finally giving up and opening the door. I feel pathetic, and as I start to remember my evening, I'm mortified.

I completely humiliated myself. Why did I have to go upstairs with Benjamin? I don't even like him. The entire time he was touching me and kissing me, I was imagining it was Logan's hands on me, his mouth tasting me. What had I said to Logan? My mind is so fuzzy, but I distinctly remember coming on to him. He'd rejected me of course. Why would he want some drunken girl doing her best to be a slut? The comment he made in the bedroom comes flooding back to me in a painful rush. *Little girls don't get to play big girl games.* That's all I was to him—just some stupid little girl. And I puked in front of him. That was not cool. He was so gentle with me this morning, though. I just don't understand him sometimes. If he was so furious with me, why did he touch me the way he did? He was so gentle and intimate. I want that from him so much. I'm sure he just felt sorry for me.

My head is pounding, and it's nearly lunchtime by the time I feel any semblance of normalcy. I feel better once I get some food in my stomach, and by mid-afternoon I think I'll live. I spend a few hours getting ahead on reading for school. I do a couple loads of laundry to get me through the week, and then I sit in my room depressed. I want to see him so much. I need to talk to him about last night. I need to explain. I need him to forgive me for being so stupid.

I know I shouldn't, but I hop on my bike and head to his place. It's cold and the ride over miserable. By the time I reach his place, my knuckles are white, and I'm afraid they'll break if I move them. I run upstairs to escape the frigid air and knock on the door. He answers. He doesn't look happy to see me, and I look away, suddenly nervous.

"What are you doing here?"

"I wanted to talk to you about last night. Or ... I mean ... I wanted to apologize about last night." I can't look at him.

I'm suddenly terrified he's going to kick me out, but he doesn't. He holds the door open but doesn't make me feel at all welcome. I enter and nervously stand by the door as he looks at me, waiting for me to speak.

"Please don't be mad at me. I was so stupid last night. I can't stand that you're upset with me."

He stares at me for a long moment without saying a word before he sighs. "Come with me."

He's obviously not happy to see me, but at least he's not kicking me out. He leads me to his bedroom and leaves me there, returning with my pajamas. He makes no move to give me privacy and silently stands back with his arms crossed across his chest, waiting for me to change. My nipples are taut just at the thought of his eyes on me. I slide my shirt over my head and throw my tank top on before wriggling out of my bra. I try to pull my tank top down over my hips as I slide my pants to the floor. Logan is still standing like a statue, watching me intensely. And though my heart is pounding, he looks completely at ease, maybe even bored. I pull my pajama pants on quickly before sitting down on the side of his bed.

He then grabs an old pair of navy sweatpants from a drawer and starts stripping off his shirt in front of me. My heart stops working when I see him fumbling with the button and zipper of his jeans. I stare at him as he stares back at me. As he pulls down his pants, I can see he's wearing black boxer briefs. His stomach looks perfect against the designer waistband, and I keep staring. I'm likely not the best judge, but he's aroused and very large, and it shows deliciously beneath the distended fabric. I can't help but remember the last time I was in this room and how good his arousal felt against my own swollen wetness. I could stare at him all night but don't get the chance before he pulls on the sweats and saunters back over to the bed. He lies down, pulling me with him.

We lie facing one another for a few minutes before he finally speaks. "Did something happen with your father today?"

Regardless of the way his body appears to be responding to me, he still doesn't sound happy I'm there. "No."

"You should have called. It's too cold for you to be riding that stupid bike around town. I would have come to get you."

I'm practically whispering. "I'm sorry. I didn't want to bother you."

"Damn it, Rowan. You don't bother me. Why do you always think you're in my way or bothering me or annoying me?"

I shake my head, near tears. "I don't know."

The fragile emotion in my voice causes him to suddenly soften and reach out to stroke my cheek.

I choke back the tears and find my voice. "It's hard letting you help me all the time. I don't want to feel like a burden, but I do. Your family has always done so much for me, and it's difficult when you have nothing to give back. I have nothing to offer you, but I take from you all the time. It makes me feel guilty. It always has." My voice is rough and strained with my choked back tears.

He closes his eyes in what I can only guess is pain. "You feel like a burden because the last time we were together, I made the mistake of using your situation to hurt you. My family loves you, and you are no burden to us. You never have been, and I had no right to say you leech off us. You didn't deserve that, and I was being cruel out of anger. I don't think that. I like having you here. I like being with you." His voice is serious, but his smile is gentle. And I smile too.

He pauses. He looks like he wants to speak but is considering his words. "Do you like Benjamin?"

"No! No! No!" I'm a damn broken record, but I'm desperate for him to understand.

He smirks at my response. "Did it feel good when he was sucking on your nipples?"

I gasp at his use of such blatant language. "No."

"You looked like you were enjoying yourself." Still smirking, and now with a raised eyebrow.

I'm silent for a moment. "It wasn't what I wanted."

"You're being coy. You either enjoyed it or didn't. Which is it?" Add a cocked head.

"It just wasn't what I expected. I mean… It was different than I thought it would be."

"It was different than it has been with other guys?" Curiosity lights up his eyes.

I look at him, confused. "What do you mean?"

"…than the other guys you've been with?"

Now I'm blushing. "There really aren't other guys."

He considers this. "So then, would it stand to reason you're still a virgin?"

I quietly answer, the heat of my cheeks scorching my skin. "Yes." I look down, not wanting him to see my face.

But he gently pulls my chin back up to look at him. "I like that you're a virgin. I think you should stay that way for a while." He looks relieved. I feel like an idiot. He seems content I'm so clueless, and I wish for the gazillionth time I wasn't such a loser. What else is new? He finally reaches over and turns the lamp off, and as I start to drift off, he kisses me gently on my forehead. "I'm sorry I hurt you. I hate that I was so cruel."

I never thought I would sleep in his bed again, and I'm thrilled.

Logan

As I lie there in the dark, I can't help but wonder how I've gotten myself to this place again. What was I thinking? I have to stop this, yet as the thought enters my mind, I acknowledge instantly that I can't. What was I thinking touching her the way I had this morning? I was furious at her for the night before and had every intention of laying into her first thing this morning, but I couldn't help but touch her. As though touching her somehow reclaimed her body from the hot Benjamin Aaronson, whom I now irrationally hate. I might as well have humped her leg like some dominant male dog.

Her bottom felt so round and perfect. I didn't want to stop. I must have had my hands on her for nearly half an hour this morning. And then I kissed her neck to make it worse. Every time I get angry with her, I end up wanting her and touching her. Why does she do this to me? And what was I thinking taking my clothes off in front of her? I was so aroused by watching her change, and I wanted her to see me, see what she was doing to me. I had no business letting her know she had affected me that way.

I want to fuck her so bad it hurts sometimes. When I don't see her, I miss her, and when I do see her, I'm tormented by her. She is all I think about anymore. I could be sitting at the drive-thru, waiting for my lunch, and I start to imagine what it would be like to spread her legs open and feast on her. Finding out she's an inexperienced virgin should have been a turn off. But it's not. I want her more now than ever before. I love that she's never been tasted, and I love that she's never tasted a man. I want to show her everything and push her to give me everything I want from her. I want her looking into my eyes as I thrust into her for the first time.

She can make this decision on her own, so why shouldn't it be me? I want her to whisper my name as she's coming for the first time. I want to roll her over and taste her in places I've never wanted to taste before, claiming every last inch of her flesh. I don't ever want another man to touch her skin again. I want her to belong to me and no one else. And I'm driving myself insane with her. I have got to get away from her, but I can't bear the idea of being apart from her. I have never wanted so uncontrollably before, and I feel like I'm losing my mind. When I finally drift off to sleep, it's to her soft breathing and my most erotic fantasies of her.

CHAPTER SEVENTEEN

Rowan

The second half of the academic year is now in full force. I've finally bought my car, an old, slightly rusted out Jeep Wagoneer. It has wood paneling and an old, worn, leather interior. I love it but rather doubt anyone else does. It's just nice to be off that damn bike finally. Even this liberating time is dampened as I start to realize the end is near. Logan will be leaving for Denver and his new place at Brighton and Brinks within just a few weeks of graduating, and as much as I don't want to admit it, I'm terrified of losing him. It's spring, and spring break is a mere two weeks away, and the passing time is starting to weigh on my mind.

Over the past couple of months, I have continued my regular cohabitation with Logan, and it continues to confuse and excite me. There are many times when it seems as though he's holding me at arm's length, and at other times, he seems so open to me—desperate for closeness. He's an enigma, and he shows nothing of what he's thinking to me. Lying to Sara has also become exhausting, and I know our deceit must be difficult for him too.

Logan will be going away for spring break with his friends to Colorado again for their annual ski trip, and I'm dreading that time. He has made me promise I'll continue to use the apartment or stay with Sara when he's away, but it isn't my father that has me so bothered. I simply don't want to go without him for so long.

Logan

I would give anything to just cancel this stupid trip. I don't even want to go, but, of course, that's ridiculous. What guy doesn't want to go away with his oldest friends on his final spring break? Oh yeah, the kind who is infatuated with his little sister's best friend. I don't even see Amy anymore but have never officially broken up with her. After New Year's Eve, I wasn't able to even pretend civility with her. I started blowing her off every time she called, and eventually, she simply stopped calling. I'm glad to be rid of her, but strangely never cared enough about the end of our relationship to even mention it to people.

I've managed to keep Rowan out of my bed, but hardly out of my mind or my fantasies for that matter. When I masturbate, it's her I see, her voice I hear, and her soul I possess. It's never satisfying, and I've become the most sexually frustrated man in history. And it's on one such frustrating evening I find myself in the most horrific of all compromising situations.

CHAPTER EIGHTEEN

Logan

It's always on Thursday nights that Rowan has her private dance lessons, and depending on the state her father is in, she arrives late or not at all. Not knowing whether to expect her or not and certainly not for some time, I find myself lying on my bed, daydreaming about all the things I'd like to be doing with her.

My mind is imagining her naked on my bed. She's looking at me, her eyes begging for me, and I'm compelled to oblige. I have to taste her before I can make love to her, and I ease her legs open from the knees as she looks on in anticipation. As I open her lips to me, I take one long delicious lick without breaking her gaze, and she gasps in excitement and need. I imagine myself studying her wet pussy before eating her. Her folds are slick and pink and swelling with desire. Her scent is intoxicating, and as I begin to feast on her bud, her hips start to move of their own accord.

Before my fantasy can take me any further, I sit up in my aroused stupor and fumble at the button of my pants, letting my hard cock loose. It's begging to be touched and stroked, and I imagine I'm stroking my cock in preparation to enter her body. I continue touching myself, indulging in my fantasy.

In my mind, I stop eating her and return to studying her every inch. I brush her clit with my finger as a shiver runs through her body, and I then run the finger down to her opening. I tickle and toy with her opening before pressing into her—only a fraction of an inch at first and then back out. Her body is quivering in anticipation, and

I don't make her wait long. I continue fingering her in and out, pushing farther each time, relishing the sight of my finger gliding in and out of her beautiful tight body until finally I push all the way. She looks down at herself, wanting to watch me fuck her with my finger as much as I'm enjoying the same view. She's quietly moaning as I continue to thrust into her deeply, and she continues watching my slick wet finger enter her over and over.

In the real world, my front door opens. But I hear nothing but the moans inside my head. I continue to stroke myself, needing my release desperately. And then I'm jerked back to reality as my only partially closed bedroom door is pushed all the way open.

Rowan

When I'd arrived at the studio, I'd found it locked and dark. It's unusual for Anthony to cancel lessons and even more unusual that he wouldn't at least call. I'd contemplated, only for a brief moment, driving back home. But as I'd been getting ready to leave no more than twenty minutes before, my father had also been preparing to leave. Besides, I always prefer Logan's company to my father's any day. Furthermore, Logan would have been furious with me if I'd gone home knowing my father was out getting drunk.

So the decision was simple, and I was left with an unexpected evening alone with Logan, something I typically don't get on a Thursday.

I make it to his place in record time. As I enter the apartment, it's quiet, and Logan isn't in the living room or kitchen. As I move down the hall, I see his bedroom door is ajar, and I hear quiet movement from within. I enter his room.

And then I gasp…

Our shocked eyes lock for a moment before I'm drawn back to the source of my gasp. It takes me a confusing moment to realize what's happening, and when I do, I can't take my eyes off his penis. His hand is still wrapped around its shaft, and he is hard and erect. He appears stunned and unable to move, and I'm stunned and unable to take my eyes off him.

As he comes to his senses, he realizes I'm not looking away from him. In what appears to be nothing more than a desperate attempt to bring me back to *my* senses, he huskily whispers out my name. "Row."

It doesn't work, and he has to repeat himself to get my attention. Finally meeting his gaze again, I'm suddenly aware I've been staring far too long, and I become immediately humiliated. Our eyes are locked on one another, and as I inhale ragged breaths he looks steadily at me, his heavy breathing and wide eyes the only signs of his own inner turmoil. I start to stutter some unknown language before finally breaking the stare and darting from his room toward my own.

I close the door to my room and stand with my back to it unable to move. Many minutes later, I make my way over to the bed and sit. I haven't turned the lights on, and I sit in darkness for a long time. I'm mortified, but through my mortification I keep going back to the sight of him. It's early yet, but I stay in my room for the rest of the night. He makes no attempt to disturb me, and I thank God for that. I don't think I could bear seeing him right now. He must think I'm the stupidest girl in the world staring at him as if I've never seen a penis before. I finally drift off to sleep uncomfortable about the coming day. I set the alarm clock early, intending to go home before he gets up, and I sneak from the apartment shortly after five o'clock.

CHAPTER NINETEEN

Logan

I wake from a restless night sleep. I know I should have gone to her last night and tried to explain, but I just couldn't get past my own embarrassment. I don't want her to see me this way—like some testosterone-driven animal. I'll have to talk to Rowan about what happened this morning, but I'm dreading the conversation. Humiliation is not an emotion I experience very easily, and I'm not a big fan. As I shower, I can't help but remember the look on her face as she was staring at my cock. The humiliation has only just started to subside, and I can't stop seeing those intense stunned eyes on my body. Were they on me for the right reason and not pure terror, they would have been an unmatched turn on.

Am I really such a cock that I lose my sense of hearing just because I have a fucking hard-on? How could I have not heard the door open? I have to admit I've fantasized, on more than one occasion, of Rowan watching me pleasure myself as I watch her do the same, but this was not what I had in mind. I step from the shower and finish getting ready, mentally preparing myself for the "birds and the bees" discussion that will ensue.

I knock on Rowan's door and get no answer, and it occurs to me, given her past history of fleeing my apartment, she likely left long ago. I enter the room and, not surprisingly, find it empty with the bed made. Irritation starts to build as I remember the last time she sneaked off to avoid me. These little immature games were going to have to stop. I suppose I'll just add that to the list of fun topics we'll be discussing next time I see her. Only problem is, I never have any idea when I'm going to see her.

I'm late for a meeting with the DA and have to rush around to get there in time. The day is long and as much as I'm not looking forward to our discussion, I'm looking forward to seeing Rowan.

But she doesn't make an appearance that evening, and I'm left disappointed. Boredom getting the better of me, I decide to hook up with my friends at The Inn for some pool and darts. On my way there, I drive by the Bistro and see Rowan's car parked out back. At least I know she's there and safe. I then spot her father's car at his shitty bar of choice. I can't help but feel a sense of excitement at seeing his car. If he's there, she'll be coming over when she gets off work at ten o'clock. I can't keep my eyes off my watch all night, annoying my friends. After a few beers and a few hours, I'm ready to leave but decide to wait until I hear from Rowan.

As much as I enjoy spending time with my friends, I still miss Rowan and yearn to see her. The time is now ten, and I should hear from her anytime within the next half hour. Even though she knows she doesn't have to call, she nearly always does, except, conveniently, when I happen to be masturbating to my fantasies of her. As soon as she gets home and sees her father's car is gone, she'll call. But she doesn't. I start to get anxious around ten forty-five when I can't reach her and I've still not heard from her. I decide to drive by her trailer just to make sure everything is okay.

As I round the corner onto Rowan's street, I see her father's ancient piece of shit car parked in the driveway, and to my horror, I see her car parked beside it. A chill runs down my back when I realize his car is partially pulled onto the lawn in an obvious drunken attempt at parking. I pull up quickly, and as I approach the house, I can hear him yelling and things being thrown against the walls. I slam open the door, yelling for Rowan in a full-on panic. The yelling and commotion are coming from her room, and I burst into the room in an instant. Rowan is curled up in the fetal position on the floor, and he's kicking her in the backs of her thighs, buttocks, and any other area he can land a foot.

He doesn't even hear me enter the room through his drunken rant, and I have him in a headlock before he even knows what has happened. I pull him backward into the hallway and out into the living room, not at all sure what my next move should be. He's struggling quite effectively, given his drunken state, and I opt to let him go and face him head on. I can hear Rowan in her room crying, and my fury hits an all-time high. I throw the first punch, hitting him square in the jaw and sending him to the floor. For good measure, I kick him in the gut.

I look down the hallway to see Rowan standing hunched over and in obvious pain in her doorway. Her mouth is bloody and her face tear-stained. I want to run to her but am afraid to turn my back on her father. He's restless, and while he hasn't made any attempts to get up, I won't give him the opportunity. I watch Rowan as she stumbles in pain down the hall toward me, glancing constantly down at her father still moaning and groaning on the floor. As she approaches me, I reach for her hand and hurriedly usher her out the door to my car.

Once safely in my car and blocks away, I pull over and turn desperately to her. She's still crying, and I have no idea how badly injured she is.

She doesn't even give me the opportunity to ask before interjecting. "I'm fine. Just take me to your place, okay?"

"Please let me take you to the hospital." My words are quiet. I know she'll refuse, but I'm begging.

"No." She doesn't fail to deliver. And the quiet resolution in her voice ends the hope I had. Not enough to stop me from continuing to plead with her, but eventually I give up, and I watch her in defeat.

She's wiped her bleeding lip on her shirt, and I touch her face, gently turning it from side to side to see if there are any other facial injuries that might imply a head injury. She allows my touch without hesitation, and when I ask her if he kicked her in the stomach or chest, she assures me he didn't. I begrudgingly take her to my apartment, wanting instead to drag her to the hospital, but it isn't my choice. She's silent the whole way there, and I help her slowly up the stairs when we arrive home.

I lead her to my room and get a wet washcloth from the bathroom. I wipe her lips and face clean. Her lip is split, but it has stopped bleeding. I then start undressing her. She doesn't object, and I'm as gentle as I can be. I pull her shirt up and over her head, finding that she's braless. I look over her stomach and small breasts carefully, finding no injuries or signs of bruising.

When I turn her around to look at her back, though, I see the trailing ends of red welts that disappear below the waist of her jeans. I turn her back around to face me. While she isn't audibly weeping, she has tears running down her cheeks. Her arms are up covering her exposed breasts, and she's shaking. I ease her arms away from her hidden breasts, pulling her into me. She relaxes in my arms, wrapping her own around me.

After a long moment of stillness, she breaks the silence. "Can I take a bath?" Her voice is so quiet.

"I want to finish looking at you first."

I continue my examination of her body. I sit on the side of my bed and slowly undo her jeans as she stands in front of me. I expect her to object, but she doesn't. She allows me to pull her pants down and help her step out of them. Again, the front side of her body is unmarked, but when I turn her, I see the swollen red marks on the backs of her thighs and calves that disappear under the panties she's wearing.

I gently pull her underwear down to see the small round cheeks of her bottom red and painful. It's apparent her injuries are localized to her legs, bottom, and mouth. I can only imagine how sore she must be and how sore she will be tomorrow. I run the palm of my hand over the round cheeks of her bottom, and her breath catches as she stops breathing. Thinking better of it, I pull the back of her underwear up over her bottom and stand up behind her.

I caress the back of her neck. "I'll run you a bath." I lead her nearly naked into my bathroom and while the bathtub is filling, I hold her and she cries. I give her privacy when the tub is filled and she has what she needs.

I'm stunned as I wait for her and can hardly make sense of the night's events, but a nagging thought won't leave my mind. He was either home already when she arrived or she knew he was at the bar getting wasted. Either way, she chose to stay there. Under normal circumstances, I would be furious with her for disobeying my rules, but on this night I just feel guilty and responsible. Were it not for what she saw last night, she would have never felt the need to be away from me. Had I not been such a chicken shit and spoken to her when it happened, her embarrassment, as well as mine, would not have affected her decisions tonight.

When I hear the bathtub draining, I enter. She has her back to me and is drying herself. I again see the welts and beginnings of bruises all over her backside.

"Is there anything I can do?" I ask her quietly.

She just shakes her head.

I get her pajamas from her room and bring them back for her. She makes no move to change in front of me, and ridiculously, I feel rejected at her modesty. After allowing her privacy to change, I help her into my bed and then join her after showering and changing myself. She falls asleep quickly, but I don't.

I hate feeling so helpless and guilty. I want to talk to her but don't want to disturb her. She must be exhausted and sore, and I can't help but feel responsible for her. I finally get up and retreat to the window seat overlooking the back courtyard. The moon is nearly full, and I stare outside replaying the past twenty-four hours over and over and over.

CHAPTER TWENTY

Rowan

I wake, and it's still dark. I'm alone in bed and wish he were with me. But he is there. As I look over toward the night sky out his back window, the blue hue from the large bright moon allows me to see his silhouette on the window seat. He's sitting parallel to the window with his feet up on the seat and his knees bent. His elbows and arms are slung on his bent knees, and he's staring off into the dark.

He would have every right to be mad at me. I never should have stayed home, knowing my father would be coming home drunk. I was actually contemplating calling Logan but was having such a hard time actually picking up the phone to do it. My father wasn't supposed to come home that early or in that foul a mood. He was raging from the second he stormed in through the doorway, and the nerve I was trying to build up to call Logan soon became the last thing on my mind.

I lie silently watching Logan. He's off in his own world, and I want to join him so badly. I start to crawl from bed and realize just how sore I am. Sleep has only served to allow my muscles to tighten and tense and my whole body hurts; I feel like one big bruise. As I move from the bed, Logan looks over at me and shadowed from the light outside I'm not able to see the look on his face. He swings his legs over the side of the window seat to face me, and as I approach, the look on his face emerges. It's impossible to read.

To my relief, he holds out his hands to me, and I step between

88

his legs as he pulls me into his arms. Even as painful as I am right now, I still love the way it feels when he touches me. He offers me safety and security, and he knows how to be gentle. It's a constant and precious reminder of how amazing men can be.

He slings one leg up on the window seat and leans it against the window. He then pats the spot between his legs in invitation for me to sit. I turn with my back to him, and he helps me find my place there. I lean back into him and can feel his heart beating into me. He wraps his arms around me and clasps my hands in his. My butt is relieved to feel the thick padding on the window seat, and I'm comfortable in his arms.

After a long time of peaceful silence, I decide to say what should have been said a long while back. "I'm sorry."

"Why?" It's barely a whisper.

"For last night … for tonight … just … everything…"

"If you want to apologize for not leaving your house when you should have tonight, then I accept. If you want to apologize for what you saw last night, well … I can't really accept."

I'm suddenly confused. As is often the case, I can't tell what his intent is.

Clearly sensing my confusion, he continues. "Last night wasn't your fault, Row. You didn't do anything wrong any more than I did. Well … actually we were both wrong. I should have spoken to you about what happened last night and not waited like a coward, and you shouldn't have sneaked off this morning—again. You do realize I hate it when you do that."

His words aren't the least bit angry, and he's only gently prodding me for my behavior. After more silence, he continues in a quiet voice. "What were you thinking when you saw me last night?"

My heart starts racing as I try to come up with something that doesn't sound completely pathetic, but the only thoughts running through my mind are: how big he is, how much I wish it was *my* hand wrapped around his cock, how much I want him to make love to me, how much I want to taste him, how big he… oh yeah, covered that one.

As the gears turn in my brain, he chuckles. "Okay. Since you're being shy, I'll start. I was confused at first, evidenced by the frozen Medusa syndrome, and then I was mortified you saw me in such a compromising position. Then I was self-conscious you wouldn't like what you saw…" He trails off, offering no other explanation for his provocative final words.

Who couldn't like the way he looks? He's beautiful. Not that I've seen that many men's bodies, but the image of his balls, heavy between his legs, and his beautiful and incredibly large, rigid penis looked so perfect against his bare stomach. Even his own hand wrapped around his shaft made him look somehow powerful and virile. Just remembering the sight of him from the night before turns my body to fire, and I'm wet in an instant.

I imagine myself kneeling in front of him, cupping his testicles in one hand and wrapping my other hand around his girth. I imagine being able to please him and seeing his pleasure as he looks down at me. I want to take him in my mouth and taste him, and I want so much for him to touch the warm wet pulse between my legs and release me from it. I'm lost in my imaginings and the vision of his naked body when I realize he's still waiting for an answer.

I'm only able to manage a weak, "I don't know," and feel pathetic, something I've gotten used to feeling around him. I want so much for him to know what I'm thinking, but I could never bring myself to say it out loud. He could never want the same from me. While his body has responded to me in the past, it was nothing more than the passing effect of his comforting me. I can't compare to the women who stare at him day in and day out. He is practically worshipped in this town, and there is nothing I could do to ever compete with that attention. I can't even manage to talk around him half the time.

I as much feel him as hear him chuckling from behind me. But then he leans down and whispers in my ear, "I was thinking of you when I was touching myself."

If I thought my body was on fire before, it was about to tear apart at the seams now. The breath leaves my lungs as I revel in his words. I can't help but spin around toward him in surprise and immediately wish I could take that move back as much for its desperation as for the fact my ass starts to throb immediately. He winces as he sees the pain on my face and gently reaches up, touches my face, and with a seductive smile, says, "Careful."

He then pulls my bent leg up and over his own leg so I'm fully facing him. He slides his hands gently under my bottom and lifts me to straddle him. The backs of my thighs rest on the tops of his, and he looks at me with his intense, dark eyes. I'm still unsure how to react and have no idea how to respond to his words. I'm stunned, and this glimmer of his reciprocation has me spinning. As he continues to look at me, he pulls my hips toward his, and I immediately feel his hard erection through his flannels. He rolls his hips up toward me to leave no question how his body is responding, and I can feel his warm breath on the side of my face and neck.

I look down, straining to see his bulge that is snug against my own cloth covered wetness, but can't see what I want to in the shadow of our bodies. He seems to know what I want and leans easily back against the wall behind him, opening up the shadow to the bright night sky.

The size of his bulge makes my breath hitch. I reach slowly down to the waist of his pants as he concentrates on me, his hands relaxed at his sides. My breath is coming in short ragged gasps. I'm waiting for him to stop me, but he doesn't. He's not hiding his emotions, and the look of longing is easily read on his face. Still, he appears calm studying my every move. I pull out the waist of his pants, catching his underwear as well and am almost surprised at how forcefully and immediately his freed cock comes thrusting upward from his pants.

I have to pull my own body farther from him just to pull the waist of his pants and underwear as low as possible, wanting to see all of him. He continues to watch me as I stare at his beautiful body. He finally reaches to the rear of his hips, arching his pelvis toward me and sliding his pants and underwear down to his thighs with one smooth move.

He huskily whispers, "Touch me ... now." And I gasp loudly at his words.

I reach out to him. I'm tentative in my shyness, but when he feels my hand on him, he inhales sharply and orders, "More."

I slide my hand around the shaft of his cock, savoring the smooth, veined skin and the look of my hand on him. His hands move to my hips in his arousal, and he pulls me back toward him. I stroke him, and he spits on his hand, interrupting me only long enough to wet his shaft for me. I continue stroking him, and his hands move up to my face.

His fingers push into my mouth, and I instinctually suck and lick at them. He suddenly stops me, pulling my hands away from him. He reaches for my waist and pulls my tank top over my head. My already tight and hard nipples intensify at the feel of the material being pulled over them. I reach back for his cock, but he gently grabs my wrists, stopping me. He's focusing on my breasts, and I can't help but look down at myself, feeling nervous.

I'm small and self-conscious of my breasts. He senses my angst and gently urges, "Don't be shy with me. I love your tits and have wanted to touch them and suck them for so long."

At that, he releases my wrists and runs his hands up the sides of my waist and then around to the front and underneath them. He gently brushes his thumbs over my nipples, and I moan at his touch. He circles around each nipple, enticing me but not touching me where I want it so much. Finally, after much intense torture, he lowers his head and sucks my nipple into his mouth. I can feel his tongue moving over my skin and the suction of his mouth is intense. He grazes his teeth over the sensitized peak, sending my body into shivers.

He moves to my other breast and continues with his erotic torture until I don't think I can stand it anymore. The heated pulsing between my legs is mounting with his every touch, and I want his hands on me and in me. But he seems intent on making me wait, and the seductive smirk on his face tells me he's enjoying every minute of my torment. Finally, once he's finished with my breasts, he takes both my hands in his and spits into their palms.

He looks at me without timidity. "Make me come."

I use my hands to stroke his length, and he makes no effort at hiding his building arousal. He takes my hands, lacing the fingers together, and he shows me how he wants it. I oblige and continue, mesmerized by his excitement. As he nears his climax, he struggles to not let his head fall back in ecstasy. He seems intent on locking my eyes with his and fights his impulse until he finally gives in and lets go of himself.

His cum is released in surges I feel on my stomach and chest more than I'm able to see. I reach down and touch my wet stomach, wanting to run my hand through his seed and feel it on my fingers. He lowers his head to my neck, and I listen as his breathing slows. I continue to stroke him while his breathing returns to normal.

When we're finally relaxed against one another again, I pick up my discarded tank top and leave him for the bathroom to wash up. For the first time in the light, I can see myself covered with his semen. I wash off my stomach with the washrag and can't help but feel the satisfaction of what I've done to him. As I start to pull my shirt back on, he enters. He's hanging long and still very enlarged, and I'm still very much hungry for him.

CHAPTER TWENTY-ONE

Logan

As I catch her half in and half out of her shirt, she blushes shyly. It's the sweetest fucking face I've ever seen, and I'm pretty sure I'm blushing too after what I just let her do to my body.

"I'm not finished with you yet," I say quietly as I walk toward her.

Her blush intensifies, and she stares at her feet not knowing how to react. I wish she knew how sexy her shyness was to me. Every blush, every furtive glance away, every time her huge, innocent eyes widen in astonishment, I go crazy—like now.

Watching the way she studied my cock and her hand on it, watching her excitement over my arousal, had pushed me over the edge. I didn't intend to allow myself to come before her, but it became quite apparent that if I was going to take my time with her, and I had every intention of taking my time, then I would have to break suit and allow my release first—and what a release. I've been craving this release since the first night she stayed here, and finally, after so much time together, she's given it to me. I wanted it to last forever.

Her inexperienced hands and hesitance made me want to push her further and further. She fed off my arousal perfectly and with very little direction knew exactly what I wanted from her. She so easily pushed me to my limit. And now, I intend to push her to *her* limit.

As I approach her, she bites her lip nervously. I help her back out of her partially on tank top and drop it to the floor. I then pull out a thick folded towel from the linen closet, lead her to the edge of the bathtub, and kneel on the rug in front of the tub where she stands. I ease her pants down and help her step out of them. Her underwear is simple white cotton with eyelets, nothing you'd see on a woman who wanted to be seen in her panties, but Rowan has a way of being sexy without trying or wanting to be.

I kiss her smooth and flat stomach from above her navel down to the area just above her panties before gently pulling them down. Even though I've now seen the better portion of Rowan's body, I've never seen her pussy before. I've spent much time fantasizing about it, and I realize upon first sight that my dreams haven't done reality justice. She is softly haired and has a well-groomed bikini line. She's stunning.

I put my mouth and nose up to the top of her pubic region and inhale deeply. Her scent is more intoxicating than I ever imagined it could be. It's her own private scent, and it belongs to me now. And I find that even though I've already allowed myself to come once, I may well struggle to slow myself with her. My excitement is already building again. As I look up, it's just to see her trembling with anxiety, and I immediately feel guilty for having gotten so lost in her already.

I stand to face her and gently touch her mouth. Her lip is still swollen, and the cut is quite evident. And as my lips meet hers for the first time, I gently use my thumb to pull her lower lip down before moving in again and claiming her lips. Soon the delicious smacking sound of our lips softly tasting and taking over each other's mouths is the only sound in the room.

After I've had her lips for many long moments, I press my tongue between them, careful not to be too rough. This is the first taste of her mouth I've gotten, and it's so incredibly sweet. She moves her tongue against mine as she leans her body into me. I feel her tight nipples brushing against my bare chest, and my erection is growing with every second. Soon, it's high between us, and her hands have found their way back down to my cock. I allow myself but a few wonderful moments of her touch before stopping her.

I grab the towel and place it folded on the side of the bathtub, providing her a soft seat for her sore bottom. I then instruct her to sit down. She does so willingly. I again kneel in my spot on the bathroom rug and place my hands on her knees, slowly pulling them apart. She tenses and locks her knees into place.

"Don't be afraid. I want you to let me taste your pussy."

Her eyes are huge, her mouth frozen in a startled "O." But she manages to find her voice. "I can't. I'm too nervous."

"I know you are, but you don't have to be scared with me. I won't hurt you, you know that. But I want you to give me what I want. And I want this."

She bites her lower lip, hesitantly gives in, and relaxes her legs. As I part them slowly, I can see how wet she is. She tries to resist me when I pull her legs farther open than she's prepared, and I press her knees firmly apart with a soft but insistent hand as she adjusts to being this open to me. I can now see her every inch, and she is soaking wet and swelling with desire.

I place my hand on her abdomen and run it down her stomach to the most intimate spot on her body. There, I spread her lips open with my fingers and study her. She's beautiful—her slick pink skin trembling at my intrusion. She's uneasy, but her body's response is all the assurance I need that she's overcome by her desire. She watches me intensely as she continues to tremble. I touch her swollen clit, and she immediately jerks and cries out in response. She watches as I lick my middle finger and then run the finger from her clit down to her opening before pressing into her. She moans softly and lets her head fall back. I gently move my finger in and out of her wet, slick opening. She's tight, and the pressure is pushing her. She starts to pant and watch my hand. Just as in my fantasy, she's turned on by watching me fuck her with my finger, and her hips start to move and push toward me.

I lower my head to taste her, and her bottom comes off the towel completely at the first touch of my tongue. She's in ecstasy and so am I. She tastes incredible, so very Rowan, and I will never forget her taste. I stop fingering her and focus on her clit. I suck and gently pull with my mouth, stopping occasionally to fuck her with my tongue. Then I lick her from hole to clit. She's watching, just as I wanted her to, and I don't take my eyes off her. My cock is hard, and I can't help but stroke myself.

I stop eating her and go back to fingering her. I slide two long fingers inside her, and the invasion is almost too much for her. But she's wet, and she keeps pushing herself forward to me. She's intently alternating her view from my fingers thrusting inside her to my hand stroking my cock, mesmerized by the view of both. She's breathing quickly and can't take her eyes from me.

She's breathless when she whispers, "I want to watch you come again. Please make yourself." That will definitely not be a problem.

I start eating her pussy again with my fingers still plunging in and out. She's starting to lose it, and I have a hard time keeping her bottom on the side of the bathtub as she pushes herself forward. Within moments, she's coming hard. She isn't loud but cries out in her release. And as she reaches and passes over her climax, my mouth leaves her hot wet center as she slides off the side of the tub in front of me nearly collapsing. I have to change my angle but keep thrusting my fingers into her.

Eventually, I slow my strokes as she kneels, her knees and legs spread wide for me. I'm still stroking my cock with my other hand, and she watches as I come, releasing myself all over her stomach. She lowers her bottom to the ground as I slow my fingers inside her and slow the strokes of my cock. I finally slide my slick wet fingers from her body, and we stay there spent. She reaches out and gently rubs my subsiding cock as I exhale deeply.

When I've recovered my senses enough, I finally find the washcloth and slowly start wiping the rivulets of my cum from her belly. Her eyes, now wide and unsure, watch me. She's suddenly tense in her insecurity as I continue cleaning her. And as my eyes meet hers, the magnitude of what we've just done somehow seems to become very real and sucks the breath out of both our lungs.

It's a sensation close to panic that passes over me, and I suddenly see her and what I've done to her so clearly. She's my little sister's young helpless friend, and I'm her best friend's older brother. Her vulnerability comes flooding back to me, and the forbidden intimacy of what we've shared is palpable between us. I'm not attracted to her less because of this realization but more. She *should* have been forbidden, but I can't bear not to have her.

I finish wiping myself from her stomach as she continues to watch me, neither of us saying a word. And finally when I'm done, I take a deep breath.

"Are you okay?" I ask quietly.

She nods. "Are you?"

Having gotten a grasp on my emotional footing once more, I look at her with a quizzical smile. "Never better." As much as I stretched her tight virgin entry and she pushed herself so forcefully into me, I have to know. "Are you sore?"

She hesitates and then slowly nods but doesn't say a word. She's still watching me, and I'm in heaven being with her here on the bathroom floor, but as she starts to wriggle, the look of discomfort becomes apparent, and I realize it's not just her pussy that's sore. She still has a bruised and sore rear to sit on, and at the moment she's sitting on the cold, hard, tile floor.

Rowan

I could stay on this bathroom floor forever, but my butt is truly throbbing now, and I'm not sure how much longer I can stay put. Fortunately, Logan moves to get up and reaches a hand down to help me. We return to the bedroom. I sit on the bed, looking slowly up his incredibly strong and beautiful body to find his eyes. They are a shadowy enigma looking back down at me. He makes no move to dress and crawls in next to me. I lean into him, kissing him, and he pushes his tongue into my mouth gently and deeply.

When he finally speaks, it's almost a whisper, and his concern and worry show in the sweetness of his voice. "Are you sure you're okay? I feel like I was too rough with you."

I was sore from his fingers but loved the way my body ached. When he slid his finger into me the first time, it was incredible, like no other touch I'd felt before. It felt tight and amazing. But when he finally slid two fingers in, I thought I was going to come unglued. It hurt and ached, and I felt stretched beyond my limit, but at the same time I wanted more.

As he kept pushing, my wetness allowed his movement to slide more easily, and my desire to let him invade my body kept building and building. Watching his fingers enter me was more than I could handle, and I started to explode. Every nerve in my body was suddenly redirected to that one place, and I really did explode. That feeling was like being on the verge of insanity. Too much, and I'd lose my mind; not enough, and I'd lose my mind; but just right, and I was in heaven.

But now, after his demanding and desperate touch has subsided, I can see the concern in his eyes, and I wish he could feel the way I do inside. If he could understand how good this ache feels, he wouldn't worry. He strokes my back and glides his hand over my sore bottom. I turn on my stomach and let his hand stroke my backside. He's incredibly gentle, and after a moment, he's leaning up and over me, trailing small kisses all along my back. He eventually makes his way down to my throbbing rear, and he doesn't hesitate a moment before continuing his trail down over each cheek of my buttocks. It's gentle and relaxing, and as I drift to sleep, he continues to let his mouth tenderly claim and caress every bruise and pain on my body. And the last thought I remember as I give into sleep is, *God, I hope there's a next time.*

CHAPTER TWENTY-TWO

Logan

I get up early, having lain awake for what seems like hours. I don't want to leave Rowan's warm body for even a moment, but in my restlessness I've made a decision, and I can't possibly know if Rowan will argue with me or agree to my new "arrangement." She's sleeping soundly when I creep to the kitchen. I start the coffee before I sit down at the table and try to distract myself until she wakes. I'm hoping caffeine will work its clarifying magic on me.

I feel guilty about what happened with her father last night, and so jealously protective of her. I can't help but wonder if she blames me as much as I blame myself. It was ridiculous of me to think I could protect her from her father. Was I really so arrogant or just stupid to think it was ever a possibility? I want to keep her near me, and my obsession with her has made it impossible for me to even try to separate myself from her right now, especially when the end of our time together is so near. So the decision is quite simple. But the logistics of it are another problem entirely, and getting her to agree to it, yet another.

She absolutely won't go back to that house. What's so complicated about that? Managing to keep our little arrangement a secret, for one. The aftermath of my moving cross-country, for another. She won't be moving to Ann Arbor until the end of summer. My apartment will be rented out to someone else as soon as I've moved out, and that leaves a stretch of three months where

100

she won't have a place to live.

I know all too well how quickly things can disintegrate with her father, and that's more than enough time for him to hurt her if she doesn't have a safe place to be. I can't ask her to stay with Sara during the entire summer break because she would without a doubt refuse, not to mention the questions this would incite from my family. And while I'd like nothing else than to drag her along to Colorado with me for the summer, that certainly would go over like the Hindenburg on more than one front.

The only plan I can seem to come up with that doesn't blatantly announce our little secret to my entire family is putting her up in her own apartment in Allendale for a time or sending her to Ann Arbor early and paying for an apartment there. Sara won't appreciate Rowan moving to Ann Arbor three months early, leaving her alone in Allendale for the summer before she follows at the beginning of the school year. But a summer apartment in Allendale will no doubt raise at least some questions with Sara and my family. And, of course, Rowan will worry about the money—not that I have any intention of making her pay for anything, and that alone will be grounds for an argument.

She'll feel like a burden to me, and it will go against that strong independent streak that is so engrained in her after so many years of fending for herself. Why she could imagine for even a second that she is an inconvenience to me is beyond my understanding. Maybe I'd feel the same way in her position, but she must know by now I'd have her no place but by me, protected jealously by me, and cared for ceaselessly by me. Then again, I would be moving away from her in only a couple short months, and the feeling of abandoning her might just rip me apart by then.

The thought of leaving her is a painful stab in my gut I've had to get very used to dealing with lately. I wonder if it will be as difficult for her as it is for me. Difficult, perhaps, but *as* difficult, I can't imagine. But then, I could never imagine being so attached to someone in all my life either.

A few short months ago, I would never have believed I could become so obsessed with someone as I have her. What happened last night was the most amazing and erotic catastrophe I've ever created. Obviously, keeping my hands off her was a battle I pitifully lost. But by having her more or less move in here permanently for the next few months, I would have to worry about keeping my dick out of her too.

That was the second of the decisions I'd made lying wide awake in bed this morning next to Rowan. I wouldn't rob her of her virginity just to leave her mere weeks later. I may have given up on keeping my hands off her, but I certainly wouldn't take that from her as well. The idea of giving into that one final desire and ultimately using her just leaves a horrible bitter taste in my mouth. She deserves far more from the man who takes her virginity, and as much as I wish it could be me, I know it can't. But the idea of it being anyone other than me nearly stops my heart in my chest. I simply can't give into the temptation. However, now that I've opened Pandora's box, I did intend to give her every ounce of pleasure she could handle between now and then... just sans sex. Perhaps it will make leaving her even more painful and torturous, but I have a very strong feeling it will be agony either way.

I finally return to my bedroom, tired of waiting for her to wake and missing the feel of her warmth. She rouses when she hears me enter the room, and she smiles sleepily and quite shyly up at me. I sit on the side of the bed and lean down to kiss her still swollen lips. The crack down the middle of her bottom lip looks painful but better than it did the night before, and I'm glad at least she won't be faced with the probing questions of her friends at school today, not to mention Sara.

When I finally break from her mouth, she looks imploringly at me, and I know a question is to come. She seems nervous and unsure about what she wants to say but finally manages to choke out the question that's been tormenting her for the better part of the last minute. "Will you make love to me?"

I knew this question would be coming soon enough, and I shake my head slowly, not wanting to upset her, but I can tell by the look on her face she's hurt, not to mention embarrassed. She looks away quickly, not knowing what to say to save her dignity, and I jump in to reassure her. "You know I want to. I'd just like you to stay intact a while longer. It's important to me." Well, that was as close to the truth as I was willing to go with her at the moment. And right now, my need to please her body and assuage her feeling of rejection is overwhelming.

My mouth finds its way down to her breasts and her taut nipples. She instantly sighs in relief, and I instantly want more. She starts to arch her back into my mouth as her pleasure builds, and I run my hand down her perfect stomach and then farther down to her wet center. I'm surprised when she suddenly stops me, especially given her recent propensity for sexual gratification. But she pulls my reluctant hand away from her body and draws my gaze up to hers.

"I want something else then."

Apparently *Let's Make a Deal* will be the game of the day.

I hesitate. "What might that be?"

"I want to taste you. I want you in my mouth. Can we do *that?*" The insecure hopefulness in her voice is a turn on in and of itself. Never mind the image I've had in my mind for so long now of her kneeling in front of me sucking me deep into her mouth. Well, I certainly wouldn't want to turn her down twice in a row. That would just be cruel.

I nod. "Are you sure?"

"Yes."

My morning just got one hundred percent better. But then I notice the swollen, split lip, and I'm compelled to warn her. "You know this might just split your lip open again."

Now it's her turn, and she chuckles. "I'm willing to take my chances."

"Well then, how would you like me, my dear? Here on the bed, lying down, sitting down, standing up? I'm at your command." I toy with her.

She blushes furiously. "Lying down?"

I waste no time sprawling myself out on my back next to her in the middle of the bed. She rises hesitantly to her knees at my side while I look up laughing at her. She smiles shyly down at me before climbing between my spread legs. She looks nervous and excited all at the same time, and I can't help but smile challengingly back at her.

"What do you want me to do?"

"Whatever you'd like."

Rowan

As I stare down at his thick, hard erection, I want to touch him but am almost too terrified to move. I want more than anything to put my mouth around him but am quite certain I'll make a complete fool of myself. Logan watches me expectantly and patiently while I battle my self-consciousness.

Apparently sensing my terror isn't going to subside anytime soon, he rescues me. "Why don't you start by touching me with your hand? We can just see where that goes. Okay?"

I nod stiffly, suddenly feeling more pathetic than I can handle. But I reach out to his shaft and am relieved when he gasps at the first touch of my fingers. I remember the way I touched him the night before, so I start to stroke him. He continues to breathe deeply and study my movements. My own arousal is building with nothing more than the sound of his relaxed and contented breath.

I spend a short time just stroking him.

"Do you want to taste me now?"

I nod slowly.

"You don't have to take all of me in your mouth. Just kiss me and lick me with your tongue until you're ready."

My whole body is shaking when I lean down to his cock. I slowly kiss my way along the shaft until I reach the tip. There, I lick around the head. Logan props himself up on the pillows and watches my every move. I continue to lick and kiss my way all around his throbbing penis, too nervous to look up at him. I reach out with my hand and cup his balls, letting them roll around in my palm. This incites another sharp inhalation of breath and with every sign of his pleasure, I relax more and more. When I finally look up at him, he's still studying me with an almost pained look on his face.

I pull back quickly. "Am I hurting you?" I ask.

"God, no. Suck me. Please. Take me in your mouth." His voice is desperate and needy.

I lean back down and kiss the underside of his head where the skin draws up in a peak one more time before sliding my lips over the head and down along the shaft. My bottom lip instantly sends splinters of pain through my lower lip, but his sudden and uncontrolled moan of pleasure drives my pain out of my mind and pushes me further.

He groans. "Just like that. Fuck, you feel so good." His voice is breathy, and his words trail off in another groan.

His moaning is all the approval I need to set my self-conscious fears aside. I start sucking and pulling him into my mouth as I slide down and back up along his cock. He continues to moan quietly and enticingly as my lips are stretched to their limit. He reaches down and runs his hands through my hair.

He begs in a quiet, breathless voice, "Look at me." I look up at his eyes to see his unrestrained expression staring back at me. "Oh

God, Row."

His panting is ragged and he's getting very close to his breaking point. I continue to torture him with my mouth and reach my hand up to stroke his slippery, wet cock. The response I get to my hand touching him is his hand winding tighter in my hair as he cries out in ecstasy.

It doesn't take long for him to start falling apart. "Oh, fuck, Row. I'm going to come."

I have no intention of stopping until he's finished, and after the second warning, he gives up trying to be thoughtful and unleashes himself in my mouth. I feel the warmth of his semen filling my mouth, and my satisfaction at having fulfilled him is overwhelming. I swallow his cum, feeling the warm saltiness of him run down my throat as he looks down at me in repletion. My own contentment is overshadowed only by my need to be touched by him, and I start to move my way up his body.

I straddle his legs just below his hips and can feel the base of his still engorged penis between the cleft of my lips. My body wants him inside me, but the look of warning in his eyes is unmistakable. Warning or not, I slide the cleft of my lips up his shaft. The length of his cock provokes my swollen nub to an almost frenzy of pleasure, but he stays my hips with his hands before I can push my wet opening down over the head of his shaft. And with one simple word, he makes it very clear what we won't be doing. "No."

Instead, he reaches his hands up to my face and pulls me down to kiss him. He rolls me over onto my back. He doesn't pull his body away from me, however. Instead, he pins my wrists above my head and starts his own torture by sliding his still swollen cock up my cleft and back down. My clit's on fire and sending shockwaves through my body. I arch my back and try desperately to line my entry up to his still hard erection, but he keeps me restrained and pulls himself back from me when I get too close. He continues on mercilessly. He moves easily between my wet cleft, and my arousal begins to mount with every glide between my lips. Before long, my panting and moaning have taken over the bedroom, and I'm nearing my release. His rhythm is perfect and is pushing me gently to the brink. My release is powerful, and I cry out loudly before I can stop myself.

As Logan releases my wrists, he continues to move with my body, his own cock still subsiding, and finally, our bodies slow. He kisses me gently and touches the split in my lip that is now starting to pound from the stretching. While my orgasm was intense, I still feel the hollowness inside me where his body should have been. It was all I could do to handle two of his fingers the night before, and I still feel the soreness his fingers left even this morning. I can't imagine how I could possibly take him pushing his full, thick length inside my body, but I know how much my body craves it from him all the same.

CHAPTER TWENTY-THREE

Logan

So much for hard conversations about hard decisions. Instead, it was another delicious interlude of my hard cock and her incredibly soft body... And let's not forget her absolutely amazing mouth. Not having sex has never been so much fun. It makes me wonder just how much I must be missing by not indulging in that one, last, forbidden act. But conversations must be had, and as much as I'd rather pull her back into my bed for more play time, this is a conversation best just dealt with.

She's eyeing me over her coffee, likely wondering why I'm suddenly so quiet. And as I watch her in return, I'm forced to acknowledge the complete shift in our dynamic. This time yesterday, I wouldn't have thought for a moment to kiss her, let alone touch her, taste her, and make her come. I'd have wanted to, but I wouldn't have given in. In the space of twenty-four hours, I caved to every last restraint, bar one, that I've had. Her pain, her wounds, and my fear for her safety were my undoing. Seeing her hurt crumbled my resolve, and I wanted nothing more than for her to feel me—my desire for her, the pleasure I could give her, my obsession for her. And here we are, sitting across from one another, regarding each other in a completely new light. The shift alone is a turn on. Knowing I can kiss her, touch her, taste her sends a jolt of energy through my body, but whatever else is changing between us, the problem of her father is not changing, nor is it going away.

So I jump right in. "You can't go back there ... ever." As she opens her mouth to speak, object, argue… who knows, I interrupt. "It isn't going to happen. There is no purpose to any of this when you end up hurt. I absolutely can't allow it to happen again. Row, I was terrified when I realized you were there alone with him. And I don't mean to diminish the experience that you endured last night, but from my perspective, you can't imagine what it was like seeing him kicking you and hurting you. There is *nothing* in this world that would give me reason to allow even the possibility of that happening again. So say what you have to say, but I won't budge on this."

She considers my words. "It's not as if I don't want to be here. I feel safe here with you, and I like being here—"

"Then it's done. There's nothing else to say about it." I interrupt quite forcefully, only just realizing how anxious I've been about this conversation.

"I can't simply move in here permanently. What would people say? How would you hide something like that from your family?"

"I don't care about any of that! It's my problem to figure out, not yours. I'm serious; you're not going back there. The only options you have at this point are my reporting what happened last night, or you moving in here permanently so that there is no chance whatsoever of this happening again! I'm sorry if you don't like the position you're in, but I'm not taking any more chances!"

I'm sure I must sound shrill and panicked, but I can't allow this conversation to get any further without the resolution I need. I'm pathetically desperate, and at the moment, not at all willing to look at the reasons for my desperation. But am I so desperate that I would actually report what happened last night, effectively damning myself and my career in the process? I have the somewhat despairing feeling I would, and I'm not prepared to deal with the why behind that either. She just has to agree.

Looking solemnly at me from across the table and obviously seeing the anxiety written on my face, she stands and approaches me. "Please, just let me think about it."

I suppose it's better than a refusal. Perhaps convincing her in a more unconventional way would better serve my agenda as well as my desires. I pull her gently down into my lap, the simple touch of our bodies releasing all my pent-up anxiety. As I start to relax, my plan of attack starts to form in my mind. She studies me for a moment longer, concern written all over her face, and I take the opportunity to latch onto her mouth greedily and hungrily, our connection flooding through me like the strongest of aphrodisiacs.

It doesn't take long for me to rearrange her body so she's straddling me. Once again, the warmth of her is snug against my hardening cock. I pull her T-shirt over her head and see that her nipples are already taut and waiting for attention. I appease her needs and spend a ridiculously long time touching, licking, sucking, and nibbling at them as she looks on enthralled. I can feel the heat continue to rise between her legs. I lift her to the table in front of me, intent on fulfilling one of my most cherished fantasies of her on my kitchen table.

As I slide her underwear down over her hips and off her lean legs, I can see the now dark bruising on the backs of her thighs and a wretched flash of fury passes through my mind. I spread her legs open to me, seeing instantly how ready she is, and my anger abates in an instant as my hunger for her takes over. The slick, wet folds of her virgin pussy are begging to be touched and stroked, and I start devouring her instantly.

CHAPTER TWENTY-FOUR

Rowan

How can this man want me? The whirlwind of events since last night are spinning me in circles, and I can't seem to wrap my brain around everything that has happened. After Logan consumed me again, I escaped to the bathroom to take a shower, and it's this smallest of emotional reprieves that has afforded me a short time to try to clear my brain. Honestly, I never expected such a reward for getting the shit kicked out of me. Gee, had I known that's all a girl had to do to get a little attention... *Attention?* Attention is what you get for wearing a push up bra; this was more than attention. What the hell was this?

Logan completely took me by surprise last night and every waking second since then. The strength of his body, the size of his erection, the incredible need between us both, watching him come and knowing it was because of me—because of my touch and nothing else. I just didn't realize how strong desire could be. And it wasn't just me! His desire was equally strong, or at least it sure seemed to me to be, but how?

Is it possible he could really be attracted to someone like me? I'm not beautiful, I'm not curvy, I'm not boobalicious, and I'm certainly not knowledgeable in any of the many ways he's toyed with me over the past twelve hours, but when he touches me and looks at me, I feel like I'm the beautiful one. But if he's really attracted to me, why won't he make love to me? That's what I want from him more than anything. I want to give myself to him and for him to own that part of me. I want him to need me so much he can't bear not to have me in the most intimate way possible. I want him that much. I just wish he wanted me the same way.

I've been standing under the hot jets of water long enough for my body to turn into a wrinkled prune, but I'm still no closer to wrapping my head around this new and incredibly erotic dynamic to our relationship. Relationship… Is that what we have? No. He's leaving so soon to start a brand new life in Denver, and I'll be off to Ann Arbor to begin a life of my own soon enough—away from insane drunk fathers and away from memories of dead mothers and away from him… My heart hurts at the very thought, and my breath is sucked right from my chest as the idea hits hard. It isn't as though it's occurring to me for the first time. I've thought about it often, but I always manage to push it away, rationalizing it's happening later, later, later… But it's not later, it's almost here—now!

My shower's done nothing but convinced me confusion really is the only way to feel, so I give up on the hot water and decide more caffeine is in order. As I look at my naked body in the mirror, I see my nipples looking rather abused and bruised, and I blush at the memory of how many places and how many times his mouth has been on my body since last night. It's hard not to think of the many past memories I have of Logan—memories that so completely conflict with these new memories of him—him with his family, playing as children, him and his friends hanging out playing video games while Sara and I played dolls and dress up. And not in one of those memories could I have ever imagined where I'd be now.

As I turn to dress, I catch the ugly black bruises running up the back of my legs to my rear, and I'm reminded of just what Logan has given up for me. He was desperate when I questioned staying with him full time. I hadn't even told him no, and he was suddenly ready to throttle me. He's gone beyond any measure I could imagine to protect me and keep me safe, so why should I balk at the idea of staying here with him? It's not as if I want to be anywhere else. I have a car now, so it's not as though I rely on Sara to pick me up for school anymore. What's more, Logan seems to like his life quiet and simple. He has many friends and always has, but he seems to like his home to be a quiet one. I've not ever seen friends or even his family pop over unannounced. He's independent and in control of his life. Maybe we could get away with it for another couple months…

As I wander back out to the kitchen, feeling overly waterlogged but refreshed, I see Logan is working on breakfast. I slide my hand up the back of his T-shirt, wondering all the while where I suddenly got such nerve as to so boldly touch a man. Oh yeah, picked up a little nerve last night … and maybe a bit more this morning. He reaches his arm around me, pulling me gently to his side before leaning down and kissing me on my forehead. I blush as that word pops in my mind again, "relationship." Is this what a relationship feels like, I wonder—close, comfortable, warm, safe, thrilling, erotic, and smelling deliciously of pancakes…

As we sit to breakfast, I decide to set Logan's mind at ease. "Logan, I'll stay here. Full time." And the look that comes over his face is all the appreciation that I need and, quite frankly, don't deserve. Relief floods over him and the tension is suddenly gone from his beautiful features.

⌘⌘⌘⌘

We can't get to the trailer to pick up my car and clothing until my father leaves, which likely won't be until the evening when he heads out to paint the town in drunken vomit. Since I have to work, Logan decides he'll take me and pick me up, and we'll go over to the trailer together after I'm off. And the moment I step out the back door of the bistro at closing time, I sense his anxiety. I know he's nervous my father will come home, and after the night before, I am too.

As we enter the trailer, he pulls me hastily down the hall toward my room. It's still disheveled and torn apart from our little one-sided boxing match the night before, and Logan sets to work immediately. Collecting clothes and any other personal items I might need goes a lot quicker than I expect; I suppose it has more to do with the fact I really don't own much of anything. And within fifteen minutes, we're out the door and loading my bags into the back of my Wagoneer. There's a better than good chance my father won't even notice I'm missing from his life. And quite frankly, I'm counting on it.

Sara calls while I'm on my way back to Logan's, asking if I want to come over for the night. I've spent less time with Sara recently than I ever have in the past, and as much as I want to be with Logan, I also really want to see Sara. It's agony not being able to share my life with Sara the way I always have, and because Logan has become such a big part of my life, I feel as though I never spend any real time with Sara anymore. I miss her terribly, and while I know I can't talk to her about any of the things I desperately need to talk to her about, I also know I need to spend time with her all the same.

After we carry my meager worldly possessions inside and dump them on the spare room bed, I tell Logan I'm going to stay with Sara for the night. He looks momentarily stunned before shaking it off and pulling me into his arms. He leans down and kisses me deeply, pulling gently on my bottom lip with his mouth.

"Well, at least your lip doesn't look too bad," he murmurs against my mouth.

Of course, I'd forgotten about my lip, but after a bit of lip gloss I'm looking as good as new, and I'm out the door.

I miss Logan the moment I hop in my car and realize I won't see him until the next day. If I'm this pathetic being away from him for one night, what's it going to be like when he's off to Colorado for his spring break skiing trip in a week? He's also going to be spending a good amount of time between Allendale and Denver these last few months of the semester, getting ready for his move and his new job. I may as well get used to being away from him. Perhaps it will soften the blow when he's gone for good.

It's late when I arrive at Sara's, but she has a late night horror movie fest planned, and we end up terrified and certain there are at least three supernatural serial killer maniacs on the loose in Allendale by the time it's all said and done.

We finally turn in, and moments after the lights go out Sara speaks. "Row, what's going on with you? You're different lately..."

I'm silent, not having any idea how to respond.

But she doesn't need a response to continue. "I just miss you. I feel like we never talk anymore, and even though we see each other all the time, there's just something missing. Like I'm missing part of you, and I don't know what part it is."

Leave it to Sara to use her best friend psychic powers on me. I'm still stunned into silence, but she deserves an answer. The problem is I can't give her one, at least not the real one.

But I try to oblige. "You're not missing anything. I'm sorry. I know I've been distant lately. I think I'm just out of sorts with the end of our senior year coming up and all the changes next year. It all just feels a bit overwhelming at times. I really am sorry. Please believe me I have no reservations about our friendship and us moving in together next year. You mean the world to me, and I'm sorry if I've been off lately." And I'm telling the truth.

I have no reservations about my friendship with Sara. I would be nowhere without her. And after all is said and done and Logan has moved on with his life, I will still need her friendship more than ever before. Whether I can tell Sara about Logan or not really won't be the issue. I'll just need her to be my constant and true friend. She's never let me down in the past, and I'm counting on her friendship to get me through the future.

CHAPTER TWENTY-FIVE

Logan

Having Rowan out of the house has given my mind all the permission it needs to run wild with my thoughts of her. I'm more than confused about her and the direction I've pushed our relationship. I'm also insane about her as well, and I know now it was only a matter of time before we ended up here. What does that say about me? What does that say about my feelings for Rowan? I know I'm protective of her, but I've known her since we were kids; of course I would care about her. I'm attracted to her, there is no doubt about that, but is it more than just attraction? Do I care about her more than I should?

I thought I might die if anything happened to her last night. I wanted to kill her father for hurting her, but my need to take care of her and my fear she might be really hurt superseded any vengeance I might have wanted to take out on him. I can't bear the idea of losing her, yet I will. Caring about her more deeply than I should isn't an option. Falling in love with her is most definitely not an option. But is it really my choice?

The next week passes quickly; too quickly. And before I know it, I'm touching her for the last time in what will be more than a week apart. The past week has been filled with her, perhaps a little studying for the bar exam, and then, of course, more of her. She hasn't spent a single night out of my bed aside from the first night she spent with Sara, which suits me just fine, since I can't keep my hands off her. I've become intimately familiar with every inch of her body, sometimes spending inordinate amounts of time simply touching and kissing every ounce of skin I can find.

I've been vacillating between excitement for our annual spring break trip and absolute despair at the idea of leaving her for a week, so it's none too surprising I'm homesick for her the second we pull from the curb. This is a trip I've taken with my oldest of friends for the past five years, and it's always a great trip. Denver has always been my second home. Sara and I grew up spending practically every holiday and vacation here. We were on the slopes by the time we were five, thanks in large part to our parents' passion for skiing and their nice little condo in Frisco. It's no doubt the reason I chose to start my career in Denver. Being close to the mountains seemed like a dream come true when I first decided to make Denver my home, but a shadow has slowly been building over that dream for the past few months.

As we make one last pit stop just before hitting the congestion of the city, I take a deep breath of the very familiar air, and on the ride through Denver toward the mountains I quietly take in the beauty of this amazing place. I do feel like I'm home here, but there is also something incredibly depressing about this realization. The mountains, usually so beautiful and inviting, seem sad and foreboding. It's as if my love for this place is slipping away from me in some small way. My dreams of living here, once so vibrant and beckoning, are suddenly foggy and filled with insecurity. The neighborhoods I've fallen in love with and planned to make my home in one day suddenly seem uninviting and foreign. I want to love this place as much as I always have, but I feel more like a petulant and resentful child instead.

After unloading the SUV at the condo in Frisco, I escape to my bedroom to unpack before we head out for dinner. I wonder what she's doing right now. I wonder if she's thinking about me as much as I seem to think about her all the time. I wonder if this time apart is as hard for her as it is for me. Then my cell rings, and the caller ID implies she must have been reading my mind. My heart races for a moment in that juvenile schoolboy sort of way I've gotten so used to, and the first sound of her voice on the other end soothes every last shred of discontentment from my mind.

"What are you doing?" I ask as I crawl onto my bed.

"Cooking a five-course meal," she responds bluntly.

"Yeah, right." I laugh for a moment. "Please tell me that's a joke?"

She's the one laughing then. "Yes. I ordered Chinese delivery."

"Good girl." I'm silent for a few seconds. "Do you remember the trip you took with us last year?"

"Yes."

"I can still remember watching you and Sara flirt with that kid just off the ski lift—"

"I wasn't flirting. Sara was flirting. I was just trying to act normal."

"How well did that work out for you?" I know full well how it worked out for her.

She laughs. "Ah, yes. I'm still not sure what happened there."

"You don't? Well, I do. You weren't paying attention to your feet, much less the skis attached to them."

"I was practically in a full-straddle split by the time I realized what was happening."

"Yes, you were. You weren't even skiing. You were literally standing there doing nothing, and your skis just kept getting farther and farther apart. It was maybe one of the funniest things I've ever seen."

"Well, that's easy for you to say. You're not the one who ended up face down in the snow in front of a cute guy and your best friend," she mutters.

"Serves you right for flirting with another man."

"Who should I have been flirting with? You? I'm pretty sure I was nothing more than an annoying child to you at that time."

"You're still little more than a child in comparison to me."

She's silent then, and I just shake my head, regretting those words instantly.

"I should go—"

"Not yet." I cut her off quickly. "Tell me what you're going to do this week."

We talk as long as we can before the guys are hollering for me to get my ass in gear and out the door. I feel more at ease than I have all day just having had the chance to hear her voice again. And when we get out of the house to the hole in the wall sports bar we visit every time we're in town, I remarkably end up having a great time. For a while, I almost feel like my old self again—engaged in the here and now, rather than feeling like I've left my brain back in Allendale. But then, it was only after talking to Rowan that I was able to relax and enjoy myself here in the mountains… So, was I really my old self again, or just living on my high from her?

When we finally close down the bar after two in the morning, I realize I have a text message from her.

Thought about sleeping in my bed but decided I'd rather be in yours. Hope you don't mind… Have a great week.

I'm a little too drunk not to respond.

So long as you leave your pajamas in your own room. They have no place in mine. Sleep tight.

Rowan

Waking to his text message is the very best way to start my day, and as much as I miss him, I feel good—really good. I'm working all week long, and it promises to be a busy week. I've picked up extra shifts and should be sitting on a fairly nice size piggy bank by the end of the week. Sara and I spend any free time I have together, shopping, eating, watching movies, all of our most favorite things. She's still wary of my recent distance, and every other question out of her mouth is some searching seeking question about my life.

"So are you seeing someone?" God bless her and her ever-invasive questions.

"Don't be ridiculous. I would tell you if I was seeing someone." I'm lying and she damn well knows it.

"Then you won't mind if I set you up with someone." She takes in the look of horror on my face before continuing. "You might like him. He's cute and he's friends with Frank." Frank's her latest and greatest.

"You absolutely will not set me up with anyone, Sara." My tone is exasperated but good-natured. She's trying to get a rise out of me.

"So *you* were just getting ready to tell me who it is you're seeing then?"

I curse her greatest gift, persistence, as I shake my head in feigned confusion, hoping it comes off honestly.

She eventually moves on and asks about how things are going with my father. She asks if anything new is going on at work. But she keeps going back to the love interest angle. Were it not her brother for whom I was smitten, I would want nothing more than to describe every last detail of my new love life with her, but I'm guessing it would be inappropriate to tell her what an amazing kisser Logan is. She gleans nothing new from me and finally gives up the interrogation and resorts to just having a good time. And we do have a good time.

By the following Saturday night I've put away a little over $600 in nice, tax-free tip money. Logan should be arriving home by the next evening, and I'm practically salivating at the thought of him coming through the door. It's quiet in his apartment; too quiet. All the windows are open as I try to air out the remnants of my latest tragic kitchen experiment, and even the sound from the streets below isn't helping to fill the void. I fall asleep early in his bed, wanting to fast forward the rest of the weekend. The sheets still smell of him, and I fall asleep dreaming of his hands and the way they feel on my skin.

CHAPTER TWENTY-SIX

Logan

I've been known to have the occasional good idea, but this might be the best one so far. I threw out the idea of leaving Colorado Saturday afternoon and taking turns driving through the night not really expecting to get much support. To my surprise, not one person disagreed. And I was high fiving myself while hastily packing for the next hour. It seems no one really felt like hanging out for the evening, when we would just be rising early to hit the road Sunday morning.

By the time we finally hit Allendale at seven o'clock on Sunday morning, my body is on fire. The seventeen-hour trip home was plenty of time for me to work my dick into an absolute frenzy about seeing Rowan again. I've missed her all week, and closing every mile between us has culminated in the most exquisite sexual tension I have ever experienced. When I'm finally dropped off at my apartment, I must look like a ravenous dog to the guys. I hop the stairs two at a time and dump my bags at the entry.

As I enter my bedroom, I see her sleeping peacefully and deeply, and my heart breathes an incredible sigh of relief being back in her presence. The early morning light shines in through the window, illuminating her in the most sensuous way. She looks stunning, and in the quietness of my room I take my time studying her, itching to touch her but enjoying my private show all the same. Her hair is its beautiful shade of auburn, shining silkily from the early morning sunlight filtering in. It's long and cascades over her shoulders as she lies on her stomach.

Her skin is smooth and pale. Her lips are soft, pink and very supple, just slightly parted in sleep. Obviously heeding my drunken text message, she is completely and utterly naked. She has her knee bent slightly up, and the angle makes the round globes of her perfect bottom all the more appealing. I can't help but imagine burying myself in her there as well and am suddenly alarmed at how fully I want to possess her, all of her, every last inch, every last entry, claimed and belonging solely to me.

I climb gently onto the bed next to her, determined to make up for my week-long absence. And as I trail my fingers over the skin of her calf, I study her face for the first sign of her waking. When her eyes open sleepily, shock and then absolute joy take over her beautiful face. She launches herself into my arms, ending our separation in an instant. I pull her body into mine, kissing her ferociously. Before long, she's straddling me, and her mouth has become greedy and desperate.

I allow my mouth to wander down to one breast and then the other, always returning quickly to her lips. I need so desperately to see her eyes, as though they calm my soul in some way. I pull my T-shirt quickly over my head as she starts fumbling with the zipper of my jeans. Our passion is healing to us both, and we are quickly carried away by it. I lay her swiftly on the bed as I pull my body up close to hers. My cock is pulsing in anticipation of her first touch, and as her hand slides under the waist of my underwear and meets the engorged head, my cock flexes and nearly jumps out of her reach. I make quick work getting out of my jeans as she starts to stroke and caress my rigid shaft. Her eyes watch mine, hungry, beseeching, and smoldering.

My hand slips effortlessly down to her hip, pulling her into mine so she can feel how hard I am for her against her pussy. I then push her hips back to the bed so I can expose all of her beautiful intimacy to me. She lets out a hiss of breath as my fingers make contact with her already soaking slit. I run my fingers down to her hole and don't hesitate to thrust two long fingers deep within her. She lets out an unrestrained cry as shock at my hasty and forceful touch fleets across her face. But she adjusts quickly in her hunger, and I start thrusting, pushing, forcing my way into her body.

Her incredibly tight passage clinches and contracts around my fingers as though her body wants to pull me within her just as much as I want to invade her. I don't let up, pounding away at her tight channel. I sink my knuckles as deep as she can take, demanding her body comply with my need. She grasps my cock, controlled by her own desperate touch.

Soon nothing but our gasps, moans, and the sloppy wet sound of our movements take over the room. She comes quickly and with clenching stomach muscles trembling with her ecstasy. I find my release fast and powerful, shooting my cum all over her glistening pussy as she continues stroking my shaft, milking my body of every last drop of it. We collapse against one another, and I'm satisfied for the first time in over a week. It's amazing how truly satisfying even this fairly innocent act can be with her. I'm exhausted from driving all night and from my hasty and vigorous petting. But I've not had nearly my fill of her, and find myself roused and ready for more within minutes.

Rowan

"Will you touch yourself for me?"

Shock. Absolute and utter shock. That is the look on my face. And while my mind is terrified and embarrassed by his question, my body betrays me and starts prickling with interest. But he can't be serious. He wants to watch me do that? I don't even know how to do that! I've never touched myself in that way. He seems to sense my hesitation and fear and coaxes his wish further on my now terrified conscious.

He leans into me and kisses me gently before continuing. "It's just me. I've seen every inch of your body, and there is nothing you should feel self-conscious of in front of me. Will you try it for me?"

I start to object, unable to face the idea of him seeing me in that way—unable, in fact, to face the idea of touching myself that way. "Logan, I don't think I can. I … just … I don't know how to … and I'm really nervous. Please, don't ask me to do this."

"I want you to try it for me. If you get too nervous, you can always stop." Still, he must be seeing the hesitation as he continues again. Persistent man! "Do you think I would hurt you?" He waits for me to shake my head, which, of course, I do. "Do you think I would ever do anything to humiliate you?" Again, he gauges my reaction with unbridled desire in his eyes. I finally shake my head again and concede to try. With a deep and shaky sigh, I commit to his little game.

With my tentative agreement, Logan wastes no time proceeding. He climbs from the bed and stands by, watching me. His eyes are smoldering sex, and I can't help but think this is going to turn into the very epitome of un-sexy. *Hope he's ready for one hell of a lame ass show.* His penis is hard and erect, and I wonder how it's possible he can find this sexy in any way—me, in all my glorious idiocy, naked, anxious, clueless, and truly the most un-sexy being in the world at the moment.

He starts instructing. "Lie on your back in the middle of the bed."

I exhale a deep breath. *So far, so good. I can handle this…*

"Now spread your legs as wide as you can," he continues.

Holy shit—no I can't! My stomach clenches in fear and panic as he studies my face. I find I've stopped breathing.

He, no doubt sensing my fast-fading commitment, leans down to my ear, quickly reassuring me in the way only he can. "I've wanted to watch you pleasure yourself for so long." His voice is warm and reassuring. "I want to see your small delicate fingers rub your clit the same way I do. I want to see those fingers inch into your tight little pussy, soaking themselves on your cum. I want to see them shiny and slick with it. Give … me … what … I … want. I promise you won't be disappointed."

Okay, so maybe this is kind of hot. As always, he's blatant in his description, and it has me hot as hell. I'm already starting to drip with wetness at the mere sound of his voice, and I realize I do want this. His words are intoxicating—his description enticing. The look of longing in his eyes is the only encouragement I need. He makes me feel beautiful; God only knows why, but he does. And on a slightly steadier sigh, I open my legs to his eyes—wide but not wide enough.

With a look between demanding sex god and patient partner, he reaches down and pulls my knees farther apart in an obscene angle. I can't help but be reminded of the poor dead frogs we pinned down to dissection trays in Biology class—their legs splayed by their oh-so flexible joints. But one look at Logan tells me he wouldn't appreciate my analogy at all. In fact, one look at Logan tells me he sees something far sexier than a dead frog on his bed. Yet, it's me that has him so intoxicated and aroused. His hand goes mindlessly to his penis as he continues to gaze at the junction of my splayed legs.

In a voice husky with desire, he continues his instructions. "Now use both of your hands to spread your pussy lips for me. I don't want even one inch of your body hidden from me."

Oh, dear God. I'm aroused at this point; there is no doubt about that, but can I really do this? He can't possibly think this view of me is going to be anything but hideous, but then our eyes meet, and the heated look in his eyes tells me instantly I'm the one mistaken. He knows exactly what he wants and exactly what he's asking for. I relax a bit more at his obvious desire for this. And as I swallow over the very large lump in my throat, I oblige and slowly reach my hands between my legs and part my slick, wet lips.

The air on this most tender part of my body tickles and arouses me further, and then there's the look in his eyes that undoes me altogether. Whatever reservation I might have had initially fades to the background of my mind. His expression is carnal, animalistic even. Absolute abandon and obsession have taken over him, and his eyes are mesmerized by the sight of my body. However difficult that may be for me to understand, it's so very obvious on his face. And I commit fully to his every wish.

He approaches the bed and sits by my feet. He leans his weight on his arm as he lounges to get a better view. My breathing hitches at his examination of my most intimate area. My body screams for his hands and for his mouth to be on me, but he doesn't touch. He continues to stroke his cock with his hand as he lounges on the bed, studying my every inch.

"Now stroke your clit."

My hesitation has left me completely, and I don't waste a moment running my finger over that tight swollen bud, sending a shiver over my body that causes me to jerk and cry out in response. God, I really do want this. But God, I want his touch more. I keep stroking my slick, wet clit while I continue to get wetter and wetter. I can feel my wetness seeping down between the lips of my vagina, and I'm suddenly embarrassed. But the sudden sharp inhale of his breath tells me he not only sees every last response of my body but also savors it.

Our eyes meet for a moment before a slight reassuring smile crosses his face. He reaches out to me, and my skin, so starved for his touch, is set on fire. When his finger touches only the small bead of my wetness that has escaped from my body, he brings it to his mouth slowly as I look on in wonder. He licks the wetness from his finger, continuing to study me.

His next instruction comes in a husky voice laden with need and unrestrained arousal. "Now push your finger into your pussy."

I slide one finger into my wet warmth. The sensation is incredible. I'm soft and smooth as silk—wet, and yet searing hot. The channel is tight and hugs my finger deliciously. It feels nothing like Logan's larger and more intrusive touch, but it's arousing all the same. Before long, he wants to see two of my fingers, and I don't waste a second before plunging another finger into my warmth. It still doesn't compare to the length and size of Logan's fingers, but it reminds me of his touch.

I thrust in and out so he can watch, and as I do, he gruffly comments on a shuddered breath. "Oh, God. You're so beautiful." As his breathing comes in spasms and his hand's movement on his dick quickens, he gives me one last instruction. "Now make yourself come."

And I do. It takes no time at all before my moans become louder and harder to control. I come intensely with my fingers still thrusting into my hole, and the fingers of my other hand still rubbing furiously on my clit. As my orgasm subsides, he climbs up my body, hovering above me on his hands and knees. He continues to stroke his dick faster and braces himself with his free arm against the headboard. As I watch without touching, his orgasm starts to build, and in one final stroke, he comes, emptying himself on my chest. He strokes every last ounce of his cum from his cock before he starts to crumble around me. He collapses to my side and pulls me into him.

One last comment remains. "Did you like making yourself come while I watched?" My cheeks warm at his words, and his question needs no response. And with a knowing gentle smile on his face, he leans into me, kissing me tenderly and slowly. His eyes are heavy with exhaustion, but he is still slow to leave my mouth. Eventually, his lips slow and finally leave mine, and he rests his head next to me.

Now it's my turn to comment. "Welcome home, Logan."

"Glad to be home, Row." And there's that beautiful smile directed at me alone. He drifts off to sleep as I enjoy the quiet and comfort of his body next to mine once again.

I lay next to his warmth, thinking about him for what feels like hours, enjoying every moment of my thoughts. I'm the beautiful woman. For the first time in my life, I actually believe it. And I don't care if nobody else thinks I'm beautiful, because in this moment, I know Logan does. Eat your heart out Amys of the world...

CHAPTER TWENTY-SEVEN

Logan

When I wake, I'm alone and finally rested. The alarm clock beside the bed tells me it's nearly three in the afternoon. I can hear Rowan tinkering around in the kitchen, which is never a good thing. But I take my time getting up, just wanting to savor the memories of this morning. She was terrified, but she gave me what I wanted. She trusted me, and it was such an incredible turn on. I need her to give me what I want from her, and I want her to know beyond all doubt when she does, she won't regret it. The trust she showed in me fed my soul and my need to have her, possess her. But in the same breath, I need her to possess me too, and she does. She gives me willingly what I need and owns me because of it.

The sight of her touching her own body in exactly the way I wanted was amazing. Her hands on her pussy were incredible. Watching every stroke of her delicate fingers was enough to unglue me. And God, the sight of her seeping her moisture while I watched so closely was my undoing. The image of her thrusting her fingers into her dripping wet pussy would make me a happy man for a long time to come. Those fingers stretched her hole, and seeing her fingers glide past the taut skin of her entrance made it nearly impossible for me not to sink my hard cock into her without a moment's hesitation.

Not making love to her is one of the most difficult challenges of my life, but I'm blown away by how incredible every other touch, taste, scent, and sight is. It's as if not making love to her and taking her pussy with my cock has heightened my desire for her in every other way. I don't feel cheated of any part of her. Instead, I feel as though I'm lucky as hell to experience an intimacy I've never appreciated as much as I do with her.

As I enter the kitchen, I catch her stabbing a frozen pound of hamburger—wonder what the hamburger did to deserve that. How is it that she never learned to cook … anything? I decide to let her flounder about for a while, content to watch her from the kitchen table while I check my e-mail. Watching her is, as always, very satisfying, and of course, amusing. Every other word out of her mouth is some sort of admonishment directed at the food she's torturing. She may have a great many talents, but cooking is not one of them. I can't believe she's survived as long as she has without a parent taking care of her. She must live out of a microwave. After her fourth "*shit!*" and a very well delivered "*fuck!*" in under a minute, I finally decide to abandon my e-mail; I've made little headway on it anyway, having gotten engrossed in watching her.

Rowan gets her first lesson in boiling water *before* adding the pasta, and I divert another catastrophe when I catch her poised to empty a ketchup bottle into the sauce I'm trying hard to salvage. I quickly replace the ketchup bottle with a handful of basil I've been chopping, and eventually, in a roundabout sort of way, we end up with spaghetti sauce or something fairly close to resembling it.

We eat in silence, and I can see by the blush of her cheeks whenever she meets my gaze, she hasn't forgotten about our morning together. I scroll through my e-mail while Rowan reads one of her textbooks. She looks amazing with her hair pulled up in a high bun and her reading glasses on. And the contentment I feel in my soul washes over my entire body, sending an incredible and pleasant shiver through me.

That is until I come to an e-mail from Brighton and Brink's office asking me to come out for a few days the weekend after next for a meeting with the partners and to meet with a real estate agent. Real estate agent? Am I really at that point in my life where I warrant the attention of real estate agents? The idea stops me in my tracks. As I look up to see Rowan across from me engrossed in her reading, my heart sinks. Dread moves through my soul, replacing the warmth I felt moments before as I contemplate leaving her yet again, and not only that, planning out this new life I will soon have with no place in it for her. What's more, it's by my own hand, sought and struggled after for years.

She looks up at me, worry plaguing her delicate features as she sees the pained look on my face. "Logan, what's wrong? Are you okay?"

I try my best to shake off these unwelcome feelings and give my best impression of a reassuring smile. She quite obviously doesn't buy it and comes to me instantly, her brow furrowed in concern. She sits in my lap, placing her hands on my cheeks and kissing me tenderly. This makes my heart sink all the lower, and the furrow of her brow deepens again in concern. She glances at my laptop and the offending e-mail before I even realize it's still up on the screen. Our breath catches in tandem, and she turns to me with a defeated look crossing her face. The look is sobering, and I understand all too well what she's thinking... and what she's feeling—one more glaring reminder our little game of house will soon be at an end.

I take her mouth with mine, shutting the laptop. I stand with her in my arms and carry her away to the bathroom. I sit with her in my lap on the edge of the bathtub. And while the bath fills, I slowly undress first her and then myself. I grab a couple of candles from the bedroom and light them as I make my way back into the bathroom to Rowan waiting patiently on the edge of the bath. Finally, I shut the lights off and close the door, shutting out all light but our candles. We settle into the warmth together, her back to my chest.

The mood has without doubt shifted, but the closeness of our bodies in the quietness of our place is soothing and calming. I turn her to face me, pulling her legs to straddle me. Her vagina is snug against my cock, and it amazes me that I've managed not to take her body in that way. She leans to kiss me gently, softly exploring my mouth with her tongue. I wait until she's satisfied and retreats before entering her mouth with my own tongue and tasting every last smooth silken surface. When our mouths finally break, her gaze meets mine in the flickering shadows of the candlelight before she leans into my chest and snuggles her face into my neck. We stay this way for an endless amount of time, shutting out everything else in the world.

But in the warmth of our darkened and quiet universe, where we are hiding away from anything that can reach us and part us, I start to think about our coming week. Every day takes us one day closer to being separated, so I tend to concentrate on our every moment together, planning it out in advance so I don't lose even a fraction of a second with her. We have to return to normal life tomorrow, classes and work, and that ever-present countdown of the calendar that will plague me daily.

The week will be busy, and our time together will definitely be limited. I want to spend every last minute with Rowan right now, knowing my clock is ticking ever closer to our deadline, so it's painful to think of losing her for even one night, but unfortunately, I will. Rowan will be staying with Sara tomorrow night as they work on their composition portfolios together, which are due before graduation. Wednesday night, we will have to face my family together for Sara's birthday dinner at her favorite restaurant.

It's always awkward being around my family with Rowan. I feel dishonest, yet at the same time, I love the feeling of her being part of my family. It's a haunting feeling, as though I know she belongs there with us, yet I can't touch her in the way that feels so right to me. I imagine being able to reach for her hand the way I want to, or brush the hair from her face, or brush a soft kiss across her cheek. I ought to be able to, but I can't. I'm trapped in this life that no longer fits, and she is the promise of what I want just out of my reach. But as real and honest as my feelings and desire for her are, I have to remind myself it isn't real for my family. Nor would it be at all understood. And quite frankly, it feels unfair.

Thursday night, I'll have to give her up again for her time with Anthony, and then she'll be working all evening Friday and Saturday night. Mom and Dad have asked Sara and me to come to the lake house for the weekend to help open it up after its long winter in hibernation. I couldn't say no, but it means leaving Rowan again, who will be working. I can't even excuse myself for the weekend by blaming it on work at the DA's office because they've lightened my load to an almost nonexistent level with my upcoming graduation just a month and a half away. So it seems a week of struggling to be together is in front of us.

At least I'll have her to myself Tuesday night. Perhaps I'll plan something interesting for that night...

CHAPTER TWENTY-EIGHT

Rowan

We're wrinkled prunes by the time we get out of the bath, and I'm content and warm. Logan takes me to bed and spends an incredibly long time massaging my entire body down with lotion until it's rubbed in completely and my skin is as smooth as silk. He starts on my backside. When he rubs the lotion on my bottom, he spends an inordinate amount of time kneading the skin and muscles there, allowing his fingers to run between my cheeks, pausing over the puckered skin of my anus.

I tense and freeze at the slightest touch there, and as I catch his face out of the corner of my eyes, he looks at me with all the seriousness in the world. He isn't reassuring me or smiling at me. His eyes are hooded and dark—challenging me to pull away from him. I don't, and as my tension starts to release, he slowly pulls one of my knees up, opening the cheeks of my bottom to him more fully. He returns to the puckered skin of my anus and starts stroking it with his fingers. He's focusing his eyes on that one part of my body, but I'm not nervous. I can see his enjoyment at the sight of my prone ass, and his rigid and swollen cock leaves no question he's absolutely okay with seeing me this way. The gentle touch of his finger on my entry feels amazing, and my skin prickles all over at the intimacy of his touch. Too soon, he moves on down my legs, and I miss the touch of him on my most secret place.

As he rolls me over, I get a very good view of how engorged and ready his cock is. It brushes against me occasionally as he works over my entire body, leaving a trail of prickly, needy skin in its path. I'm turned on, as he must know, but he avoids touching the most sensitive areas of my sex, which only makes me crave his touch there all the more. And when he finishes, I start in on his body.

I torture him the same way he's tortured me, by refusing to give him my touch where his body wants it the most. I do, however, allow my breasts to brush up against his bare skin as I lean over him. He inhales a ragged breath at the touch of my nipples against his skin. He examines my every movement as I run, stroke, and massage my hands over his body. His skin is warm, and his muscles flinch at my touch as he relaxes further and further. I end with his feet, just as he did with me. But he's far more ticklish than I am, and before I know it, I've found my secret weapon.

His entire legs jump as I run my fingers up the soles of his feet. And I start to torture him. He chuckles at my game before he bolts upright and pins me to the mattress with his strong arms and the weight of his body. I'm trapped, and the glint in his eyes tells me that's exactly how he wants me to be.

But rather than allowing our seduction to continue, he pulls us both up to the head of the bed where we stay in each other's arms for the rest of the evening. It isn't really late, so it's a long and pleasant night of TV in bed. Logan leaves only briefly, coming back with a bowl of ice cream and a couple spoons. We devour our treat while catching a sitcom that has us both rolling in laughter. Our time together feels so real—so normal. Blocking out the inevitable end to our relationship is the only way to tolerate it. There's that damn word again—"*relationship*." And it *is* a relationship—however destined to die it might be.

Eventually, we fall asleep. And as I'm fading into unconsciousness, I notice the wetness between my legs still lingers from my want being unsatisfied earlier. My dreams are equally wet. They involve fingers invading my body agonizingly slow and touching my warmth there. Over and over for an eternity, they blaze their slow path toward my deepest part. But as my unconscious eventually meets my conscious, I realize these aren't dream fingers at all. And I know these fingers so well. They fit me perfectly, and they are only concerned with my pleasure.

Logan

My dreams are fraught with losing her, and it's desperately painful. When I wake in a panic, I'm almost certain to find her gone from me, but she's still there—sleeping soundly beside me and breathing quietly and deeply. I have to have her. I have to claim her. She belongs to me, and I have to take her in the only way I can. And in the dark, my hands feel their way along her warmth. She's wet, and my fingers slide into her easily. She's on her stomach, and at my first invasion of her pussy, she mindlessly pulls her leg up to give me better access. She's still sleeping soundly, but the quiet moans escaping her mouth tell me she'll wake soon enough. I move millimeter by slow millimeter into her channel, taking her slowly and gently over and over. When she's awake enough, I roll her over and bury my face between her legs.

Her scent belongs to me, and I lick greedily at her wetness, wanting every last bit of it. Her moans have increased, and she's fully awake and fully aroused. I spread her folds and suck and nibble away at her clit while my fingers invade her tight sheath. When she comes, it's with my name uttered helplessly on her lips. And soon she's taking her own sweet time with my body, first with her hand and then her mouth. She sucks deeply and circles the head of my cock with her tongue. She moves down to my balls, licking gently and sweetly. She cradles them in her hands as she starts nibbling and licking at the base of my cock. Within moments, her lips are parting over the head of my swollen dick again, pressing down over me, and taking all of me deep into her throat. As I come, she drinks me completely, relishing my flavor. And then we steal away to sleep again.

The next morning, we get ready for the day together. I watch her as she stands naked in my bathroom blow drying her hair. She's never worn much makeup, and I study her as she brushes a small amount of mascara over her long lashes and then glides her lip gloss over her pink lips. We're having coffee in the kitchen before long, watching one another over the rim of our cups. This feels so right, and I wish I could box her up with the rest of my belongings and take her to Colorado with me.

I have a full day in Grand Rapids as I prepare to hand off my projects to the new summer intern that has been brought on board to replace me. And it's long after Rowan has left for Sara's that I finally get home. I'm relieved to have stayed so busy and am more than happy to couch potato it up when I finally get home. Dinner delivery ordered, I open a bottle of wine and settle in front of the TV. I should be studying, since I'll be busy the next couple of nights, but it's the last thing I want to do. I finally get bored enough to move and soon have the guys rounded up for a couple games of pool at The Inn. Very irresponsibly, we close down the bar at two in the morning, and I know I'm going to regret it tomorrow morning. As I enter my apartment, I grab my cell phone and start typing. I really need to stop drunk text messaging Rowan in the middle of the night.

I miss you. Sleep tight.

CHAPTER TWENTY-NINE

Rowan

Composition portfolios done early, apparently some of Ronnie's procrastination rules were heeded, we decide to go catch a movie. Since it's Monday night, the lines are short, and we load up on popcorn with double butter and enough candy to keep a preschool in business for a month. We find our seats and laugh for an hour and a half straight. Sara is animated all the way home about next year and how much fun we are going to have. It's hard not to get caught up in her energy, and I actually start to believe her until Logan pops into my mind.

I really do want to believe everything Sara says about our future, but the pain of knowing Logan won't be a part of this future is numbing. She can't possibly understand how hard it is for me to think about next year without him. Hell, I can't stand thinking about this summer without him, let alone the rest of my life. I can't help but thank God Sara will be with me next year. Part of me is worried Sara will just remind me of Logan, and I'm sure that's true to a point, but Sara is my oldest friend, and I wouldn't know how to face next year alone. I'm not sure I could stomach the idea of going off to Ann Arbor without her; the loneliness of being away from Logan would kill me.

Our night ends late, and when we get home it's straight to bed.

⌘ ⌘ ⌘ ⌘

When I wake, I see I have a text from Logan. I wait for Sara to leave for the shower before reading it. And I instantly smile with gratification when I do. He was thinking of me ... apparently at two-thirty in the morning ... but nevertheless, thinking about me—just me. We set off for school a half hour later, and I'm anxious to get through the day so I can see Logan. He texts me while I'm in class, letting me know we're going out that evening. Going out! Like a date going out? And I spend the rest of the day in a daydream of him. I can't wait to see him, and I practically speed all the way to his apartment when I'm finally finished with my last class of the day. Stupid really, when you consider he's not even home when I get there. But I set out getting ready for the night.

I try to curl my hair, but only half will hold, and I end up looking lopsided—fail. I try to put makeup on but end up looking like Elvira—fail again. After washing my face, reapplying my normal dose of cosmetics, which is very little, and finally pulling my hair up in a bun in an attempt to hide my experiment with the curling iron, I start going through my closet for something to wear. It's warm out for early April in Michigan, so I settle on a white cotton sundress with navy stripes which hits right above my knees, a coral colored cardigan and white deck shoes. I appraise myself and decide I look far too nautical for the middle of Michigan, but I like the beachcomber look.

As I start to pin back a few stray hairs from my bun, I hear Logan come in, and moments later, he enters the bathroom. He looks at me, taking in my clothes and bun. It's a quizzical look, and he tilts his head to the side as he's studying me. Perhaps the nautical look is out this year, and I just didn't get the memo—wouldn't surprise me in the least.

"You don't like it?" I nibble on my bottom lip, suddenly self-conscious. He sees the uncomfortable look in my eyes and approaches me, instantly pulling me into his arms and leaning down, pulling my lip from between my teeth into his mouth.

"I like it very much. You look beautiful. It just makes me question our plans for the evening."

At that, he turns and starts stripping while he reaches into the shower and turns on the jets. I stare after him, wondering if he's going to explain further or if I should change. It's clear he has no intention of elaborating.

"So ... should I change?" I ask.

From the shower, he leans out and with a smirk says, "Oh no.

Please don't do that. I'm changing my plans to suit your outfit."

Hmmm. What, I wonder, does that mean? I leave for the kitchen, pouring a small glass of wine to calm my nerves. When he emerges ten minutes later, it's my turn to appraise. He's wearing absolutely, fabulously, worn jeans with a pair of flip flops, a faded-out mustard colored T-shirt with his college emblem on the front, and a cream colored, zip-up, cable knit sweater. He looks like a bloody Ralph Lauren model! He does beachcomber far better than me, and in a third of the time it took me. I'm muttering inwardly. Damn naturally beautiful people.

Curiosity getting the better of me, I pry some more. "So, will you tell me where we're going?"

"Well, I had thought we'd go to Grand Rapids to the new dinner theater and then dessert down in the village afterward, but as I said, your outfit made me rethink that idea." At that, he grabs his keys, a couple blankets from the foyer closet—*interesting*—my hand, and we are out the door.

When we reach his Jeep, I try again. "So, you still haven't answered my question."

He looks at me as we both climb in. He then takes my hand, looks at me a moment longer, and then replies, "No, I haven't."

We set off, leaving Allendale minutes later. However, we are not leaving in the direction of Grand Rapids. We head west instead. There's little out this way for nearly forty minutes, and then it occurs to me: he's taking me to Grand Haven. I smile inwardly. It's one of my favorite places to visit. It's near where the Harringtons' lake house is on Spring Lake, but it isn't Spring lake that is so impressive about Grand Haven. On the other side of town from that lake is Lake Michigan and the seaside harbor. It's a beautiful, eclectic area, and I love it.

Ronnie takes Sara and me to the boutiques down by the harbor on occasion during the summer, and we shop and feast the afternoon away in the quaint village. I always love visiting Grand Haven when I can. And in growing anticipation, we get closer and closer until I can see Lake Michigan coming up before us. We park along one of the side streets of the harbor area.

As Logan helps me from the Jeep he pulls me up in his arms and whispers in my ear, "I thought you'd look far more appropriate here. I hope you won't miss the dinner theater too much."

Hand in hand we stroll down to the harbor and to Main Street, filled with its boutique shops and quaint restaurants. There's a street festival of some sort going on, and the look on Logan's face tells me he's not surprised by this.

"So, was this the other idea you had in mind?"

He confirms with a smile. "Yes. This is their Farmers' Market. Too early for good produce, but still, lots of good food, music, and shopping. Then, if you're not too tired, I thought we could drive out to the lighthouse at the beach and take a walk on the pier."

Embarrassingly, this is my first real date, and I have a feeling every date in my life will pale in comparison. We continue strolling through the crowds of people. We look like any other real couple on the street, and it's easy to pretend we are exactly that—a couple; just a normal happy couple spending time together—were that only true. He never lets go of my hand as we meander from shop to shop, one vendor table to another, and one street band to the next.

When we stop to listen to music, he pulls my back into his chest and holds me possessively. He rests a hidden hand inside my cardigan and strokes my nipple through the thin fabric of my dress. He nuzzles my bare neck as waves of desire shoot through my body straight to my center, and soon I feel the all too familiar wetness begin to build. We eat our way from one end of the street to the other, savoring every dessert and delicious treat we can get our hands on, and by the time we return to the Jeep, a couple hours have passed and the sun is starting to set.

As I reach for the car door handle, Logan suddenly stops me, pushing me up against the car instead. The side street is blessedly empty except for us. My chest is against the door of the car and Logan presses in behind me. I can feel his hard length against my back, and I know instantly how much he's been waiting to get me alone. He leans down to my bare neck and starts nibbling the spot where my neck meets my shoulder. His mouth makes its way around to the other side, made easy by my upswept hair. His hands work their way down to the hem of my dress as he slides it up my backside.

The cool air on the back of my thighs entices me but not enough to stow my nervousness at being so exposed in a public place. When my hem is secure at my waist, his hands travel to the top of my underwear and slowly, oh-so-slowly, start working them down my hips. I'm incredibly turned on but also terrified someone will walk around the corner at any moment. As it is, there are people passing by the entrance of this quiet little street on their way down Main

Street. They pay us no attention, and Logan continues. As he works my underwear down over the cheeks of my rear, he sinks to the curb behind me. He eases my underwear down my thighs and then helps me to step out of them entirely. His hands grasp my cheeks as his mouth finds the soft skin of my bottom. He kisses and massages the skin of my buttocks, first one cheek and then the other as I stand exposed in front of him. I'm soaking wet at this point, and I'm so addicted to his fingers that I would do anything to feel them on me. But he's intent on focusing on my backside at the moment.

To my sudden horror, a middle-aged couple rounds the corner toward us, but as swiftly as they appear, Logan stands behind me, pulling my hem back down and pocketing my underwear. Before the couple even has time to look up and notice us, he's reaching for my car door as though he's doing nothing more than being a chivalrous gentlemen—if they only knew. As the couple approaches us, they nod a pleasant evening greeting to us, and Logan smiles and returns the gesture.

He returns to his side of the Jeep and climbs in, winking at me. Once seated, he looks at me with a mischievous grin on his face before starting the car and pulling out into the street. After we're on our way, he reaches over and takes my hand, pulling it up to his mouth and brushing his lips across my knuckles. I watch him, completely enamored. We drive for only a few minutes before reaching the lighthouse.

He turns to me with the same mischievous smile. "Are you up for a bit more play?"

And here I thought we were just sightseeing. Who am I to turn down more fun? I meet his challenge. "You betcha."

We stroll toward the pier, again hand in hand. Logan has the blankets in his arm, and I wonder exactly how those are going to come in to play. Hmm. There's that word again, "*play.*" And what an exciting word it is. The pier is deserted this time of year, and twilight is just settling in. The sound of the water lapping the concrete walkway is the only sound aside from our footsteps.

We near the lighthouse tower that sits halfway out on a concrete pier between the land and an old historic house. Walking around the lighthouse, Logan finds a place on the far side, away from the view of land but well illuminated from the lamps that line the pier. Here he stops. Turning to me with eyes smoldering with need, he sits on the concrete ledge that runs around the circumference of the tower.

It creates a short bench, which is about a foot high from the ground, and as Logan sits he pulls me toward him with his hands on the backs of my knees.

As usual, he takes the lead. "Lift your dress to your waist." I oblige, never taking my gaze from his as he regards my naked sex. "Touch yourself." As I do, he asks, "Are you wet?"

"Yes." It's all I can manage in my weak and shaky voice.

Only one final request is needed. "Spread your lips and feed me your pussy."

At that, my heart lurches in anticipation, and he guides me up between his knees, where he lifts one of my legs, planting it on the ledge next to him. His face is now in the perfect position for me to do just what he wants. I part the lips of my vagina with two fingers and push my pelvis to his waiting mouth as he takes one long, deliciously slow taste of my wetness.

The first touch of his tongue drives my hips closer to his face, and before long I'm thrusting my sex to his mouth, moving my hips. My unoccupied hand finds the side of the lighthouse wall to support myself, and as I lean my cheek against the cool surface of the building, I continue thrusting against his lips. I'm in control of this act, and it's a heady feeling.

I fuck him and hump against him in the way he usually does to me, and his mouth tells me it's everything he wants in this moment. As I near my release, my legs start to shake. He reaches around my hips, clutching my bottom and fiercely pulls my pussy to his mouth, sealing himself to me. He sucks deep and hard on my clit as my orgasm overcomes me. Incredible. I sink down to his lap, and he strokes my hair as my breathing returns to normal.

CHAPTER THIRTY

Logan

Beautiful. Everything about her. Her willingness to try everything I want her to, her bountiful insecurities, and also her less bountiful confidences. I love her intelligence, though she doesn't see it in herself. She has a quiet sarcasm that pops out when you least expect it and constantly leaves me laughing. She's compassionate in a way no person who's suffered the abuse she has should still feel. And beyond all that, the damn way she keeps me coming back for more and more and more without ever tiring of her.

I wonder if this night has been as amazing for her as it has been for me. The dichotomy of experiencing her in such an innocuous way as strolling down the sidewalk hand in hand compared to the utter heat of having my face fucked by her on the pier. Every man in the world should be so lucky to have this amazing dynamic in a partner. She is my partner—completely and totally mine, and I'm as much hers.

Strolling back toward the land, again hand in hand, I refuse to think about our parting so near in the future. It consumes too much of my thought, but not on this night. Too perfect a night as this doesn't need to be sullied by our pain. I've brought the blankets for a reason, and I intend to push my dread of losing her out of my mind with one final roll in the sack ... or better stated, roll in the sand. As we near the beach off the edge of the pier, it's clear privacy won't be an issue tonight. It's deserted and dark on the stretch of sand that extends into the distance. The bluffs on the landside afford us all the solitude we could need—though there is no need whatsoever as our car is the only one in the parking lot.

We veer off the path rather than heading back to the car, and I see I've caught her interest, catching her sideways glance to me. I find a relatively flat stretch of sand, away from the lapping waves, and I lay both blankets down to give us a nice soft bed under the night sky. I lead her to the middle of the blanket, leaning my mouth down to hers. I pull her tongue deep within my mouth, sucking it with my mouth and lips. As I lay her down on the blanket, she looks up at me, desire and intrigue showing in her eyes. I spend time with her mouth some more, kissing and tasting her before I pull her body on top of mine. I undo my zipper and set my cock free. It brushes her vagina, and a slight moan escapes her lips. I know her desire so well, and she starts pushing against my cock in want and need.

I still her hips and whisper huskily into her ear before nipping her earlobe. "Turn and put your pussy in my face."

She registers what I want and slowly, perhaps a bit hesitantly, she complies. Soon I see the round globes of her ass framed against the night sky, and for the second time in so many minutes, I take her clit again. She wastes no time taking my cock into her mouth. And her strokes and tongue take me to orgasm in no time. I fuck her with my fingers thrusting swiftly as I pull her clit into my mouth. She comes on shaking knees before collapsing to my body, using my groin as a pillow and her warm entry against my chin.

As she regains her strength, she rights herself against my body, and I pull the side of the top blanket up and over us. We lie in silence, our bodies snug to each other, enjoying the quiet sound of the surf lapping the shore. And long after we curl up together, I break from her body in reluctance, standing to pull her up to her feet. It's time to head home.

We have a good forty-five minute drive, and it's nearing ten o'clock already. She looks tired but content as I help her back into the Jeep, leaning to her mouth for one last taste before we head home. She starts to doze on the trip as I mindlessly stroke her hand with mine. When we get home, I lead her upstairs to bed and pull her dress off. I unfasten her bra as she shrugs out of it with a stretch and yawn. I quickly strip out of my jeans and shirt and join her. We are out in moments.

⌘⌘⌘⌘

I'm up early and out the door before she wakes the next morning.

141

I have an early morning meeting with my advisor to review my graduation requirements before I head to Grand Rapids for another day at the DA's office. Sara's birthday dinner is this evening, and I have a lot to get done before I can meet my family and Rowan at the restaurant. At lunch, I call to check in with Rowan to see what she's up to, and I'm instantly happy just to hear her voice. I apologize for not being home when she woke that morning, before assuring her I'll see her that night. When five o'clock finally rolls around, I head out the door and rush off to meet my family.

I enter the restaurant, a great little French place in the heart of Grand Rapids, and I'm directed to my waiting family. My parents stand to greet me, my mother kissing my cheek and my father shaking my hand. I hug Sara, wishing her a happy birthday before casually taking the chair next to Rowan and perhaps not so casually saying hi to her. My parents order a bottle of wine, and Sara steals drinks from my glass every time my parents look away. They're not fooled, but begrudge her this small treat; she is eighteen, after all.

We talk and eat and talk some more. When the conversation turns to my next trip to Colorado, Rowan stills beside me, and her mood shifts—perhaps not perceptible to anyone but me, but it's an obvious settling of her spirit. When Sara starts talking about hers and Rowan's plans for next year, my mood begins to shift. Rowan makes it understood she notices as she crosses her leg and allows her foot to hook behind my calf and caress me—terribly bold of her. I'm impressed. I steal a look at her, smiling gently. I'm far more grateful for her touch than she likely realizes. We both look up to see a quizzical look cross my mother's face before we both glance away, blushing. *Oops.* My mother lets it go quickly before returning to Sara's excited chatter about school and Ann Arbor.

Sara and Rowan will be getting an off-campus apartment of their own when they move to Ann Arbor, and my parents are thrilled they'll be together. My parents trust Rowan's judgment and know she'll be a good and faithful friend to Sara. They know just how much Sara cares for Rowan as well. And an idea settles into my mind as I listen to their conversation.

I still have to deal with the aftermath of my moving away to Colorado and where Rowan will stay for the summer, but if I can get my parents to go along with this little idea of mine, I might just have that problem solved. I'm resolved to speak with them about it as soon as we're away from Sara and Rowan. I don't want to get Sara's hopes up, and knowing Rowan will understand my ulterior motive, I want to give her no chance to argue.

Sara asks her to spend the night so they can "*study*." This is, of course, code for hang out and do nothing productive at all, and Rowan agrees as disappointment hits me like a fist to the stomach. Rowan drove herself, so once dinner is over, Sara is anxious to be on her way. The last I see of Rowan that night is her backward and somewhat lingering and begrudging glance as Sara pulls her from the table. I'll miss her tonight as I always do when we're apart, but I'm thankful for the opportunity it has afforded me to set my plan in motion.

Once they've rounded the corner and are out of view, I open my mouth to speak, but before I do, my mother, perceptive as always, launches an inquisition. "Honey, are you okay? You seem different lately... I don't know why, just different."

"I'm fine. I'm just busy and have a lot to do before the move."

"Is there anything you need to talk to us about?" Damn leading questions, and her stare is penetrating.

As I glance around, trying not to let my unspoken emotion register on my face, I respond. A bold lie, but a response all the same. "Nope. I'm fine. Really."

She still has the penetrating stare. But she gives it up and turns and speaks to my father. "Aren't you glad Row will be with Sara next year, Marcus? I feel so much better knowing they'll be together." And as my father agrees, her eyes snap right back on me, gauging my reaction to her words. *Shit!*

I look away nervously but not before my eyes catch hers one more time. She isn't upset, just inquisitive and perplexed. That's my mother. Not much gets past her, especially when it comes to the emotional part of being human.

But I have a mission, and I intend to stay on course. So I continue. "What would you think of letting Sara stay at my apartment for the summer? Of course, Row could have the second bedroom. They'll be living together come next fall anyway. It might be a fun way for them to spend the summer. They're going to be on their own come next fall. Think of it as a trial run for next year."

My mom's eyes narrow and watch me—still intent on trying to read my mind. I give the performance of my life and coolly look right back at her. Like I said, this is a mission, and an important one at that.

My father weighs this and speaks while my mother still tries to work me over with her Jedi mind tricks. "I don't know. What do you think, Ronnie? I wouldn't have a problem with it. They'd still be close, and quite frankly, there's little difference whether we rent it out early summer or late. Ronnie?" And still she's studying my face. "Ronnie?" My father again, finally capturing her attention.

She finally responds. "I don't have a problem with it as long as you're okay with it. It will be nice to keep them close but give them their freedom. Maybe this will help me adjust to the separation next fall... I have to let them go eventually, after all." And again, eyes boring holes into my brain. She's the one who should have been the lawyer.

My plan worked out perfectly, so I need only sit back and let it run its course. My parents will tell Sara, and Sara will, of course, tell Rowan. If I'm lucky, it will never get back to Rowan that it was my idea. My fear is she'll feel bad for my concern or ... what? I don't know what. I just don't want to take the chance she'll turn this down. And the more she thinks it's coming from Sara and my parents, the more willing she will be to go along with it. That seems backward. She's my lover. Yet she so readily and easily disagrees with me. Shouldn't it be easier for me to convince her of such things than others? But then, it never has been easy to get her to go along with my ideas. I doubt I'd want her any other way though. I like her feisty and determined, so long as she's pliant and agreeable in my bed.

CHAPTER THIRTY-ONE

Logan

I don't see Rowan again until late the next evening when she gets home from her lesson with Anthony. She comes in wearing a zip-up sweatshirt over her leotard and tights and a pair of yoga pants. Her hair is still up in a high bun, and she looks amazing. Her porcelain pale skin is shown off so perfectly when her hair is pulled up this way. The delectable lines of her neck make me instantly want to taste her skin, and I'm ready for her the moment she approaches me on the couch.

I pull her to my lap so she's straddling me, and I can feel her warmth as she presses against my hard, anxious cock. I pull her hips hard to meet my erection and lean into her neck. Soon her sweatshirt is on the ground, and I have only to peel her out of her leotard to get to her nipples. They are taut and tight, ready to be touched. But as I pull the straps of her leotard down her shoulders, she stays my hand.

And with a bite of her lower lip she explains the interruption. "I'm sweaty and smell disgusting."

Humph. I'll take her smelling any damn way I can get her.

But as I return to her straps, shaking off her comment, she stops me again with a small smile. "Please. I'm too self-conscious when I'm this sweaty and gross. Can I just take a shower first?"

Hmm. Rowan in the shower... Don't mind if I do.

I say nothing, swiftly lifting her from my lap and marching her off to my bathroom. Having started the shower, I return to de-clothe her, peeling her yoga pants to the ground. Her leotard and tights are all that remain between me and the body I so desperately want to touch. Having been admonished for touching her too much when she's sweaty, I decide to respect her space—but only so long as I enjoy myself in the process. I start directing my most favorite show. Rowan ... naked Rowan.

"Turn around," I challenge, hoping she's having a self-confident day.

After appraising me for a moment, she turns slowly around. Her leotard cuts fairly narrow on the rear, and the contrast between the light colored tights and the black leotard gives an impressive view of the roundness of her cheeks. It's a struggle not to approach her and pull her leotard and tights down in one swift move to leave her naked in front of me, but I want to see her do this for me.

"Now, slowly pull your leotard down. Leave your tights on."

She obeys to a T and before long, I'm admiring her impressive ass through the opaque material of her tights. Her cheeks are visible under the tight fabric, and I swallow my desire painfully, wanting nothing more than to touch her.

"Now your tights—slowly. Bend over to your feet when you pull them down."

This gives her a moment of pause as she nervously plays this one out in her head before complying. I want to see her exposed to me—every last inch of her. She starts peeling her tights down, bending completely as she pushes them down to her ankles.

When they are off her feet, she starts to right herself, but not before I stop her. "Spread your feet apart, keep your legs straight, and touch your ankles."

Again she's weighing my words and trying to visualize exactly what she's getting herself into. After a moment, she steps her legs out to the side and bends back down to her ankles. I can now see every inch of her ass, anus and all. The beautiful lips of her pussy are oh-so-visible between the junction of her legs, and I want to reach out to her so bad it's a physical pain in my groin.

Instead, I do the next best thing. "Now reach down and spread your pussy lips for me."

She hesitates only a moment before parting her lips with her fingers, so I can see the pink slick skin of her folds. Her entry is begging to be touched—begging to be fucked. Again, she can't hide the wetness that has escaped in her need. My cock is throbbing for her, but the lady wishes for a shower, so she'll get a shower. Afterward, I will absolutely put her through her paces for making me wait.

"You sure you want a shower?" I taunt, but before giving her a chance to answer, I approach her and touch the small of her back. "Get in. We wouldn't want to waste water, would we?" At that, she finally rights herself, gives me my favorite shy smile, and steps in the shower stall.

I grab the towel she's left folded on the floor next to the tub and go to the bathroom counter to wait. I strip my clothes off and leave them heaped on the floor and wait as patiently as my cock will allow.

A few minutes later, I see her hand reach down to the place her towel should be. Not finding it there, she peers out from behind the curtain at the towel I hold in my outstretched hand, and another precious smile creeps across her face. I'm a few feet away from her, forcing her to step out naked into the space between us. As I smile mockingly at her, she returns it with her sweet, innocent one. I desperately want to feel her naked body against mine after two days apart, and I don't have to wait long. As she closes the space between us, I pull her tight into my arms, not wanting even a millimeter of space between us. Her body feels amazing, albeit dripping with water from her shower.

I finally pull away from her and hold her at arm's length to look at her. Her chest is rising and falling, slow and deep, as water still trickles down her skin, and she continues to watch me expectantly. I know she's turned on from the pre-shower show, and as I lean down to kiss her, I find my own neediness is going to be hard to control. I thrust my tongue deep into her warm mouth, finding it impossible to satiate my need to overcome her body. She runs her hands over my back and down to my hips where she pulls my body to hers. I guess she's needy too.

She doesn't waste a second before she begs me for the one thing I won't give her. "Please make love to me." She desperately wants this, and the pain of my restraint is excruciating.

I lean down and kiss her again and let her hands explore my body. When she reaches my hard erection, she wraps her hand as far around my shaft as she can and starts to stroke. This is my heaven, and I know it will be nearly impossible not to fuck her.

As the intensity of our kissing heightens, so does her demanding touch. She wants to be fucked very badly, and in an attempt to keep myself from throwing her on the floor and giving her what she wants, I turn her body to face the counter and mirror, taking my place behind her. I start to kiss her neck while my erection teases her back and hips. I watch her beautiful face in the mirror with wonderment that I've missed her so much after only a couple days apart. I caress her breasts as she watches my every move. This isn't enough for her, and she keeps reaching back for my cock, wanting me to give into her wishes.

I move her hands back to the counter as a resigned look comes over her face, and she lets out a slow deep breath. Understanding is now upon her. "You won't make love to me, will you?" The disappointment is clear on her face.

I slowly shake my head from side to side without saying a word. The look of hurt on her beautiful face is evident and painful to see. She must know by now my attraction for her is very real and very powerful, and there is no reason to feel rejected. But her expression tells me she has no idea.

"But you're obviously not saying we can't be together at all?" Her brow furrows as she asks the question.

I shake my head. "I've already tried that approach enough times to know I would fail miserably."

She can't help but object. "But I want it to be you."

I watch her steadily for a moment before I try to calm her fears. "What if I promise to make it up to you in other ways?" She returns my gaze with her own confused look before I continue.

Rowan

"Shall I tell you how it would feel to make love to me? Perhaps that would appease your need?" He has the most amazing seductive voice.

He doesn't wait for my response before trailing his lips down the side of my neck, never taking his eyes off mine in the mirror.

"The first thrust would be severe, but you'd welcome it greedily. In fact, you'd instantly want more." His voice is aroused and throaty.

He continues to taunt me with his tongue around the nape of my neck, never losing sight of my eyes.

"I wouldn't make you wait more than a moment before I thrust inside you again. You're wetness for me would let me go deeper, and with each thrust your body would accept more and more of me, until you'd taken every last inch deep inside you."

He's now on the other side of my neck, eyes searing holes in my brain. The head of his hard, thick cock is brushing my lower back, taunting me further. I want to turn and grab him and make him fuck me just like he's describing, but the seduction is just too pleasurable.

"The pain would be extreme but equally gripping. Your body would rise to meet mine every time I drove into you, and before long you'd be thrusting your body against mine as much I was thrusting into yours. Your hunger for release would start to overshadow your pain, and as your clit started to swell with need you'd beg me to fuck you harder … and I would."

I'm now panting, and my legs feel like rubber. I can't take my eyes off his, and with every brush of his warm breath on my neck and ear, my desire reaches a new height. I want to feel his hands all over my electrified body, and I don't think I can take much more of his torture.

"I'd pound you until I was certain I must be hurting you, but the look in your eyes would tell me it was exactly what you needed."

The fingers of his hand are now trailing down my back and sending shock waves up my spine everywhere they touch.

"Your pussy would tighten around me like a vice, and when you finally came it would be harder than my tongue or fingers could ever make you come."

His fingers are now sliding between the cheeks of my bottom.

"Your body would spasm as my thrusting continued through your orgasm. I wouldn't waste time after you'd finished to let go of myself."

He's now moved himself directly behind me and uses his other hand to gently but firmly lean me over the counter. My cheeks open to his still lingering fingers, and he makes no move to pull them away.

And then he finishes his seduction. "As I finally reach my peak, I'd come deep in your tight pussy and claim your body for myself."

At that, he brushes his finger over my exposed anus as a shudder washes over my body. He watches me closely as I gasp for breath.

He studies my eyes for what seems an impossibly long time before leaning over me and whispering in my ear. "I want you to let me taste your ass while you make yourself come."

I gasp again, suddenly terrified and electrified at the same time. My self-consciousness is screaming at me to run, but my body, so starved for his attention, is locking me in place, wanting nothing more than to give him every part of me. He doesn't wait for my response before he slips his hand between my thighs and pushes them farther apart.

"Now bend all the way over to the counter," he whispers calmly.

I'm bent at a nearly ninety-degree angle at the waist. He then kneels behind me. I'm mortified and can't believe I'm so exposed to him in this way. He starts stroking my anus again, relaxing the tightness I feel there. But before I'm able to fully relax myself to this sensation, I'm struck by a new sensation when his mouth touches the gathered skin. His lips are warm and gentle as he kisses and licks the most vulnerable part of my body.

He stops momentarily. "Make yourself come, baby," he murmurs against my bottom. He reaches up and guides my hand down to my sex, where I start to rub my swollen clit.

He starts exploring me with his tongue, pushing past the rim of my hole. He shows no sign of hesitancy, and my arousal starts to build at his obvious satisfaction. When he urges me to push my finger into my wet pussy, I don't hesitate a second. His mouth is suddenly off me as he takes in the view of my finger sliding in and out of my hot entry. The pressure of his mouth is replaced by his finger as he gently but forcefully presses it into my bottom. This new sensation causes my muscles to tense and sends a sharp wave of pain through me until my muscles relax again.

Once my body loosens to this new invasion, he starts to finger my bottom slowly as I keep fingering my other entry. I can feel his finger passing over mine through the thin wall of my vagina as he continues his gentle thrusting. His breathing has quickened, and it doesn't take long for me to reach my climax. As I come, he removes his finger and returns to kissing and licking my puckered hole gently.

As my legs start to buckle, he stands swiftly and turns me in his arms. He kisses me fiercely and forcefully, taking over my mouth with his tongue. His hard erection is trapped between our bodies, and I desperately want to relieve him of his need.

Apparently, he's thinking the same thing as he whispers in my ear, "Let me fuck your beautiful mouth."

He hardly waits for an answer before pulling me to the doorway of the bathroom and backing me up against the inside of the door frame. I barely have time to wonder about his odd choice of location before he continues his assault on my mouth. I reach down to touch his engorged penis, and my lightest touch causes him to pull back and concentrate on my hand. As my hand starts to stroke up and down on his shaft, his breathing begins to hitch, and the muscles in his stomach start to quiver and contract. He finally grabs both of my wrists and pulls them swiftly up above my head and holds them to the frame of the door.

He orders me down to my knees, keeping my hands pinned to the door frame above my head. "Put your rear up against the door jamb."

I scoot back into position, my calves straddling either side of the doorway. As I look up at him in anticipation, he runs the fingers of his free hand through my hair before gently pinning my head back against the door frame as well. I suddenly understand the odd location. He's got me on my knees, against the door frame with my calves straddling the door and my head braced against the frame as well—perfect height for his cock in my mouth and nowhere for my mouth to move except open to accept however much of him he chooses to give me.

I'm suddenly nervous as my head and upper body are locked in place. He senses my fear and his face softens. "Don't worry. I won't go too far. If you start to feel like it's too much, just pinch my hand with your fingers." He gives me his reassuring, gentle smile. "Now, open your mouth."

I obey slowly while looking up at him. His eyes bore holes into my brain as he begins pushing his hips forward, entering my mouth and stretching my lips taut. Just as he assured me, he only pushes his length partially into my mouth, and I start to relax. He pulls out and plunges back in, again taking care not to push too far—still, he's filling my mouth and stretching my lips to their limit. My mouth starts to fill with saliva as he continues his thrusting.

Watching him from my vantage point is erotic and intimidating at the same time. I feel owned by him in the very best sense of the word—cherished. He continues his thrusting, never once taking his eyes from mine. This must be how he moves his body when he makes love, and I relish the idea of this invasion being directed toward other entries to my body.

His pace quickens, and my ability to withstand the force and building saliva in my mouth starts to waiver. While his thrusting remains controlled, the power behind it is insistent and unforgiving. As his breathing becomes more ragged and desperate, I watch him and expectantly wait and hope for the taste of his release. My fear starts to build as my mouth becomes over-full with my gagging saliva. And when I think I've finally hit my limit, he comes—filling my mouth, his cum mixing with the saliva. I gulp him deeply and desperately, inhaling through my nose and relieving the claustrophobic fullness of my mouth.

He releases my hands and my head, bracing himself against the door jamb as he finishes emptying himself. I can taste his uniqueness on my tongue. I grasp the backs of his thighs and pull him farther to me as his shudders subside. I peer up at him as I continue to gently suck and lick around the head of his penis. His eyes are closed and his breathing heavy as he leans into the door frame. His face looks exhausted. He slowly opens his eyes and smiles warmly down at me as I finally release his cock from my mouth. He chuckles quietly, and there's his warm smile again.

Reaching a hand down to me, he pulls me up to my feet and into a tight embrace, burying his face in my neck. He holds me there for what seems a most enjoyable eternity before finally lifting me into his arms and carrying me back to his bed. He climbs in after me and pulls my body up against his, leaving not an ounce of space between us. He falls quickly asleep, and soon after, I drift off too—satisfied and complete.

CHAPTER THIRTY-TWO

Logan

The next evening, I leave work early so I can pack for the lake house and be on the road by five o'clock. That's a lie… Truth: I leave work early so I can get home in just enough time to play with Rowan's body in the shower before she has to go to work. Packing, on the other hand, ends up being a last-minute side note that takes about thirty seconds. I end up forgetting underwear but bringing five pairs of socks.

Once at the lake house, I'm more productive than I've ever been. It's the very best way to deal with missing Rowan. But come Saturday evening, when our work is done for the day, I'm distracted and impatient. I want to call her when she gets off work, but it's nearly an hour away, and I'm more anxious than I care to admit waiting for the time to pass. I've been leery of my mom's suspicion ever since Sara's birthday, and I have no doubt she notices my odd behavior. But at ten-thirty, I dismiss myself by saying I'm going for a walk—odd behavior or not.

As soon as I'm out of earshot of the cabin, I dial Rowan, waiting in anticipation to hear her voice. And when I do, my stress and anxiety release immediately. I wonder if I have such a strong effect on her too. I walk for a long time along the shore, strolling along the well-worn paths of the shoreline. We talk about nothing at all important, just needing to hear the sound of each other's voice.

"I tried to burn down your apartment again," she comments.

I hum in response waiting for an explanation. When it comes to

Row and cooking it never ends well, but the stories sure do make for a good laugh.

"I don't know what happened," she muses. "But it came out black... And then the fire alarm went off... And then I had to climb on top of the dining room table to fan the fire alarm..." She went silent then.

I'm absolutely certain there's more to it than that. "And...?" I prod.

"And then I lost my balance, broke the light bulb with the handle of the broom and put a hole in your drywall with the handle too," she finishes quickly.

I start laughing as my mind plays out this scenario in my head.

"You're not upset?" She sounds legitimately worried.

"No, Row. I'm also not surprised." I can't seem to stop chuckling, and every time I let my mind wander to the visuals, my eyes tear and I start laughing again.

"Stop laughing at me!" she cries incredulously.

I keep strolling on as my laughter fades away, and I'm more content than I've been since my shower with her the night before. As we talk on, I confess I'm now on day two of my underwear and will be going commando by the next morning. It's now her turn to laugh.

By the time I can see the cabin again, all of my stress and anxiety are gone, and though I'll miss her until I see her again, I'm finally happy. I can't wait until the next night.

"Promise me you won't cook anything else until I get home tomorrow night, and I'll promise to cook you dinner. If you burn down my kitchen, all deals are off."

She hums and I smile as I hike up the sloped lawn toward the cabin. "Promise," she says.

We disconnect quickly after that, and as I hop up the steps to the porch, I'm smiling like a fucking idiot. But then I step onto the porch, and I see my mom waiting for me on the porch swing. Weariness sinks in.

She smiles when my eyes meet hers, and I move to join her on the swing, suddenly quite curious of her good mood. Not that my mother is prone to bad moods. She's an elementary art teacher, after all, and known for being fun and energetic. As I sit, she puts a hand on mine.

When she speaks, she leaves no room for comment. "It's nice to see you smile, dear. I don't have any idea what's going on with you right now, but if it makes you smile this much, you won't hear any objection from me."

At that, she stands and starts to stroll back toward the front door. Once there, she pauses and looks at me once more. "You know your happiness is more important than anything else to your father and me, don't you?" She then disappears inside, leaving me a bit dumbfounded and confused by her comment.

I stay on the swing for a while longer, thinking about her words. I'm perplexed at her intent. Of course, I know my parents want me to be happy. Why did she feel the need to tell me that? Does she think I've been unhappy? Or does she think I will be? Is she wrong? Of course not. I *will* be unhappy. When I leave Rowan for Denver, I will, without a doubt, be unhappy. For how long, I have no idea— a week, a month, forever? Does she know I'm dreading my move to Colorado? Does she know why? She's perceptive, I'll give her that, but just how perceptive? I know she must be suspicious given my behavior recently and how I've acted around Rowan, but what can she really know?

For a fleeting moment, I consider confiding in her, but regardless of her words there's no chance she would be happy to hear about the secret I've been keeping for the better part of the school year. There's also no chance she would accept the liberties I've been taking with Rowan. Her words are kind, and I get it. She wants me to be happy, but she has no idea what makes me happy. If she did, she wouldn't be nearly so generous with her well wishes. Of that, I'm certain.

I eventually retreat to bed and fall fast asleep. I wake the next morning to Sara's music playing way too loud and her dancing around the kitchen with Rufus in tow. The dog is barking in excitement, and Sara is doing her best to follow the dance moves to some random hip hop romance movie on the TV... You know, *West Side Story* for the twenty-first century. She's failing miserably and looks ridiculous, but holding true to Sara form, she could care less.

"Look ... look ... look! I almost did that move. Did you see that?" She's practically yelling in her excited flurry. "I should have been a dancer. I could ... yeah ... I could totally be a rock star at this!" She's short on breath for her exertions, and I can't help but laugh.

As her older brother, I know I should be irritated with her, but

I'm not quite able to get the image out of my mind of her pathetic attempt at, what's it called—Crunk—with Rufus trying to join in the fun. Her face is scrunched up in her focus as she tries to follow moves she has no hope of ever copying, but she just … doesn't … care! She pulls off ridiculous better than anyone I know.

We eventually get down to work, and I again engross myself in my tasks. I collect the branches that have fallen in the yard and pile them high on the fire pile before cleaning the gutters and then mowing the yard. When we're finally done for the day and ready to head home, I'm practically pulling out of the driveway before my car door is even closed.

I stop at the grocery store when I hit Allendale and stock up on everything I need for the meal I promised Rowan. The checkout line is slow, and I silently curse the dawdling cashier for keeping me away from Rowan for even longer than I've already been away from her. When I finally come through the door with my groceries, Rowan is working on homework at the kitchen table. Her hair is pulled up in a high ponytail, she's wearing the reading glasses that make her look so fucking sexy, and her skimpy tank top and ever loose pajama pants. I no longer have to wonder what she hides under those baggy pants as I've seen every inch of her figure, but they remind me of the early days of our time together, when I wondered incessantly about her body.

She helps me put away the groceries, and as she does, I start to peel her clothes off her. As she reaches to put an extra box of pasta on a high shelf, I pull her tank top up and over her head before she can object. And as she bends to drop a box of dishwasher detergent under the sink, I slide her pants and underwear to her ankles, kissing both cheeks of her ass as I do. She's now naked and eyeing me suspiciously. But she wastes no time playing my game and starts stripping me of my clothes as well.

When we're both naked and the groceries put away, we set about cooking. I'm hard as hell the whole time watching her move around the kitchen. And she's spending an awful long time focusing on my cock rather than anything else, including watching where she's going. And when I catch her running into the kitchen counter because she's staring at my penis rather than minding her feet, I can't help but laugh. She blushes furiously before blaming me for her little accident.

I manage to pull off salmon fillets, though having an erection for the past hour is fast becoming excruciating. And as we sit to eat, I struggle to think about anything but her and what I want to do to her body. Her breasts taunt me from across the table as I try to force myself to eat. I'd like to say the salmon was good, but as I was so focused on her tits I can't really say what it tasted like.

Once dinner is over and the table cleared, I pull her back to my shower and we end our weekend the same way we started it. I wash her body as my erection brushes, nudges, and quite frankly, tries to invade her anywhere and everywhere it touches. She finally reaches for me and starts to stroke up and down on my shaft, lathering soap as she goes. It's the touch my body has been waiting for, and once she's done washing and rinsing me, she kneels and takes me deep in her mouth. I'm beyond eager and keep inadvertently clutching her hair in my fists and pumping her mouth hard, too hard. Every time I try to rein in my thrusts, I fail miserably and find I'm right back to fucking her mouth harshly and invasively.

Her eyes are uneasy but trusting as always. I finally give up and pull from her mouth, not wanting to scare her more than I have already, or worse yet, hurt her. I offer a quiet apology as I shake my head in frustration at myself. I'm again reminded of just how much I loathe the feeling of humiliation.

She stands watching me, and I offer her what explanation I can give. "I'm just coming undone. I'm sorry. I can't stop, and I don't want to be too rough with you. But I'm either going to fuck the hell out of your face or your pussy and neither is okay."

She raises a good-natured eyebrow in mock contemplation, and at her smile I start to relax once again. But I'm terrified to touch her. Rowan naked in my kitchen for over an hour after an incredibly long weekend away from her was too much torment for me to handle, and now my restraint for her is perilously close to non-existent. She stands quietly by, waiting for me to give her some sort of direction while I will myself to get a grip.

After thinking and watching her for a long time, I come up with a plan—likely ill-advised, but a plan nonetheless. "I'll make you a deal. If you promise not to fuck me, I'll let you tie me up and have your way with me. However tormenting it might be… At least then I don't have to worry about being too rough with you or doing something I'll regret."

Again her eyebrows raise, and I'm suddenly afraid this might not have been my best idea ever. But she's in a good mood and ready to play. She holds her hand out to me, and as I reach out to shake hers, she winks at me. Quite the vixen tonight, isn't she?

CHAPTER THIRTY-THREE

Rowan

The phrase, *"don't write a check your butt can't cash"* is suddenly running through my head. I'm innervated and electrified at Logan's suggestions, but what the hell do I know about tying a man up and having my way with him? What does that even mean? *Okay, I can do this.* Besides, he's used to me making an ass out of myself, and it's never seemed to bother him before. Let's just hope this time is no different.

So, with the tables turned for the night, I lead him out of the shower by the hand. I dry our bodies, and his engorged cock jerks every time I brush against it. He's not kidding. The pained look on his face tells me he's struggling to behave in any sort of decent manner. Maybe I should tie him up sooner rather than later.

I lead him to his bed, and he lies down in the middle with no direction whatsoever. I spy my toe shoes peeking out of my bag on the chair by the bed and quickly pull the satin ribbons from each shoe. The material is silky smooth but strong, and I can only hope this constitutes an appropriate restraint. And as I approach the bed and Logan sees what I carry with me, his incredibly harsh breathing tells me I'm definitely on the right track.

He holds his wrists up to the headboard, and I start securing him to the slats with the satin ribbons. Once done, I look at him— insecurity written all over my face. I have no idea what he expects me to do, and I'm suddenly feeling excruciatingly inadequate. As I start to fidget and panic that I've gotten in way over my head, Logan, as always, rescues me.

"Come here and kiss me," he says quietly, seductively.

Well, that's easy enough. I lean to his mouth and kiss his soft warm lips. When I pull back, he smiles.

"More," he demands.

I don't hesitate. This I can do. I take his mouth again and start to explore with my tongue. As I glide my tongue over his bottom lip, his breath hitches. I start to relax the more I taste his mouth and feel his passion. I move down his chest as he watches me. I touch his chest, running my fingers over his nipples. They're rock hard, and I lean my mouth in to taste him. I lick trails across his chest before nipping his nipples lightly between my teeth. He gasps and I bolt upright afraid I've hurt him.

He reassures me that I haven't. "Don't stop. Your mouth feels so good." His voice is breathy and aroused.

I return to his nipples and let my teeth catch on them as I graze my mouth over his pecs once again. When his breath hitches once more, I'm more confident it's for the right reasons. I sit up and let my fingers trail down the side of his chest, brushing so closely to his exposed underarms. His skin trembles and he pulls against the ribbons securing him to the bed. But his eyes are hungry and focused on mine. He lets his focus shift to my exposed breasts, and he licks his lips subconsciously at the sight of my naked chest.

I lean up to him, but this time I pull myself up higher on his body. I don't press my breast to his mouth, but I let it linger above his face. It takes only half a moment for him to lunge up to my nipple, pulling it deeply and harshly between his lips. The strong and incredible suction makes me cry out. I'm not sure if it's pain or pleasure or falls somewhere between, but it's intense, and I don't even consider pulling away. I don't want him to stop.

After he's left my first breast bruised and raw, I offer him my other, and he just as aggressively devours that nipple as well. Once he's lessened his grip on my nipple and has taken to laving around it with his tongue, I pull away and return to his body. This time, I start a bit lower, and at the first touch of my tongue on his stomach, his muscles start to twitch. I start to brush my fingers along the tops of his thighs. His body is tight and straining against the restraints. He's ready for my mouth, and his eyes implore me dangerously.

I move between his legs, and he opens them wide for me, and I take in his incredible body from this most amazing view. His eyes are dark and carnal, and they belong so perfectly to his beautiful face. His chest is well formed, and his nipples are still hard as pin heads. The strength of his arms is easily seen in his up-stretched body. And trailing my gaze down his trim stomach, I'm taken aback by the quivering of his tight abdomen. His stomach leads perfectly to his hips and his incredibly large and engorged cock that juts up between his hip bones. His thighs, also strong and lean, are as tense and tight as the rest of his body.

As I meet his eyes once more, he begs, "Please. I can't wait anymore."

Not one to be cruel, I lean instantly to his cock and part my lips to take him within my mouth. He cries out at my first touch, and his hips start to thrust upward to meet my mouth. I pull back and start to stroke his balls in my hands, and he drops his hips back to the bed. Once he's back under control, I return to his cock again. I push my mouth over the head and down his shaft. My mouth is filled, and I open my throat to allow more of his length. I force my throat to stay open as I continue to sink his cock to its hilt into my throat. I suck deeply, while his moans intensify, before I turn to using my hand on his cock. I rub up and down his shaft, while I pull the sensitive head of his cock into my mouth.

Soon he's panting and fighting to keep his ass on the bed. His heels are dug into the sheets of the bed, and his legs are pushing and straining hard against it. When he comes, it's with hot streams of cum to the back of my throat. He cries out loudly and harshly as his body curls in on itself. As he pulls his head and chest up, his wrists strain against and threaten to break the restraints on the headboard or perhaps the headboard itself. His orgasm continues to rack his body, and his stomach muscles ripple as they work.

When he finally collapses back to the bed, I crawl up his body and straddle his hips. My wetness touches his still engorged cock. My need is so strong it's difficult not to slide along his length and push myself back down onto him, but I heed the terms of our agreement and control my own need to impale myself on him.

But he's not quite as trusting of my motives, and a look of warning flashes harshly across his face. "Untie me."

"Do I have to?"

"If you want to come you do," he retorts, or was it a threat?

"Well, you don't need your hands for everything."

He eyes me suspiciously. "That's true. Did you have something in mind, my dear?"

I do, but I have no idea how to be so bold. So I just beat around the bush, hoping he'll catch on. "Maybe like Grand Haven?"

He relaxes, understanding I have no intention of having sex with him. "What about Grand Haven? We ate some good food, we listened to some good music, we did some shopping. It was a lovely evening. It was one of my favorites ever, actually."

I can't disagree with that. He's feigning confusion like a pro and enjoying my discomfort immensely.

I take a meek stab at the truth. "I was thinking about *after* the Farmers' Market."

But he refuses to give in. "Oh, you mean the walk we took at the pier. Or were you thinking about watching the stars on the beach?"

Two can play this little game. I give him my best impression of a bored smirk before pushing off from his stomach and moving to leave. But he's fast, and before I know it he's wrapped his legs around me, playfully pinning me to him.

He looks at me with his penetrating stare for a long moment before giving in. "Fine. Have it your way. Were you thinking lighthouse style or beach blanket style?" And there's that magnificent smile again.

"Up to you. You're much more skilled in these things than I am..."

"And I wouldn't have it any other way. I enjoy shocking the hell out of you every time we're together. But if the choice is mine, lighthouse all the way, baby. I loved having my face fucked by you."

Cue magnificent smile again, and I melt. I also get wet at the mere memory of the lighthouse. But the technicality of the act starts to set in, and I'm suddenly worried I might have to be a contortionist to pull this stunt off.

Logan, as always, seems to be reading my mind and instantly reassures me. "Don't worry. You won't suffocate me. Put your knee at my armpit and your other foot up to the head of the bed. You'll figure the rest out from there."

He loosens his hold around my waist with his legs, and slowly, nervously, I start working my way up his body to straddle his face as he watches me closely. I do as he says and brace myself on one knee and one foot, holding the headboard for support. He's correct. It puts me right at his mouth, and in a similar fashion to the lighthouse, I start to thrust against his mouth. With a hand braced against the headboard, I move. I push with just enough pressure for him to get a good hold on my clitoris but not so much to make him uncomfortable.

His mouth may be occupied, but his eyes are all I need to see to know he's enjoying himself immensely. But I miss his hands and his fingers, and the more my body builds toward orgasm, the more I crave that touch, that penetration. As I near my release, I reach swiftly to one wrist and pull at the ribbon, freeing his hand. He knows what I want and wastes no time sinking two fingers deep within me as my body starts to shudder. As my orgasm subsides, I pull my body back from his mouth as he continues to move his fingers in and out of my pussy. God, he's good at this.

I stay in place until he slowly withdraws his fingers for the last time. He reaches up, releasing his other wrist, and then swiftly lifts me by my hips and replants me on his lap as he sits up to meet me. He kisses me gently and slowly. He tastes of my scent, and I love that he enjoys my taste so much. It makes me feel so cherished and beautiful.

We stay this way for what feels like an eternity. He's now calm and satisfied, and I take my time kissing my wetness from his chin. He caresses my back and bottom—running his hands gently over my skin. His cock is nestled between the lips of my sex, but he makes no move to pull himself away from me.

When the phone rings, it's an unwelcome interruption in more ways than one. As I make my way out to the kitchen for a glass of water, I see Logan on the phone and can tell he's speaking with someone from Brighton. They're confirming his flight arrangements for the following Thursday when he will be traveling to Denver. Logan is cordial, but the look on his face is anything but. I return to the bedroom, not wanting to hear anything more. Minutes later, he crawls in next to me and pulls my body into his.

Wanting to fall asleep and forget the last in a long line of reminders that Logan will be leaving soon does nothing to actually help me get to sleep. I lie awake for what feels like hours, unable to shut the feeling of loss out of my mind. He's not gone, yet I miss him already. I know how painful it's going to be. Far more than I ever imagined it would or could.

And as he rolls toward me, he whispers in my ear. "I hate this. Being away from you…" He trails off as he shakes his head.

He must be fighting his own demons. But his comment is

bittersweet. I want him to miss me—I really and desperately do. I want him to miss me as much as I will miss him, but in the same breath, I don't want him to hurt as I do. I can't stand the idea of him feeling this pain. This is his future. He's wanted this for so long. And my future has been equally sought after.

I was ecstatic when I found out about my scholarship. It's hard to land great ones, especially in the arts. This particular program only gives out one per year, and it was given to me. It was more than I ever hoped for. I still remember the day I received the letter. Sara was with me when I opened it, and we both sobbed. It was the best moment of my life. It was the very thing I needed to help me understand life would move on from my shitty old trailer and my asshole of a father.

Imagining life after my mother passed away was impossible. It was hard to look forward to the next week, let alone a happy future. This scholarship symbolized all of that. It put to rest my long-held fears that I would end up alone in Grand Rapids, never escaping my father and doomed to slave away a meager living for the rest of my life. It was truly the first time I was happy since my mother had passed away. And now it seems to symbolize nothing but loss.

I finally drift off to sleep dreaming about her—my mother. These dreams are always sad, and I always wake missing her as if she was only taken away from me yesterday. This night is no exception, and when I wake us both crying out for her like a child, I start sobbing pathetically as Logan pulls me into his arms, hushing me and stroking my hair.

The next morning as I get ready for the day, Logan watches me closely. I'm numb and emotionally drained from my dreams. And as he approaches me from behind as I stand at the bathroom sink staring at myself, he wraps his arms gently around me and nuzzles my neck with his mouth.

His lips find my ear, and he whispers, "Do you want to talk about it?" I shake my head, and he exhales a deep, concerned breath.

As he looks down into my eyes before leaving for the day, my emotions get the better of me again, and I start to furiously blink away the unwanted tears that suddenly hit me. He exhales another deep breath, and I know it's helplessness he feels. He wants to fix my pain, but he can't, and he hates it. I kiss him swiftly and move away from him before my tears can destroy his mood more than they already have. And when the door finally closes behind him, I start to numbly move through my day, carrying the haze of my sadness with me.

CHAPTER THIRTY-FOUR

Logan

The week moves faster than I want, just like all others, and by Wednesday night I'm packing, and we're spending the last of our intimate time together. It's erotic and intense but also tinged with dread because of another long weekend apart and the knowledge that every day takes us closer to our final moments together.

We don't speak a word to each other as our bodies move, and my hands and mouth explore every secret part of her. I grip her skin possessively, harshly, and she gives in willingly to everything I want.

My flight is early the next morning, and I have to leave long before Rowan even needs to get up, but when I rise in the pre-dawn hour, she's already stirring, and she watches me sleepily as I walk toward the bathroom to shower. When I emerge twenty minutes later, she's still awake, curled up to my pillow.

I don't bother dressing right away, and she watches as I move around the room, packing last-minute items and laying clothes out. When I catch her staring at my cock, I smile at her and wait for her focus to shift up to my eyes. She blushes instantly when she realizes I'm watching her.

I approach the bed, already aroused and pulsing with desire that will have to wait until the long weekend is done. I shake my head in frustration as I look down at her, and I sigh when I sit beside her on the bed. Kissing her, however, is something I can definitely make time for. I taste her mouth and lick her tongue, driving us both

166

insane for a few minutes before finally breaking away and standing to dress.

She smiles when I glance at her as I'm slipping my shoes on. "Did you remember your underwear?" she asks sweetly.

"You know you're completely responsible for that."

Once dressed and ready to leave, I return to her lips and torture us both for a while longer before begrudgingly breaking away to leave. It's going to be a long weekend—a lonely weekend.

But Sunday does eventually arrive, and when it does, so, too, does my excitement to see her...

⌘⌘⌘⌘

When I open the door, Rowan practically screams in excitement. I'm exhausted, but seeing her bounce off the couch toward me wakes me up in an instant. She looks practically animalistic as she runs toward me, and sensing that her prowess could easily knock me over in my tired state, I drop my bags just as she reaches me and pounces into my arms.

I carry her to the bedroom as she straddles my hips, and I'm hard just imagining the way she'll touch me. It will be perfect. It will be everything I need from her, and as I lay her down under my body, she gazes up at me, her face softening as she reaches for my cheek.

"You're tired," she comments quietly.

I smile down at her. "I'm not too tired for you."

She bites her lower lip looking guilty, but then I grind my erection between her legs, pressing harshly into her sex. She reaches down, fumbling with my button and zipper, and the moment my pants are undone, she pushes them and my underwear down, setting me free.

Her eyes watch mine, hungry and beseeching. We've been apart for days, and the separation has been as difficult as it always is. And with this separation comes the intense need to be together in every possible way. And she asks the question I dread—her expectations always set this one act. Making love. She wants it. And God, so do I. Every day with her, every touch, every look, every taste erodes my resolve just a bit more. But she sees the rejection in my eyes before I've even a chance to turn her down yet again. The weariness of her thoughts is clear in the depths of her eyes.

"Why won't you make love to me? Please, just tell me."

There is no answer to this question that will satisfy her, but she also deserves the truth. I'd rather she understand how her importance to me and my respect for her are at the heart of my

167

decision rather than sending her away brokenhearted and dejected.

So I open a page of my innermost heart and give her a glimpse of what it means to be completely and utterly obsessed with her. "You can't imagine how hard it's going to be for me to let you go. I've become … attached to you … very attached," I say as I reach out and stroke the porcelain skin of her cheek.

"Then why not? Don't you want to? Is it something about me or something I've done?"

"No! That's not… I want to make love to you as much as I've ever wanted anything in my life. This isn't about what I want. Hell, it's not even about what you want. It's about what's right." The confusion in her eyes tells me I'm not making any sense, so I trudge on. "I can't keep you. You don't belong to me, and someday you will belong to someone else." I can't keep the pain of this thought from registering on my face. But still, I trudge on. "You deserve a man who will take you and keep you, not a man who will have you and leave you. I can't be the man who does that to you."

This evening, after so many away from each other, has just turned to hell. Tears sting her eyes as she struggles to maintain her composure. I've rejected her once again, and the reasons don't soften the blow even a fraction. I wish she knew it was all about her. Every last decision I've made has been about her; whether they were right or wrong, *her*. She struggles against her tears and fights to find her voice. She finally gives up and, in tears, leaves the room. She leaves me, numb and in shock, sitting on my bed.

My gaze trails after her, and I want to call her back. I pray she'll return to me so I can comfort her, touch her, fix her, fix us. But she doesn't come back, and I know why—because there is nothing to say. God, I want to hit rewind and start this reunion over again. At my core, I want to keep her safe, content, and satisfied, and my heart screams at my head in protest. *I can't keep hurting her.*

All I want is to give in to her wishes. Show her how much she means to me. But my head knows what my heart doesn't understand—she deserves better than that. She isn't mine to take. Our paths are simply too far gone from any common direction. The obstacles are insurmountable. And this weekend in Denver, meeting the partners and touring the area with a real estate agent, has confirmed this fact harshly again in my mind.

I sit on my bed for what feels an eternity, not wanting to smother her but wanting to know she's okay. Eventually, I move. I find her sleeping on her bed, and as I sit and she wakes, her puffy red eyes remind me of her hurt and remind me of my own agony as well. My heart lurches in my chest as the pain she feels hits me like a ton of bricks. I pull my body up next to hers, needing to comfort her.

"This is hard for me too." I want to share her heartache as I reach out and stroke the soft skin of her cheek.

The porcelain skin trembles under my light touch and her eyes fill with tears, threatening to spill yet again. I lean to her mouth without hesitation and kiss her gently. I want to take away her hurt, and I take my time as I cover her lips with my own. When her mouth becomes greedy, I know she's stowed her pain for the time being in exchange for the passion we find so easily together. But the moment I think she's set aside her sadness, the gears shift in her mind yet again.

And when she speaks, she breaks my heart. "I can't do this anymore," she whispers with a strained look on her face. And my own agony clutches my heart and squeezes until I think I can't stand it any longer. She continues. "I'm sorry. It just hurts too much. More than I ever imagined it could."

I can't move; I can barely breathe. I'm not ready to lose her. I can't lose her. I don't know how to lose her. But the light in her eyes has suddenly dimmed. Her beautiful face, now slack and defeated, just stares over my shoulder. She won't look at me, and as the reality sinks in, it hurts—physically, emotionally, every last muscle of my body aches for her.

She is gone from me…

I stand up on shaky legs; my own tears sting my eyes at this sudden and unwelcome rejection and loss. She's not angry at me. She's just done. I've hurt her too much. I've taken too much of her and refused to give her what she needs. To her, making love is everything it should be; born of her young, idealistic mind, it's love and nothing more. It's what she has been trying to give me for so long now. It's the emotion, the intimacy, the surrender of herself to me. And it's what I won't give her. It translates loud and clear in her mind. I've withheld my love and emotion and every last bit of myself she needs by refusing her. And regardless of whether my intentions were valid and honorable, it's broken her heart for the last time.

When I return to my room I lie awake, staring at the ceiling for hours. I drift off to sleep in the early morning hours, and I dream of Grand Haven. I replay every moment of our time there and how much I enjoyed her that night. We were just a couple, like any other. It was real, and it was incredible. And when I wake, I'm content for half a moment until I remember just how far I am from that reality.

As I rise and make coffee, I discover she's gone for school already. I have no way of knowing at this moment, but this will be our new co-existence for the next couple of months—Rowan conveniently side-stepping any interaction with me. Why should I think she'd be any less capable of evading me than she does her father? She's well-practiced in the art of avoidance, and the next long weeks promise to be agony.

CHAPTER THIRTY-FIVE

Rowan

The days slip by like a grotesque ticking clock. *Tick tock tick tock.* The days slowly become weeks, and as much as I'm dreading the loss of Logan, it looms ever closer with each passing minute. The whole painful countdown is all the more agonizing because I'm angry, uncharacteristically and inappropriately angry, at Logan. I want him desperately in one breath and hate him in the other. I've used my hurt to punish him. He doesn't deserve it, I know, but it's somehow easier to hate him than to hurt all of the time.

I've taken to spending nearly every night I can with Sara. I'm also working far more hours and evenings than I ever have before, and while I'm struggling to keep up with my last semester of school, I don't care. It's the very best way to avoid Logan. On the rare night I don't have plans to stay with Sara, I show up late from work and retreat to my room without so much as acknowledging Logan's existence. I feel his eyes watching me pass through his home—he watches, but he never speaks to me. I feel terrible for how I'm treating him, but he's giving me my space. He's giving me exactly what I've asked for. It's what I wanted, isn't it? I'm sure he regrets ever meeting me, and sad as it may be to admit, I think that's probably for the best. The odd time or two I've been forced to actually speak with him have been the most strained and uncomfortable conversations of my life.

Sara hits me up about moving into Logan's apartment for the

171

summer a couple of weeks after I broke it off with Logan. I'm hurting constantly and bouncing back and forth from resentful anger to absolute sadness. It's almost laughable when she asks, given my current situation, were it not such a glaring reminder of just how dishonest I've been with her.

"Come on, Row. It'll be fun. They don't even want us to pay rent."

She obviously sees the hesitation in my expression. Staying at his place is hard now, and once he's gone I'm terrified it will be nothing but a gut-wrenching reminder of what I've lost.

"I don't know. It seems like a lot of effort just to turn around and move again a few months later." My eyes shift from hers in my guilt, but not before catching hers drop and her face slacken. I'm hurting her.

She hasn't missed my sullen, depressed mood lately, and I know she worries. "Please, Row." And then she unloads her wounded heart in my lap and leaves me wanting to beg her forgiveness. "I can't stand not knowing what's going on with you right now." She has tears in her eyes, and they threaten to spark my own. "You're so far away from me, and I hate it. I can't help fix what's going on in your life when you won't talk to me, and … I know if you wanted my help, you'd tell me about it. I know that, and it hurts. You've never shut me out before. Please just at least let me be here for you." Now her tears are falling, and so are mine.

I feel awful. I feel guilty. I've set her friendship aside in exchange for my own sorrow. I'm hurting one of the most important people in my life, and I hate myself for it.

I manage nothing more than "Okay," in my voice that is fighting hard not to break down into sobs.

Sara has every reason to hate me, but she inexplicably doesn't; she's just concerned. I can't help wonder if I would be so gracious if the tables were turned. I'm more blessed than I deserve with her. I know I'm bitter as hell pretty much all the time, but even I, in all my piss poor attitude, have to admit I'm being a monstrous bitch, and staying in Logan's apartment is without doubt the best place for me to be, even if the thought is excruciating.

In truth, I suspect Logan is the one behind this whole scheme, but I have no other real options lest I destroy my relationship with Sara. I won't survive the next year without her, and I can't allow myself to push her away in my pain. She doesn't deserve it.

Over the next weeks, my ever-watchful best friend worries incessantly about me. Most days, it's hard just getting out of bed in the morning, let alone reassuring her I'm fine. She asks, but I'm sure she doesn't expect to get much response from me at this point, and eventually, she gives up asking and does her best to just support me. And she does.

Patiently and quietly she sits by day after day waiting for me to talk. But I can't talk to her about this, and it just furthers my sadness. Still, she's happy I've agreed to move in with her for the summer, and it seems to bring her some degree of reassurance.

Every day is a struggle, and I wonder if it will ever feel better. Ending my relationship with Logan was my choice, and I know it was the right decision. However, there isn't a day that goes by where I don't reconsider and have to fully fight the urge to beg him to take me back. But the fact of the matter is there is nothing to go back to—a relationship destined to die from the start. A relationship built on coupling more than anything else—and coupling in the most juvenile of terms at that; I am, after all, still a virgin. He just didn't want me enough, or did he respect me too much; what was the excuse he fed me? It all feels the same, and it hurts. It doesn't really matter how you slice it.

But truly hating him is an impossibility, and through all my bitterness and anger I still love him desperately and painfully. *Love.* That wasn't supposed to happen. Then again, the past half year should never have happened. I remember the first night I spent at his apartment. Never in a million years could I have imagined going from awkward encounters standing in his kitchen in the middle of the night to finding myself in his bed, to ending the most satisfying and amazing relationship I could ever have imagined. And I want to regret it. But I don't. Instead, I would give anything to go through it all again … perhaps with a happier ending.

⌘⌘⌘⌘

I bow out of Logan's graduation ceremony as gracefully as is possible, though I'm sure the Harringtons find it strange I should miss such a big day in Logan's life. Logan, on the other hand, is ever present on my own graduation day, and as Sara and I take our turns receiving our diplomas, it reeks of finality to this last school year, and I'm not sure I'm ready for the life that lies in front of me.

My father manages to make it to the occasion, though the stench of last night's booze is following him. I'm far past being embarrassed by him, and as we approach the Harringtons after the ceremony, Marcus holds a hand out to him genially. Logan appears to be seething with hatred, and as my father's stale cigarette and alcohol stench reaches the group, a few noses wrinkle. Okay, I take it back; I'm embarrassed. Still, they're pleasant as I stand by nervously and uncomfortably rocking on the outside edges of my wedge sandals.

Having given up hating my father with his eyes, Logan is now concentrating on me, not paying attention to any of the pleasantries around us. Logan's parents are congratulating me generously and graciously. Marcus puts an arm around me and gives me a good squeeze before kissing my cheek. Ronnie pulls me into a tight hug, crying the whole time. These aren't new tears, though; she's been going on since Sara and I woke up this morning. Logan's family looks at him expectantly, waiting for him to congratulate me as well, and with the eyes of his entire family watching, he takes both of my shoulders in his hands and leans down to kiss my cheek gently.

His lips linger a moment too long, and I blush furiously as his lips meet my skin that has been so deprived of his touch for so long. My knees weaken as the breath leaves my lungs, and as my breath hits his neck so very close to my mouth, he inhales sharply. My body has been on fire from the moment he closed the space between us, and as his lips leave my skin, my body cries out for more.

"Congratulations," he says quietly as he pulls away.

My nod is barely perceptible, and when he releases his hold on me, I'm left once again with his absence—and the depression that goes along with it. The loss of him floods back to me in an instant, and my eyes well over with tears. I turn from the group trying to hide my eyes, but not before Ronnie notices the tears slide down my cheek. And as our eyes meet, hers drift to Logan, who is now holding Sara in a tight bear hug. I avoid our small group, pretending to see something else of interest across the room, but moments later I feel Ronnie's hand on my arm.

She pulls me into another hug, but rather than congratulations, she offers me support. And in a tone laced with compassion and at least some degree of understanding, she whispers in my ear, "You'll be okay, kiddo."

At her words, my tears fall freely, and I excuse myself to the restroom. Tears aren't hard to come by on this day, and I'm guessing I fit in quite well. To add insult to injury, Marcus invites my father and me to join them for dinner at a nearby restaurant. My father has no intention of turning down a free meal or free drinks, and so I'm to suffer with more Logan today.

As we're seated, Logan takes the seat across from me. He focuses on me while I struggle to make the most minimal of eye contact with him. I revel in his presence, yet I suffer at the same moment. I dread the end of dinner when it will be time to part from him again, but I feel like I'm coming unglued at the seams the entire time we're there.

My father, holding true to form, starts drinking early and doesn't stop until the end of the meal. He's drunk by the time we're ready to leave, and the humiliation I felt earlier at his presence has now been quadrupled.

Marcus suggests I drive him home, but as Logan starts to object my father pipes up in a rather loud, slurred, and belligerent voice. "Doesn't even live with me anymore. She probably can't even remember how to get there…"

And as Sara and Marcus start questioning what he's talking about, Ronnie pipes up quickly, saving me any further lies. "Well, Sara, the two of you do spend a good deal of time together. I'm sure it just seems as though she's never around."

Before anyone can comment further, she's out of her chair ushering us all out the door. Logan offers to drive my father home, and I bristle at the thought of them together. And as I eye him warily, Ronnie again interjects and agrees Logan should take care of it. Hasn't she turned into quite the puppeteer today? Logan gives me a small nod and a final quiet "congratulations" before escorting my stumbling father to his Jeep.

Given my father's reception to Logan, I would guess he doesn't have any recollection of the last time they were together, but where my father's memory might be lacking, Logan's certainly isn't. He hasn't stopped glaring at my father all day. I'm worried about Logan being alone with him, but it seems the choice isn't mine to make. I can't quite comprehend what Ronnie knows, but she, without a doubt, has her suspicions.

The day ends with Sara and I crashing in exhaustion, and at least one of us excited for summer and the rest of our lives. I sure wish I could share her enthusiasm.

CHAPTER THIRTY-SIX

Logan

I feel so terribly guilty for not having foreseen just how truly devastating the end of our relationship would end up being to both of us. I care so much for her, but all I do is cause her heartache. I wish now that our relationship had never crossed the line it did, but at the same time, I can't imagine not having had her. The pain of my presence and my touch was so evident in our interaction today. I miss her insanely, but I cause her nothing but grief when I'm around her.

And as I start to pack up my boxes for the move, I start to see more and more withdrawal from her. She escapes to Sara's the better portion of the time anyway but with the boxes comes more absence. I get it. It hurts. It hurts me too.

Rowan has agreed to move in here with Sara, and for that, I'm relieved. But I have still to work out the details of moving her in here *after* I leave and disguising the fact she's been here all along. It shouldn't be hard, considering her entire life's possessions can easily fit in the back of her old Jeep, but she won't be able to spend the night here on the night before I move out.

My family will be here helping me pack up that evening, and then they'll be arriving early the next morning with Sara's furniture to unload before Dad and I head westward in the moving truck with my Jeep in tow. I couldn't quite come to terms with buying a house in Denver given my current hatred for anything more than a mile from Rowan, but I did find a great house for rent in the LowDow neighborhood. It's an easy commute to downtown Denver, and I've always loved the area—eclectic, old homes, mature trees.

Mom will be staying behind with the girls to help them move and organize. I'd suggest Rowan stay with Sara the night before, but Sara will be busy here helping me. She needs to just disappear for a night, hopefully somewhere safe and quiet where I can join her after my family leaves for the evening. I can't bear the idea of not spending time with her on my last night in Michigan. And though I know I'll be treading on thin ice with her, I have to see her one more time. There is so much to be said, and I need at least the chance to undo some of the hurt I've caused her.

So when I finally catch up with her at the beautiful old hotel that sits on Grand Haven's bay late on the evening before my departure, I'm disheartened to see her state.

"Why did you ask me to meet you here? I mean, here of all places..." She can barely look me in the eye, and the look of bitter agony is evident in her face.

"One of my most favorite memories was being in Grand Haven with you. I just wanted us to be here together again." I shake my head subtly.

She's right. Of course, I understand why it's hard to be back here, and I suddenly feel like a complete asshole for dragging her back here once more for an encore. This will be no encore of our previous night spent here. Instead, it will be one more reminder of our time together and the fact it's now over. Why did I bring her back here of all places? What was I thinking? I haven't seen her smile in over a month, and when I thought of this place, all I could think of was how much we smiled. The memory of that evening—the Farmers' Market, the pier, the beach, it reminded me of us. But that time is over, and this place is now just an unbearable reminder. God, she's right.

My eyes drop in guilt. "I'm sorry. I shouldn't have brought you here. I just wanted someplace quiet and out of the way that we both enjoy, but I should have realized this wasn't a good idea."

And that same sad face is all I get in return. Sad isn't even the right word. Her face is simply slack and emotionless—her eyes dead of their usual spirit. I haven't seen that spirit and twinkle for so long, and the loss of it has destroyed my ability to feel joy anymore. I'm just a dead carcass of a person, and I should have known this place would just torture us both. But I do my best to salvage the evening.

It's late, but I've not eaten all day and suggest dinner down on the bay. She reluctantly agrees, and the trip down is uncomfortable and devoid of any conversation. She spends the entire meal picking at her food and not eating anything. She stares off at the water, unwilling to look at me. When we return to the hotel, she closes the bedroom door in the suite, making it clear she doesn't want anything more to do with me. But I can't let it end like this.

As I knock on the door, I half expect her to tell me to fuck off, but she answers, and with a weary sigh she lets me come in. But she stands impatiently, refusing to look at me, waiting for me to speak, and quite obviously wanting to get rid of me.

So I take a stab at softening her heart. "I've missed you. I wish it didn't have to end like this. I can't bear that you hate me so much."

She says nothing for a moment, letting her emotions wash over her face, twisting it in agony at my words and what they mean to her. When she speaks, her voice is a mere whisper, softened in defeat. "I'm not mad at you. I can't stand this." Her voice falters, and her composure disintegrates.

Her tears well over and flow; she doesn't even attempt to restrain or compose herself, and at the sight of her pain my breath and emotion hitch in my throat as I feel every awful stab of it. She continues. "It hurts so much." And that's when she comes apart altogether... And I do too.

As she sobs, I grab her up in my arms and hold her tightly and desperately to me. I hold her, afraid to release her even slightly, terrified I won't get the chance to hold her so close again. Her arms are around me, and I lift her gently to the bed and lie down next to her. For the moment, the constant anxiety that has plagued me for the past six weeks is completely abated. And while I know it won't stay gone long, I revel in this short reprieve. Her body is in my arms where it belongs, and I soak up this momentary relief.

Her mouth finds mine, gentle at first and then insistent and demanding. And I'm desperate to take away the pain of the last many weeks apart. I know I have to give her up tomorrow morning, but I'm powerless to think about tomorrow right now. I've been so starved of her that I've lost all sense of reason. I want to claim every part of her that has been withheld from me for so long. And I start pulling her clothes from her body aggressively. She matches my insistence as she strips me of my clothes as well, and soon we're naked and alone together once again.

I mount her body and spread her legs wide with my own. I nestle between her legs, feeling her warmth and moisture licking seductively at every spot where I make contact with her pussy. I want to taste her wet folds and take over her pussy with my fingers, but I need her eyes more. I've been so harshly punished of her eyes for so long. The windows to her soul she has so openly shared with me in the past have been so devastatingly withheld from me, and I need to see her again. She looks back at me, panting as I take in her eyes. They're desperate and finally alive to me again. I drink in her gaze, finally ending the month-long deprivation.

It doesn't escape my attention that my cock is nestled between the slick wet folds of her sex. Her breath is hitching, and mine is as well. She needs all of me. And God, I need all of her too. Her eyes are on mine, and without speaking a word she's asking me to submit to her wishes one last time. She's asking me to give her the one thing I've denied her for so long; she's asking me to love her fully. And I need her to love me just as much. There is no way I can let her go without sharing this with her. It has to be me. It's supposed to be me. And in one instant, my long-held resolve crumbles in defeat.

I take in her eyes one last time and thrust hard to my hilt inside her virgin entry before even consciously being aware I've made the decision to, but I was powerless to deny her the instant she opened up to me again. And as shock and recognition of what I've just done sink in, I look to her eyes for reassurance. What I see instead is pain. Oh God, what have I done to her?

Rowan

Pain sears through my core, tearing away at me as his body invades mine. The fullness is overwhelming—the agony so unexpectedly sharp and intense. He's searching my eyes with horror etched all over his beautiful face. He starts to leave my body, and I panic. I clutch at his hips trying desperately to keep him—wanting to savor the experience.

He stills within me, our heavy breathing the only sound in the room. He clutches my cheeks so tenderly in worry and wonder. He remains buried in me as still as a statue ... waiting—ready to pull away at any moment and leave my body forever. He has to belong to me. I could bear this hurt from no other man. He owns it, and I desperately fear the loss of it.

And in fear of his loss, I encourage him further. "Please, don't stop."

He looks at me in shock as though I've struck him across the face.

I plead again. "Please." I need him, pain and all.

And slowly, heat from the permission I've just granted him touches his face. His eyes relax and his shoulders release their tension. He starts to move.

The first withdrawal is agonizingly slow, but I know he won't stay gone from my body for long; the look in his eyes tells me he's resigned and lusting intensely after this fate. The fight is finally over. He's given in, and there is nothing left to hold back from me. The second invasion is as slow as his withdrawal—his gaze never leaving mine. The throbbing ache is steady and unrelenting as his cock fills me farther and farther and stretches me to my limit and then past it. When he's deep within me once again, he stops and waits patiently, so patiently, giving me time to adjust. And eventually I do. The next thrust comes faster and with one swift move. And each thrust after becomes more and more demanding. And as his pace quickens, so does my body.

The pain eventually fades to a dull throb as he continues to enter my tight passage and then retreat over and over again. Every jolting thrust of his cock innervates the nerves of my channel and touches me in such a way that my body starts to crave his pounding force. I rise to meet his cock over and over, forcing him to drive deeper into me—not fearing the intense invasion in the least, though I know it will hurt.

My orgasm starts to build incredibly, mixing with the throbbing ache in my groin, and it's something completely new and intense—unlike any climax he's shown me so far. I know it won't be long before his thrusts will finish me off completely, and as I finally come, clutching his shoulders close to mine, he continues to take my body over and over until he's crying out his own release, burying his face in my neck, and clutching me in his arms. He loses himself deep within me, coming inside me, and emptying himself as his orgasm pulses through me.

He stays buried in my neck as his gasping slows, and he finally meets my eyes again. I can see fear taking over instantly—concern at what he's done. I want to reassure him, and I reach out to touch his face. His skin is smooth and warm, his face so vulnerable in his panic, his mouth so tender and beckoning. I lean to him, taking his mouth before he can express his worry. At the touch of my lips, he starts to relax, and he rolls us both to our sides. We kiss endlessly. I want to give him no time to question himself. He made love to me—finally and oh-so-incredibly. The pain felt nearly unbearable, but I was instantly addicted. To imagine we've given up so many hours of this for the sake of appropriateness. But even as I revel in our act, I feel him withdrawing in guilt.

With one quick kiss and a stroke to the cheek, Logan rolls away from me, pulling himself from my sore vagina as he goes. I gasp at the sudden loss of his body, instantly wanting him to be back within me. The concern in his eyes tells me he carries a world of regret on his shoulders, and it hurts. I want him to be okay with this as much as I am, but instead he insists on torturing himself. He stands from the bed, letting me soak in his beauty.

His bottom is firm and the cheeks perfectly round. His legs are long, lean, and perfectly proportioned. His shoulders are strong and taper down to his toned waist. He is so beautiful and so damn perfect. It takes my breath away. I'm struck by the sudden remembrance of him from earlier in the year. I used to revel in his presence, imagining what a man such as him must look like naked, what he must taste like, what he must smell like. And all through my imaginings, I could never guess how intimately I would come to know him. I've mapped out every inch of him over these past months, conquering and claiming his body as though it were my own. But as I watch him now, his guilt is palpable, and he is once again distant. I watch him retreat naked and beautiful to the bathroom, my heart dropping inch by inch by inch on the heel of his footsteps.

CHAPTER THIRTY-SEVEN

Logan

As I stare at my body in the mirror, I struggle against anger at myself and complete satisfaction of finally having experienced her fully. But what plagues me is what I've taken from her. She may not think she cares right now, but I've just taken something I can't give back, and the evidence is all over my still engorged cock.

As I wash her blood from my penis, still vacillating between complete repletion and utter despair, she enters. She looks worried and nervous and positively stunning. Catching my attempt at removing the evidence of having taken her so forcefully, she instantly reassures me she's fine. I offer a weak smile, but the look on her face tells me she isn't buying it.

She starts the bath and returns to me while she waits for the bath to fill. Her touch calms me as she wraps her arms around me, and when the bath is finally full she turns the light off, leaving only the dim bedroom light to filter in through the partially open door. And as we've done in the past, we shut out the world and retreat to our own private world of warmth, darkness, and each other.

As she sinks into the bathtub, she stills as her raw and abused pussy hits the water, reminding me just how sore she must be. I secretly admonish myself for being so rough with her. I gave in pitifully, and with no restraint whatsoever; I took over her body completely.

After impaling her so aggressively, I tried to go slow, but she was willing, so very willing, and I soon pushed her to the pace I needed—fast and hard. But she felt amazing. Tighter than I could ever imagine, and she rose to the challenge wantonly. I've made love to her—finally and wholly, I've had her in every way I've wanted and needed. And I want more. I want to own her, and the idea she will someday share this with someone other than me is hard to swallow.

She must and she should move on with her life, but it hurts all the same. Could I rewrite our lives and the directions we're going, I would do so in an instant, but I can't stand in her way, and my own path has been laid out before me for so long—signed, sealed, and delivered. She's too young and has yet to experience her life and her freedom. She will likely change her mind countless times about everything she holds as truth in this moment; it's just the way youth works. She's not ready for forever... even if I am. And I am. I would seal my future with her for the rest of my life if I could. My need for her is that strong. Or is it my love for her that is so strong?

Love. That was never part of the plan. But I love her. There is no doubt nor question in my mind at this point. But that doesn't help either of us. How could I have let this happen? I was satisfied with my simple boring life and with my simple boring girlfriend before Rowan came along. Then it wasn't enough anymore; nothing was enough except for her. Now I've taken her virginity, which never should have belonged to me. And hard as I try, I can't regret it. It was the most precious gift she could have given me, and she did so willingly and eagerly.

Rowan

As the water cools with our bodies, Logan helps me from the bath and dries us off. My arousal stirs at his touch even though the throbbing between my legs tries to restrain me. He accompanies me back to bed and then crawls between my legs. He places soft kisses on my thighs and stomach before parting my lips and kissing the swollen and raw folds of skin. His kisses are sweet, patient, not meant to lead anywhere, just to tell me he understands I'm hurting. He watches me carefully, gauging my comfort. And when he's kissed every painful inch of my sex, he turns off the bedside lamp and pulls me possessively into his body. There he falls into a restless sleep, murmuring and flinching at my slightest movement.

I don't find any rest either, knowing the alarm clock will plague me for the remainder of the night. I settle in and listen to his deep breathing, hypnotically setting my own breaths to match his. He's so perfect in every way—strong, sure, and protective, yet caring and tender. I trust him beyond all measure and have found security and a gentle touch that I no longer knew existed.

Having experienced his support and touch, I've realized how much this security was missing from my life. It's now all I crave, and it's slipping through my fingers. His life is running its own course. I'm sure it will be amazing; he's a Harrington, after all. He will be happy, and I hope someday I will find my own happiness. But it's hard to imagine at this moment, a dark and lonely moment, there will be light after Logan. He's so near but slipping away by the second.

As I stroke his cheek he stirs, and I'm overcome by my need to join myself to him again. Come morning, I will lose him and be forced to deal with distance, and worse yet, lasting and permanent absence from him. I must savor every last moment of him I can. And I start stroking his chest, running my fingers through the fine hairs that cover him, and nuzzling his neck.

He rouses and pulls me in closer. I kiss his neck and move up to his face. As he clutches my cheeks with his hands and kisses me softly, I know of one certainty: he cares. I mean something to him, and though I can't guess if it's nearly as significant to him as it is to me, I trust it matters. And he shares my dread of being parted.

I'm still so sore, and his cock is so large and invasive. Yet I can't let him go without having him again—just once more. I have no idea how to make love to him, but my body, always so desperate for him, will surely figure it out. I raise myself up above him. And as I pull myself to straddle him, his hands clutch my hips and stay my movement. I plead one last time for what I need. And he gives in … one last time.

Logan

As her pussy makes first contact with the engorged head of my penis, the sharp inhale of her breath tells me she's hurting but determined. She slides down my length, failing to restrain her cries as the pain tears through her. I fight the urge to push her off me and save her any further hurt. She wants this, and I understand why.

She takes all of me until she's sitting squarely and firmly against my hips. She stays still for some time waiting for her body to adjust to me. And when she's ready, she slowly begins to make love to me—gently and sweetly. I hold her tight to my chest with one hand on her back and clutch her face close to mine with the other. And as she begins to slowly move along the shaft of my cock, I give her the only thing I have left to give her.

I whisper every word she needs to hear and I need to say. I tell her how beautiful she is. I tell her she amazes me. I make sure she knows she is the most precious person in the world to me. I make sure she understands what losing her means to me and how impossible it is to imagine my life without her. She continues to make love to me slowly and surely as I murmur in her ear, clutching her body close to mine as she pushes her pelvis down against my own. I whisper on a hushed breath everything I want her to keep and take with her. Her silent tears drop to my cheek as she rocks our bodies. I hold nothing back from her except the three words that are simply too much for me to say and will bring her nothing but grief. I pray she knows those words even though I can't give them to her.

We stay firmly together, moving together while her tears touch my skin and I struggle to restrain my own. And when everything I have to tell her has been said, she gives me my release. For the second time this evening, I empty myself deep within her, wanting to possess her in that incredibly intimate, and quite frankly, inappropriate way. I want her to feel my cum within her body, and I want to leave my seed in her, like some territorial animal. I have no right to be so careless with her, but it's too late. As my pulsing orgasm subsides, she takes her own. This moment is quieter, more intimate, and more precious than any other moment I've spent with her.

She collapses to my chest, and I stay within her, not wanting to lose the feel of her warmth. Her tears continue to slowly run to my chest. I keep her fast to my body for many minutes before kissing her warm mouth as I pull my length from her tight sheath. I continue to kiss her as I shift her to the bed, enfolding her in my arms. And there we stay, waiting and dreading the morning. My sleep is tortured and agonizing, but the morning does come eventually. And as I wake, I find a note in her stead. She's slipped out once again. She knows how much I hate that. For the last time, she defies me, and it's bittersweet and so very Rowan. I open the note from her.

Logan,

I'm sorry I left early. I hope you won't be upset with me. I just couldn't stay. Thank you for everything you've done for me. I know you've questioned yourself every step of the way, but I never have. Be happy and well and forget me fast.

-Rowan

Numbness slowly takes over my heart as I read the last words she'll give me. My new life is standing in front of me. Finally, after so many months of dreading it, it's here, and she's gone. The emptiness is nauseating, the numbness is paralyzing. I have no idea how to continue being a person. My life, so meticulously planned out by me, is suddenly my worst enemy, and I hate myself and pity myself all in the same breath.

I stand in the shower letting the overly hot water scour my skin painfully. Her scent is washing away from me, and as it does, her every last detail flashes across my mind, and every part of my being resists and fully denies she is gone.

CHAPTER THIRTY-EIGHT

Logan

When I return to my apartment, I manage to make it upstairs and get coffee started before collapsing on my bed in misery. I don't want to think, I don't want to feel, and I sure as hell don't want to remember. I try to close out the world by closing my eyes, but all I see is her face. Opening my eyes is no better. I'm surrounded by our space—the bed we've spent so much time in, the window seat where she first touched me. The entire apartment has her invisible stamp on it. What was once mine has been so thoroughly taken over by her, and now she's gone. It's tormenting, and I want to escape. But escape is no better. For every mile I put between us will just break my heart further.

When my family arrives, I mindlessly set about lifting, carrying, un-assembling, and re-assembling, until there is nothing left to do except leave. But leaving is hard. Leaving is always hard. It's not as if I thought I'd have no feelings about moving halfway across the country, but when this decision was made I hadn't fallen madly in love with a woman entirely too young for me whose life is moving in the complete opposite direction as mine. So what I already knew would be hard became damn near impossible. But it's time—unavoidably. My mother sobs, Sara is ready for me to leave so she can take over my apartment, and I stand by numbly—unable to cry, unable to do much of anything at all. Once my father and I are on our way, I turn my brain to autopilot and stare mindlessly out the window at nothing at all.

The miles fall away slowly as I continue to stare, brain dead, out the window. When we finally stop for the day somewhere in the middle of Nebraska, my father turns to me and says, "So, are you going to tell me what's got you so bent out of shape? Not like you to be so out of sorts, but you haven't said so much as two words to me since we left Grand Rapids."

I owe him an explanation, but my mind is so defeated that coming up with any appropriate excuse is impossible. I just don't have it in me to invent excuses. I end up shrugging. "I'm fine."

He knows better but leaves me in peace. Once checked into our hotel, my father is hungry for dinner, and we end up eating boring food in the hotel restaurant. I try to make small talk, but it's hard to even get words to come out of my mouth. It's painful trying to pretend to be normal. I eventually give up and sulk like a child. I do my best to numb my brain with wine, but even slightly tipsy I'm miserable. Being slightly inebriated, though, makes calling Rowan seem like a fine idea all of a sudden. But being still slightly sober also gives me enough common sense to know that would just be cruel to both of us—much like developing a relationship that would be doomed to failure. When we return to the room, I collapse on the bed craving the peace of sleep. And before long, I've found it.

We're back on the road early the next morning, and by mid-afternoon we're pulling into my new driveway of my new house in my new town to start my new life. I liked my old life. At least I did once Rowan entered it. Life with her is truly all I really want anymore. As we unload and unpack I let my mind drift to her. I imagine she's here with me, smiling at me in that most amazing and radiant way—her eyes alight with joy at a shared life together. We're unpacking, but it's *our* new town to start *our* new life … together. It's the most pleasure I've felt since making love to her in the early morning hours of the day before. It feels like so long ago, yet she's only been away from me for a short while.

We work late into the evening, taking time only to order pizza and scarf it down. We have all the furniture unloaded, in place, and re-assembled by the time we finally call it quits at midnight. The next day starts early, and we finish unloading all the boxes before lunch. By late afternoon, I'm dropping my father at the airport to catch his flight back to Grand Rapids, and I'm finally alone in this place. And I don't want to be here.

My job will start on Monday, leaving me the entire day tomorrow to wallow in my self-pity. And that's exactly what I do, rising occasionally from the couch to put something away. I wander to the nearby liquor store and buy a bottle of wine. Again I spend the evening drowning my sorrows in a bottle, only to find I have to fight my restraint to pick up the phone and call her. But I manage to keep from dialing each time I'm overcome with my need to hear her voice. And by the next morning I'm arriving at Brighton and Brinks to a very warm reception from my new firm.

My office is amazing with incredible views of downtown Denver and the mountains beyond. It's everything I'd ever dreamed of, and I curse myself for thinking this was what I wanted. Fortunately, I'm brought on a jury selection team almost immediately and put to work; I don't think I could stomach my life right now were it not for work. And as I delve into my case and research, I find my first measure of peace since leaving Grand Rapids. It hardly keeps Rowan out of my mind, but it makes being away from her more tolerable in some small way.

⌘⌘⌘⌘

Days start ticking off the calendar, and I stay as busy as possible, putting in ridiculous hours at work to avoid being alone with my thoughts more than I have to. But every night I end up fighting my despair the second I lay my head on my pillow. It's then I miss her the most—when my brain stops moving for the day and the memories of her are allowed to flood my mind, causing agonizing grief.

It's been nearly three weeks now since I last saw Rowan, and I'm desperate for the torture to end. It must at some point, but it hasn't faded an ounce, and I can't help but wonder if it ever will. I can't imagine her sharing this pain, and I wonder if it's as awful for her as it is for me. The idea of her suffering this too only makes my own anguish all the more palpable. I pray she's doing better than I am.

CHAPTER THIRTY-NINE

Rowan

I hate my life. The six weeks since Logan left have been the hardest I've experienced, overshadowed only by the memories of my mother's death. Ronnie and Sara seem intent on dragging me everywhere and anywhere, trying to perk me up, but I'm hopeless. I want them to believe I'm fine so they'll just leave me in peace, but I can't pretend I'm not in hell. Smiling makes my mouth hurt; laughing is impossible.

So when Ronnie suggests a shopping day in Grand Haven, I inwardly groan but outwardly try to be a good sport. The trip there fills me with anxiety. I dread the images that will plague me from my last time there. I want to see nothing of that time as it will be more excruciating than I can stand. But the images and the memories are everywhere. We eat lunch in the harbor on the very same street Logan and I enjoyed the Farmers' Market only a few months ago. It's warm and sunny, but my heart is cold and dark. The lighthouse is visible a few miles down the coast, and I swear if Ronnie suggests a drive out there, I'll scream. All I want is to be at home in bed, sleeping. It's my only safe haven—though even my sleep is often interrupted with memories of Logan.

He's doing well, so Ronnie says over lunch when Sara asks, involved in a big case and staying very busy. Her eyes are on my face as I refuse to look up from the spot I'm studying on the table. I don't want Ronnie to see the pain in my eyes, and I know she's searching for it. I'm glad he's okay, but I want to hear nothing more about it.

The reminders hurt, and in some ridiculous way I resent him for being okay. I'm not okay. Why the hell should he be? It isn't fair, and I resort to throwing a temper tantrum inside my head while I focus on the worn and scratched surface of the table in front of me.

When Ronnie drops Sara and me off later that afternoon, I have a letter waiting for me from the admissions department at the University of Michigan. They need a copy of my social security card for their records, and my guts clench at the realization this will mean a trip back to home sweet trailer park. If Logan were here, he'd kill me for even considering it… But he's not here, and I have little choice but to go. It's mid-afternoon on a Tuesday, so my father should still be at work. There's no time like the present, and I tell Sara where I'm off to before running out the door.

When I arrive and enter the trailer, I'm taken aback by the state of the place. Not that our trailer was ever anything to write *Better Homes and Gardens* about, but I have never seen it in this state. There is garbage strewn about from room to room. The stench is overwhelming; many months' worth of Styrofoam take out containers, fast food bags, and old pizza boxes litter every piece of furniture and every square inch of floor space. Well, if I didn't want to stay any longer than necessary, the smell of this place was all the motivation to work quickly I would need.

I proceed first to my father's bedroom closet. And while I find a collection of gratuitous porn magazines that are more terrifying than they are sexy, a handgun—again frightening given who it belongs to—and a strange collection of old rusty nails, what I don't find is my social security card.

As I wander back out to the living room, my eyes land on the side table that sits next to my father's old smelly recliner. It has two drawers, and I've seen my father stash many an odd piece of paper in there. It's as good as any place to look. The trailer is small, and while cluttered all to hell, there simply aren't that many places my social security card could be hiding. I approach the side table, and doing my best to touch only what I absolutely must, I start rifling through the contents of the drawer. I find more overdue bills than any grown adult ought to have, numerous scraps of paper with bizarre notes and messages written on them, and a rather large amount of receipts from the nearest liquor store. Again I strike out finding my social security card, and as I slam the drawers shut I unleash a slew of expletives at the poor old side table.

Giving up is sounding like a better idea by the minute. There may not be very many logical places to keep the card, but unfortunately, there are a good deal of obscure and unfathomable places it could be hiding. Being here is unsafe, and I can just imagine Logan laying into me, but the idea of Logan yelling at me for risking my safety just brings on the all too familiar stab of pain … and a bit of resentment. What can I say; anger has become a very effective means of coping with my loss of him. I often find my daydreams of him becoming charged with fury at him, fury at myself, and fury at life in general for pulling us apart from one another. And my fury now compels me onward. Onward, in this case, means the file cabinet in the kitchen that the microwave sits on.

As I enter the kitchen, I find it's in an even worse state than the remainder of the house. What looks like a city dump in the living room is a full-on explosion of garbage in the kitchen. Every inch of the counter is consumed by dirty dishes and rotting food. The stench is a solid mass that hits like a blanket smothering my face as I plummet into it. There are mice feces all over the counters, and I'm suddenly very attuned to the scurrying sounds that surround me.

I approach the file cabinet ready to hold my breath and dive into one more disgusting filth pit, but as I tug on the dusty old handle it doesn't budge. Awesome. Locked. Of course, it's locked. I let go of another inanimate object tirade before completely throwing in the towel, and as I storm back into the living room still cursing, I walk right into the meanest man in the world. He looks more demon than man at the moment, and given the nearly empty whiskey bottle in his hand, I'm guessing he's beyond the point of any sense and reason.

As I stumble backward into the kitchen, he grabs me with one hand around my throat and virtually throws me back into the living room. I hit the side of the recliner and fall over it to the ground. I'm on the opposite side of the chair from him, but trapped in the living room with no way to skirt around him quick enough to get out the front door. As I pull myself up from the floor, he moves around the recliner and grabs me by the throat once again. He squeezes tight, and I'm suddenly overcome by images of myself being choked to death. The sting of the constricted air passage sets my brain to panic mode, and just when the pulsing vibrations of hypoxia start to take over my brain, he punches me hard on the temple. The very best thing I can say about being punched is that it forces me out of his suffocating death grip.

I fall back, hitting my head hard on a wall shelf behind me, but not hard enough to knock me out completely. I'm almost upset I'm not unconscious at this point. I thought people weren't supposed to feel pain when their bodies were in fight or flight mode. Instead, I can feel every last ache and throb. My eye feels like it's outside of my socket, the back of my head feels like it's going to explode, and my throat is still burning with fire.

As I fall to the floor on my knees, grasping the back of my head, his foot makes first contact with my gut, and what little breath I'd regained from being nearly choked to unconsciousness is forced back out of my lungs, leaving me gasping loudly and desperately for air. And before I can regain any use of my lungs, the next kick lands in nearly the same place.

I now crumble to the floor, unable to support my body any longer. As kick after kick lands, I continue to beg my body to take in air, but with every second I'm losing a fighting battle, and what little air I manage to gulp down is horribly expelled from my chest every time his foot makes contact with my abdomen. With every kick, I'm getting further and further away from consciousness. And as my consciousness fades, so, too, does the pain, and I'm only slightly aware of the thudding sound that his foot makes as it meets my body.

Suddenly the dull thudding stops, and I can feel myself being pulled by my ponytail across the carpet. The carpet is burning my face, and I'm losing hair in ripping clumps as he pulls me along. But every sense is dulled, and while I know what I should be feeling is excruciating, I'm struggling to feel anything at all at this point. And a very sad and defeated part of my mind is resigned to the fact this likely means the end must be near. Logan's face comes to the front of my mind, and as my father's torment continues I focus on Logan. I know now I won't see him again, and I regret in a way that is nearly unbearable that I ever let him slip away. But relief is coming soon.

Death will take me and end the pain and sadness I feel for my loss, and I'm thankful the suffering will be over soon. I hear the zing of scissor blades as he pulls me upright by my ponytail. I'm hanging limply from my ponytail, the hairs tearing from my scalp as the weight of my body is too much for the thin strands to bear. And as I wait for the stab of the scissors, wondering where he'll mutilate me and how he'll kill me, I hear instead the scissors releasing me from the hanging force of my ponytail. Once he's cut through my ponytail, shearing off my long hair, I collapse back to the floor. In my numb haze, I wonder why he cut my hair off. Perhaps he wants me as ugly and repulsive as possible in my casket.

He throws the scissors against the wall, yelling every awful thing he thinks about me. He then returns to me and pulls me to an awkward sitting position by the remaining hair on my head. My arms are slack at my sides, and I can't even move them. There's a warm burning in the lower part of my diaphragm that I'm sure is bad news. And as I gaze foggily up into his monstrous face, I block it out and focus on Logan. His smile. I will miss it above all else. This will be hard on him. I can feel his anguish already. He'll feel responsible, and I won't be here to reassure him he's not. As my father's face comes back into focus, I hear him call me a particularly ugly string of epithets before backhanding me across the face so hard my head sails into the very same file cabinet I was kicking mere minutes ago.

My vision blurs with every passing second and darkness is crowding in from the periphery of my sight. I crave the darkness, the end, and I spend the last of my consciousness remembering my favorite parts of life—my mother, meeting Sara, the day I found out about my scholarship, Grand Haven, and every other amazing night I spent with Logan. And as I drift off to the dull incessant thud of my limp body being kicked repeatedly, the pulsing electric buzzing in my brain returns.

And my world fades to black...

CHAPTER FORTY

Logan

I've been immersed in pre-trial research on a fairly high profile case for the better part of the past few weeks, and it's been a relief to keep busy. My life revolves around work, and I leave no time for anything else because everything else means misery. Work at least gives me something to focus on other than Rowan.

One of the partners has become determined to set me up with her daughter, and while I dodge the question as often as I can, she doesn't seem to be taking the hint. I can't help but wonder how long it will be before I'm ready to meet people, date, or even start a relationship. The idea of being with anyone but Rowan is offensive and sickening, but at some point that feeling must go away. At some point I have to get past this, don't I? But not yet. Not even close.

I sit in my office overlooking the skyline of Denver and zone out, thinking about her for a while. Immersion in work only gets you so far. Sometimes she enters my mind, and I'm powerless to do anything but give into it and enjoy the memories—even if only temporarily. But the joy of her memory ends when reality creeps back up on me, and it's then the depression hits the hardest. But this Rowan memory spell is interrupted as my phone rings, jolting me back to reality. I pick up, resenting the asshole on the other end of the line who has interrupted my fantasies.

"Hello." I fight to keep the irritation from coming through in my voice, but I'm sure it does.

"Hi Logan." The voice is choked up and emotional—exhausted

even. It's my mom.

"Mom, what's wrong? Is Sara okay? Where's Dad?"

"Logan, it's Row. Something's happened. She's in intensive care. Yesterday afternoon ... I should have called sooner. I'm sorry, it's just ... it's just been so hectic. It was touch and go last night, and Sara is so upset and won't leave the hospital. Um..."

My heart is thudding in my chest, and my ears are buzzing. I'm ready to pass out, but I have to hear the rest, and I'm too weak to even interrupt her.

"Her father did it. Just ... tried to kill her. She's got a couple cracked ribs, but the worst of it was the internal bleeding. She has a lacerated liver and spleen, and they had to resect part of her abdominal aorta. She was in surgery for hours last night before they could get the bleeding under control. She had to have a blood transfusion, and they almost lost her a couple of times during the operation before they could control the bleeding. But Logan, they think she's going to be okay."

They think she's going to be okay? She *has* to be okay!

"Now that she's stable and her blood volume is good, they're going to take her off sedation later tonight and let her wake up when she's ready... Did you hear me? The doctors say she should pull through. All their tests show the internal bleeding is now under control, and the cracked ribs didn't shift, so her lungs are fine. She's going to be hurting for a while but ... they're optimistic she'll make a full recovery."

My mother has barely taken a breath since she started talking and neither have I. I'm holding my breath in stunned silence, my heart screaming in pain. I say the only thing I need to say before hanging up quickly. "I'll be on the next flight. I'll let you know when I land."

And as I hang up, I catch her last comment. "I thought as much. We'll see you soon."

I walk hastily and numbly from the building without speaking to anyone. I speed to the airport without stopping at home to pack and dump my Jeep in long-term parking. I stop at the ticket counter, hoping God will cut me some slack. And he does. The next flight out is in an hour and will require only one fairly quick layover in Kansas City. I should be home by mid-evening. And as I slump into my seat on the airplane forty-five minutes later, the first tears start to prick my eyes.

Once in KC, I call my mom and let her know my flight number

and arrival time. She hands the phone to Sara who's waiting with her at the hospital, and Sara spends the next couple minutes sobbing into the phone as I try not to join her. I finally ask her to hand the phone back to Mom, and when she does, I discover my mom is now crying too. I finally give up and tell her I'll see her soon.

As I sit waiting to board in Kansas City, my mind starts to get away from me again. I can't imagine what Rowan endured, but it must have been hell. What was she thinking going back there? What if she had died? I don't think I could survive that. I'm in love with her, completely and utterly. How could I have ever left her? My life has been hell the past month and a half I've been away, and now I've nearly lost her. I'm not supposed to be apart from her, yet I live halfway across the country and am only returning because she nearly died. How truly fucked up has my life become?

The last leg of my flight is excruciatingly long, and my anxiety builds with each passing minute. I want to see her so desperately, but I'm terrified to see her. Seeing her hurt is hard. Seeing her when I don't know if she'll want to see me adds fear to my pain. And by the time I de-board in Grand Rapids, I'm trying to gulp down calming breaths of air to calm my body.

My father picks me up at the curb, and in less than ten minutes we're pulling in at the hospital. More calming breaths on the elevator ride up, and when we emerge Sara tackles me and the sob fest starts all over again. My mother eventually pulls her off me and embraces me in a warm hug. She whispers that Rowan is sleeping, but I can go in and sit with her for a while. Sara immediately jumps up to go with me, but my mom quickly pulls her back and nods slightly at me to go on in. Thank God for my mom and her intuition.

I'm trembling as I approach her door, and as I make my way through and into the small room, I get my first glimpse of her, and I have to grasp the door frame of the bathroom door just to stay standing. She's pale, her skin has the pallor of a dead person, ghostly white, and I have to remind myself she's going to be okay. She looks so frail, and it adds to her terribly vulnerable appearance. This isn't her. I fall apart and sink into the chair beside her bed.

I cry. I cry for her pain and what's been done to her. I cry for my own pain and the sadness of losing her. And as my tears slowly start to dry on my cheeks, I look to her again. I want to touch her so much, but I don't want to disturb her. So I stare at her—taking in every last detail of her.

Her hair has been chopped off, her left eye is swollen and bruised, and her right cheek is abraded. Her throat shows dark bruises where she's obviously been choked. She's gowned, but I know beneath her gown the beautiful body I used to worship so incessantly is covered in bruises where she was kicked and bandages and sutures where her body was opened up. Her slender fingers and frail hand are dwarfed by the tubes of the IV line attached to the top of it. She's breathing gently, and her face, though bruised and injured, is peaceful. She's beautiful—broken and battered, still the most beautiful woman in the world to me—the only woman in the world for me.

I stare at her for what seems like forever. I study every bruise, every swollen spot of skin, every cut and abrasion, and as I look at every visible part of her body, I curse myself for ever leaving her. I want to wake her so desperately. I want to hear her voice and see her eyes. I want to kiss her and promise her I'll never leave her again, but it would be a lie. My obligations are elsewhere... And I ache for her deeply and agonizingly. There is no denying I'm once again complete in her presence. This is my place. I belong to her and my place is by her side. And the absoluteness of that statement is profound, and it begs to rewrite my life.

CHAPTER FORTY-ONE

Rowan

I didn't expect to wake up. In fact, it actually comes as quite a
surprise when I open my eyes and don't see the pearly gates.
Instead, I'm looking at a terribly white and boring-looking
ceiling. The stench of the trailer, though, is blessedly gone, replaced
instead with the tell-tale antiseptic smell of a hospital. This ceiling
doesn't match the dirty and faded ceiling of the trailer either. Bonus
for me. But I feel numb, and I can't understand why I'm alive. I
shouldn't be. I'm sure I should hurt, and I can feel where my body
should hurt: my cheek, my eye, the area below my left breast that
wraps around to my side. But the pain I know should be there is dull
and faded. My brain is likewise dull. I feel lucid, but so incredibly and
comfortably tired. It's euphoric... It must be drugs. I like these
drugs. But in addition to this blessedly content feeling, I also feel
safe, and I feel warm. I try to move my hand, but my hand doesn't
respond to the signal my brain is sending it. I wonder for a moment
if perhaps I'm paralyzed, and then I decide I'm not sure I care
enough to worry about it—drugs, good drugs.

The first face I see is Sara's. She looks beautiful as always, though
puffy and splotchy from crying. Wow, I must look like hell for her
to be this upset. When she sees my open eyes, she starts sobbing and
shrieking, and as the room fills with nurses I start to think perhaps I
should have just kept my eyes closed for a while longer. The doctor
that enters ushers everyone out of the room, including the nurses,
almost immediately before she takes a seat by the bed. She

introduces herself as Dr. Ahmari, and she instantly has me at ease when she says she's *"the only heavy set, middle aged, Indian doctor in Michigan"* so I should feel very privileged she's my doctor. I do.

She's kind and motherly, and as she goes through all the different injuries I sustained, I'm glad to have her there as I start to cry. My pain medication starts to wear off, and I'm suddenly nervous. The ache in my side where my ribs are broken and where my many internal injuries were repaired is building, and it hurts. Bad. Dr. Ahmari gives me another dose of pain medication as we talk, seeing the discomfort on my face. She assures me the hurt is normal, and I shouldn't expect it to go away immediately. The cracked ribs will take a considerable time to heal and will cause me the most pain, but she thinks there's a better than good chance I'll be ready for dance in the fall.

She's going to schedule time with a physical therapist to help keep my strength and flexibility up while I heal, and she has no problem with my training with Anthony as soon as the physical therapist gives the go ahead—though she cautions that Anthony will need to follow the advice of the therapist to avoid any injury to me. I'm relieved I'll be able to train, at least, and should be back up to par by the time school starts. My education depends on it, after all, and that's really the only thing I have going for me at this point.

Truth be told, I've been desperate to get through the summer so I can throw myself into dance and forget about the past year. I'm looking forward to school as much as I have in a long time just for the distraction and the escape of it. I have to fill the void Logan left in some way, and Allendale has just been one awful memory after another.

As Dr. Ahmari stands to leave, she pauses at the door and turns back to me. "You know, Rowan, you're a very lucky young lady to have survived this. You lost a lot of blood, and your blood pressure kept dropping so low during surgery that I thought we'd lost you for sure. We almost did a few times. Take good care of yourself." And as an afterthought, she adds, "Oh, and apparently I'm not the only one who's been waiting patiently for you to wake up. The detectives have been showing up regularly to see if you're ready for visitors."

That's just what I need. But it brings up an interesting question. What the hell happened to my father? The last I saw of him, he was quite intent on killing me, yet somehow I'm alive. While I ponder this, Dr. Ahmari fills me in on the police action in the hospital, which revolves around me, of course. She wants to know if I'm up for speaking with them. I can't see any reason to delay the inevitable, so bring on the cops. This should be fun.

Sara rushes in as soon as the doctor leaves and pulls me into a painful but welcome hug. She starts crying yet again, and I wonder how much she's been doing this over the past couple days. But before I have time to ask, two detectives enter the room and ask Sara politely to leave.

"Oh, come on! Seriously?" She's miffed, and with a reluctant and very annoyed look, she turns around and leaves the room again.

The detectives are patient as I recount the events of two days ago. They record my statement and take notes endlessly while I talk, interrupting only occasionally with questions.

When I'm finished, they have more questions. How many times has he been violent with me, what other injuries have I sustained, why didn't I tell anyone, how did I avoid this happening more often than it had? My answers are simple and straightforward. "He's been violent more times than I can recall, and I've sustained plenty of injuries but never to this extent. I didn't tell anyone because, at first, I was too young to know what to do, and when I was older I didn't want anyone to know, and I avoided him by disappearing when I needed to thanks to good friends who were always happy to have my company." I can't help but sardonically think that Logan would somehow find himself responsible for every single one of their questions—amazing how he can hold himself so responsible for me.

The detectives are nice enough to fill in the blanks of my memory. Apparently my father had lost his job that morning, which is likely the cause of his little tirade. And he did not give up trying to kill me. Instead, he heard nearby sirens, and assumed, incorrectly, they were for him. He fled the house at some point and ran into a tree two blocks away. He was arrested and booked for a few different charges, not the least of which was drunk driving.

When I didn't return to the apartment where Sara was waiting to drag me to a movie, she started trying to call me. When she couldn't reach me, she came to find me. And she did find me—lying in my father's kitchen, unconscious, barely breathing, and with my hair shorn off. She called 911, and I was in surgery within the hour. The police suspected my father immediately, given his past record and the fact the attack happened in our house. They figured out they already had him in custody pretty quick, and my statement is what's going to keep him there.

The detectives assure me they'll stay in touch before finally leaving and letting Sara back in the room. She comes bursting in again, and now it's my turn to cry. I owe her a debt of gratitude I can't even conceive of and I certainly can never repay. God, I love my best friend. This is the first time since I woke that we've had a chance to actually talk for longer than thirty seconds. It's mid-afternoon, and I've only been awake for a couple hours, but I'm already exhausted. Sara is in no mood to keep quiet any longer, though, and she's bursting at the seams to talk my ear off. She tells me all about the day she found me—every last excruciating detail. She's choked up and emotional, and it's hard to listen to her talk about how painful it was to see me that way and waiting during my surgery. We both cry as she tells me how upset her family has been the past two days, and then she mentions Logan's name.

My gaze snaps up to hers, my eyes wide and begging to take in more information. He arrived last night. He was in here with me for more than two hours while I was sleeping. He left the room in tears, according to Sara, the first time she ever recalls seeing him cry. New tears are pricking my eyes, and I have to fight to breathe as my chest tightens.

I croak out the only question I want an answer to, hoping I don't sound too obvious or desperate. "Where is he?"

"Oh, he left early this morning. He said he had to go talk to the DA he used to work for. He called a while ago and said he was on his way to Detroit on business but would be back when he could be. I think he left Denver in a bit of a rush, so maybe he's trying to make up for lost time? I don't know," she says with a shrug.

Sara seems oblivious to my torment, and I try again to act normal. *Holy shit! He saw me like this?* I cringe at the thought of what I must look like, and while I'm almost terrified to look, I ask Sara if she can find me a mirror. Now it's her turn to cringe as her mouth screws up in a half smile, half horrified grimace that says, *Are you sure you want to see this?* But I have to know just how bad it is, and I nod my head at her questioning look.

She rifles around in her purse, comes up with a compact, and hands it to me—again very reluctantly. *Oh, holy shit!* I look worse than bad. I look dead. I look like a Halloween costume gone bad. I look like a child who's gotten hold of the scissors before anyone could stop her. I look freaking ridiculous!

Sara offers the kind of support only she can get away with. "I'm not gonna lie. It's perhaps not your best haircut, and you could definitely do with a bit of makeup..." She flashes a sarcastic smile.

I can't help but laugh. Oh, were it not for Logan having seen me this way, I probably would be amused right now along with her, but the idea of Logan spending two hours with me looking like this: swollen face, freak show haircut, carpet burn on the cheek, and my neck black and blue, is horrifying. No wonder he was in tears when he left. Did anyone actually check to see if they were tears of laughter? How could they not be? I'm atrocious. Sara quickly reassures me that Ronnie's stylist has agreed to pay me a visit the next day to do what she can with my hair. The rest will just have to heal on its own apparently.

Sara stays as long as she can before the nurses usher her out so I can get some rest, but I'm not tired. Suddenly, I'm wide awake and the last thing I want to do is sleep. A nurse comes in asking how I'm feeling, and I have to admit the pain has been building slowly since all the chaos of the day died down, and I'm relieved when I feel the soothing effects of the morphine drip. That's nice. Maybe I'll actually be able to do something normal, like watch TV or read or daydream about Logan with the soreness kept at bay, and then ... I'm asleep. Good drugs.

⌘⌘⌘⌘

When I wake the next morning, it's to see Dr. Ahmari waiting for me to rouse. She examines me, and when she's removing the bandage on my upper abdominal area, I get the first glimpse of my stomach. I'm one gigantic bruise. Dark purple and blue bruising covers nearly every inch of my stomach. The sutures are actually staples and one incision sits a couple of inches below my left breast, while the other is situated above and to the left of my belly button. The incisions are both many inches long. They apparently had to open a considerable area to locate and stop all the bleeding. And it looks exactly as you would expect. The skin is puckered and bunched under the staples and is scabbed over in places. It just adds to the horrific sight of my body.

I choke back the tears at the sight of myself, thinking my body suddenly looks foreign to me. I don't recognize any part of my torso at the moment. The cracked ribs are throbbing, and with every breath I take it feels as though the ribs are being pushed outward and trying to force their way out of my chest. The pain is bad. But

Dr. Ahmari has scaled back the morphine. She wants to move me over to prescription pills I'll be able to take home with me when I'm released. Release? Now she has my attention.

"So when will I be released?" I ask hopefully. And while Dr. Ahmari doesn't tell me the answer I want to hear, which is right now, she does make me happy when she says tomorrow.

Ronnie's hairdresser shows up about noon that day and does a remarkably good job. I end up with a short pixie cut somewhere along the lines of the classic Audrey Hepburn look, but I'm no Audrey. Given what she had to work with, I've decided she's a genius. I look normal, facial swelling, bruising, and abrasions notwithstanding. But it's unarguably the first time in a few days I've felt some semblance of normalcy. If I can just stay away from a mirror!

Every time the door opens, I expect to see Logan come in, and I'm both ridiculously nervous and eager to see him. I know it will only reignite my pain for him, and it will hurt all the more when he returns to Colorado, but after the last few days I just want him near me—even if only for a minute. I know I'll regret it later, but I just need one more minute of his time now. But he doesn't show, and come evening when the Harringtons finally go home for the first time in a long time, I give up thinking I'll see him. I know I could ask, but of course, I can't do that without sounding too overly interested in him.

A nurse comes in shortly later and takes my vitals. She starts going through all the things I need to accomplish before I can be discharged. Apparently you have to graduate from patient to normal person in order to get out of a hospital. And apparently that means I have to go poop on command like a dog, which I don't want to do. I also have to walk to the end of the hall without assistance, which I again don't want to do. I've been out of bed since that morning, taking myself to the bathroom to pee, but the end of the hall is a long way away ... I think. I haven't actually been out of my room since waking up in it two days before, but still, I bet it's a long ways away. And then going to the bathroom... It just doesn't sound like a whole lot of fun right now, so I think I'll take a pass. But the nurse isn't buying it.

She insists I have to have a bowel movement before they'll let me leave. Pooping on command has never really been my thing, and the idea of using my tummy muscles, or any muscle in my torso at all right now, is very unpleasant. The few times I've had to cough have been agony, and I can't imagine going to the bathroom is any better. But short of busting myself out of this joint, I'm going to have to break down and make this happen. I think I hate nurses. And by the end of the night, I've dubbed mine the poop nurse.

She's incessant. She wants me to go home. I get it. And I'm sure it's all for my own good, blah blah blah. But I hate her all the same. After much soul searching, a laxative, and a malicious silent curse at my poop nurse, I'm finally a good little hospital patient, and she signs off on my discharge requirements, but I still hate her. We're not going to be friends. But I get to go home tomorrow, or more accurately, to the Harringtons'.

They've asked me to stay at their home for a couple of weeks while I recover so Ronnie can keep an eye on me. I'm relieved. Not that Sara would make a bad caretaker, but I've avoided spending more time than I have to at Logan's apartment. I live there, but it's so filled with memories of him that I escape as often as I can. Fortunately for me, I've been working lots of hours and have kept somewhat busy with Sara. But being laid up in bed for the next week or so at his apartment would be hard.

I drift off to sleep that night wondering what it will be like to see Logan again. It's the most confusing feeling in the world. I want to see him so much I ache for him, but at the same time I know it will bring me nothing but pain. Who knows, maybe he's had to return to Denver already and isn't coming back to Grand Rapids. I have no way to know, and I'm frenzied just thinking about him.

CHAPTER FORTY-TWO

Logan

I sit silently in the chair, waiting for her to wake. I've been anxious to see her again for the many days I've been in Detroit, and I've been craving this moment like no other in my life. Restraint will be difficult, impossible perhaps, but I have to be near her now.

I arrived back from Detroit just this morning, and Rowan has been at my parents for two days now. They have Rowan in Sara's old bedroom, and she's sleeping soundly on the bed. Sara and my mother are out shopping, and my father is at the office. I assured Mom I'd look out for Rowan while they were away, but I couldn't disguise the anxious look on my face as they left. My mother's leer tells me she's noticed my odd behavior, but I've given up caring about that anymore.

When her eyes open and I see her beautiful gaze on mine, I melt. It has been far too long since I've seen her amazing round blue eyes. I've forgotten just how blue they are, and I instantly sigh as though I've been holding my breath for the last long months apart. She gasps as she registers my presence and tries to sit up quickly before she winces and drops back to the bed. The pain on her face has me up and moving to her side instantly, and I climb to the bed sitting next to her. I'm afraid to touch her, afraid to kiss her, afraid even to move, lest the mattress shift and cause her more pain. She's always been delicate to me, and now in her injured state she's like a crumbling fall leaf I'm so desperately trying to save.

She reaches over for my hand and clasps it as tears flood her eyes. I can't tell if it's happiness or sadness or full-on despair. And I'm instantly fighting back my own tears with a clenched jaw. After long moments of this struggle against my emotions, and when I finally feel like I'm in control enough to speak without crying, I ask the only question I can think to say, regretting its stupidity immediately. "Are you okay?" Duh.

"I am. I'm sorry. I'm just really emotional, and I ... didn't know if I'd see you before you went back to Denver, and I just ... um ... I'm sorry. I've just missed you."

She's practically stuttering in her unease, and I understand exactly how she feels. I lean gently to her mouth and kiss her warm lips, unsure if she'll accept my mouth. But she doesn't stop me, and as her lips part in acceptance of me, I slip my tongue just slightly past them, tasting her mouth cautiously before withdrawing. The paleness of her skin shows her blushing cheeks all the more noticeably. I sit back, watching her, unsure how she's feeling. Her eyes are wide, and I can't get a grasp on what she's feeling. She seems stunned, nervous even.

When she speaks again, she surprises me once more. "Do you regret me?"

I stare back shocked at her question while she waits as patiently as she can. It's obvious by the look on her face that my answer is a hinge in her mind that can tip her heart one direction or another. She has worried about the answer to this question for a long time, and she isn't going to let the answer slip by her. Her vulnerability in this moment is painful to see, and I can make or break her with this one answer.

But this is easy. I tell her the truth. "Never."

"Not even having sex with me? I know you didn't want to..."

I smile gently at her. She's so anxious, paranoid even, that I'm going to say something that will leave her heart wounded. I do my best to put her at ease, but I can see by the look in her eyes she's wary. She has every right to be.

"From nearly the first night you stayed with me, I wanted to ... very much ... constantly. But I also wanted to do what was right for you. I promise making love to you is not something I could ever regret. On the contrary, it was ... amazing—more than amazing."

I lean to her lips again, taking her cheeks gently in my hands. This time, I push my tongue farther into her warm silken mouth. I kiss her long but soft. I let her explore my mouth with her tongue, and the relief she feels floods back to me. My own relief is quite obvious; in my over-passionate and desperate response I'm practically attacking her lips, trying to go slow, trying not to be rough, but I'm failing in my want to be close to her.

I finally pull away, needing the separation to keep myself from consuming her. "Did I hurt you ... when we made love?"

She shakes her head, smiling gently, but she says nothing.

"You left before we even had a chance to talk about this."

I've been obsessing about what her first time was like for her since the moment I withdrew from her body. I know I left her body hurting, but not being able to talk to her, see her, touch her, has left this lingering concern in my mind. Of course, she's okay. It's not as if I thought taking her virginity wouldn't come with pain, but I've missed this—talking to her, hearing her reassurance, just seeing that she's okay. I've needed this. And I don't want to stop now that I have her. I want to talk. I want her to share every detail with me. If it makes her uncomfortable, to hell with it.

"What was it like for you ... making love for the first time?" I ask her quietly.

She looks embarrassed but contemplative at the same time. She finally answers. "It hurt." Her expression is suddenly shy. "A lot. But ... it was also incredible. Better than incredible. I can't describe it." Hesitation still laces through her words. "It just filled this void that was missing in me for a really long time with you."

Her vulnerability terrifies her as much as I may love it. And her gaze flits away from me at her sudden exposure. She's stuck lying on her back, fairly immobile, and while she takes her time avoiding my eyes, I let my gaze travel over her. I want to touch her hair... what's left of it, at any rate. Who knew she could be so beautiful with a pixie. She's like a brunette version of some pixie-sporting Hollywood actress, only completely and perfectly Rowan—petite, alabaster skin, big round eyes, slight but oh-so-feminine curves, and that incredibly tight pussy. She's made for me.

And as she finally allows her shy eyes to drift back to mine, she catches the sly and somewhat hungry look in my eyes. But her gaze is uncertain, and I'm left reassuring her. "Don't worry. I have no intention of taking advantage of you in your current state. I think your doctor might kill me if I did."

"Yes, she would. She likes me, after all."

"Who wouldn't?" And at that, I give her a wry smile and a wink. I'm glad, at least, this conversation is looking up, so I decide to test it once again. "You're not … um … pregnant are you?" I ask with a raised eyebrow and a grimace. The question has popped into my mind on more than one occasion over the last month. And now seems as good a time as any to get it out—not that Rowan carrying my child isn't a complete rush, but it's just a rush better saved for later in her life.

"No! No! I'm not. Not! Not at all, not."

Well, just in case that wasn't clear enough, I decide clarification is in order. "You're sure? It's just, I didn't use any protection and…"

"I promise. I started my period the day after you left and again when I was in the hospital. I'm definitely not. Not. Not. Not."

And relief floods over me. "I mean, talk about screwing up your scholarship. I'm sorry. It was so reckless of me. I just couldn't stop—couldn't think at all really." I have a slight smile on my face at the memory. And the smile reaches her face too.

"Speaking of your scholarship, what has the doctor said about this fall?"

"She's giving me a good prognosis. She thinks with enough physical therapy, strength training, and easing back into my routine, I can be ready to go by this fall." But her expression shifts as the idea processes in her mind. "I'm worried about it though. What if I can't keep up or get back to the place I was before this happened? I mean, I can barely move, and I hurt all the time. It's hard to imagine doing the things I did before this happened. I'm just not sure I can be ready by fall." She worries out loud.

I reach for the soft skin of her cheek, hoping to make her feel better. Her eyes are wet with unshed tears, and I can tell just how concerned she is about this.

"Row, you're going to be fine. I know you. And I know you can do this. It's going to be hard work, but you do hard work better than anyone I know." She doesn't look convinced, so I lay down next to her with my head propped up on my elbow and my other arm draped low on her stomach where I think it's safe to touch her. "I know you hurt right now, but you have to give yourself time. You will feel better. It might be slow, but it will happen. I'm sure it feels bad right now, but you can't apply the way you feel right now to the next two months or your life."

She nods slowly. Maybe I'm getting through to her. And as her eyes linger on mine, I slowly reach for the top button of the pajama shirt she's wearing. She watches me but doesn't stop me. And as I slowly undo the buttons, the first signs of her bruised flesh show through the parting fabric. When all of the buttons of her shirt are undone, I pull open the top and take in the mess her father left—beautiful but painful to see. I'm once again fighting back the tears that are suddenly threatening to spill.

Her skin is smattered with bruises from her stomach up to her chest, and the angry and pinched skin of her incisions is knotted and red under the staples. Her neck is still bruised in that horrific pattern that shows exactly where his hand choked her. Her breasts were spared from most of the kicks, and they are as beautiful and pale as ever, save for the small pink nipples that are taut and hard as her body responds to my intrusive gaze. Her lower abdomen was saved as well from most of the abuse and is trim and flat down to the pajama pants she wears.

I want to touch her so desperately, and if the look on her face is any indication, she wants me to touch her, but there is no way for me to do this and not hurt her. I reach out to the soft skin of her belly and caress it for a moment before buttoning her shirt back up. She lets out a long and somewhat defeated sigh as I work my way up her buttons. I know exactly what frustration she feels. She would probably accept my touch right now in her aroused state, painful as it might be, but I can't stand to do that to her. So we're back to abstinence once again. I lay my head next to hers as she drifts off to sleep, and I listen to her deep relaxed breathing, letting my own body relax for the first time in a very, very long time.

CHAPTER FORTY-THREE

Rowan

W hen I wake, it's to a slight rapping on the door as Ronnie
enters. Logan is gone, and I'm alone on the bed.

"Time to get up, dear. It's dinnertime. Sara and I got take out from Gino's on the way back, and Marcus will be here any minute."

Ronnie gives me one final appraising look, worry etching her usually vibrant face. She must decide I'm okay as she finally gives me a gentle smile before leaving. As I wash up for dinner, I look myself over in the mirror. The hair is growing on me, not literally... It's easy to take care of, which is good considering raising my arms too high always sends a sharp pain through my side where my ribs are healing. My skin is always pale, but it's nearly drained of all color right now. My eyes have dark circles under them, and I'm more exhausted than any eighteen-year-old should be. Lip gloss does nothing to improve my state, so I give up and slowly make my way downstairs to the dining room.

As I enter, I see I'm the last to arrive, and everyone watches me with sympathetic looks on their faces as I move slowly to my place at the table. I'm directly across from Logan, and he gives me an intimate, warm smile without hesitation or restraint. I can feel the warmth of my cheeks as a sudden blush takes them over, but I quickly realize no one is paying us much attention.

Marcus and Sara spend the better part of the meal in a heated, albeit good-natured, debate about politics, while Ronnie referees.

Sara is a chip off the Ronnie block, which means she's passionate, vibrant, and loud when she wants to be. Marcus is strong willed and level headed. Neither ever gets offended or upset, and you can tell they thoroughly enjoy these sparring matches. Logan is known to go his rounds with his father too, but on this night he's very content just watching me.

He does little to hide his attentiveness to me, filling my water glass so I don't have to get up from the table and grabbing what bowls I need so I don't have to reach too far. Ronnie is the only one who seems to notice his attention, but he doesn't seem to care at all that she's watching him closely with an intrigued and subtle smile on her face. Instead, his gaze remains on me, waiting patiently for me to meet his eyes whenever I can bear it.

When Marcus and Sara finally call a truce, Marcus asks Logan when he'll be headed back to Denver. My gaze snaps unwittingly up to Logan's as he looks back at me with concern.

In barely a whisper, he responds. "Tomorrow morning." But as he sees my face drop instantly, he continues quickly. "I'll be back in a few weeks, perhaps a month. I have to be back in Detroit soon so I won't be away for long."

He's looking intently and reassuringly at me when his father asks, "Something interesting going on in Detroit then, I take it. A big case?"

"Something like that." Logan returns his attention to me. "I'll talk to you about it soon. Once I know more about it."

Marcus nods in agreement before letting the conversation drop. We end up playing Scrabble for a couple hours before Sara finally stands to leave for the night. She's taking me to my first physical therapy appointment tomorrow, and after confirming when she should pick me up, she gives me a quick kiss on my cheek, elbows Logan in the shoulder, and hollers her goodbyes over her shoulder.

Ronnie excuses herself and Marcus for the night, pulling Marcus along with her. Logan and I are finally left alone again, and my body is suddenly anxious and electrified. We settle in on the sectional in the family room, some obscure drama playing out on the TV. Rather than pulling me into his body as has always been Logan's custom with me, he moves behind me in the corner of the deep and comfortable sofa, straddling my hips and resting a hand on my waist. He lets me move my body back to his at my own speed before he gently wraps his arms around me and nuzzles against my neck. The warmth of his breath on my skin, starved of his attention, sends a quiver through my entire soul.

I've discovered I ache terribly by the end of the day, but on this night I could care less. The electricity coursing through my veins staves off the pain better than any painkiller can. I've missed this touch and this closeness. I came to depend on it so much when we were together, and when I lost him I was starved of it. Now I can feel his warmth, his firm body against mine, his scent. And I'm finally content again. Pain or no pain, I'm complete.

But I'm complete in this moment. What about tomorrow morning when he's gone again? Can I survive another month without him? And then what? Then how long do I have to wait to see him? Does he want to continue this pseudo-relationship in this way indefinitely? Can I do that? Could I ever be happy with that? The first time I ended our relationship, I knew the answer to that question. No! I knew that his loss would kill me and being with him was simply torturing myself, but now after so long away from him, I'm tired of being alone and I just miss him too damn much to fight it. I just want to feel this contentment. But the reality of tomorrow is there whether I want to acknowledge it or not.

These fleeting encounters won't make him happy any more than they will make me happy. He'll eventually want a relationship that is truly present in his life, not sporadic. What makes me think he hasn't already started seeking it out? He's beautiful, and whether he chooses to attract attention or not, he's always gotten it. If it hasn't happened already, it will happen soon enough, and with me half a country away what choice will he make? What choice should he make?

Painful stabs of jealousy rack my fragile body at the thought of him with someone else. And as my jealousy takes over, the images of another woman in his life start stabbing my heart. I see him longing for her, I see her touching his body, and I see the hungry look in his eyes before he consumes her. It's as if I'm watching all the many times we've been together, but it isn't me. It's some faceless, nameless woman who is probably far more beautiful than me, and it hurts. Is this what it's supposed to feel like to lose something you hold so dear?

I don't want to do this to myself tonight. I desperately want to stop this torture before it takes me over. Why can't I just shut this part of my mind off? I've had too much of this pain for the past few months, and I curse myself for allowing it to come between us now.

I wallow in it, trying to hide this most unwelcome shift in my mood from Logan, but he always seems to know what I'm feeling. He tightens his hold on me and nuzzles closer to my neck.

He traces the edge of my ear with his nose, grazing and tickling my skin before he whispers in my ear, "Why are you suddenly so tense? What's wrong? Are you hurting?"

Yes! But not from the pain he thinks. I turn slowly to him, unwelcome tears stinging my eyes, and at once he stills as concern consumes him. He grasps my cheeks in his hands, searching my eyes desperately for some sign of what's going on inside my head, and as the first of my tears spill over, I bury my head in his chest, craving his warmth and his strength.

He won't let me hide from him, and he pulls me back from his body determined to make me open up. "Don't push me away, Row. Please. I can't leave you like this again, running from me, hiding. I know this is hard, but please just hang on... I..." He trails off wanting to say more, but what? Is he afraid he'll hurt me? Afraid he'll piss me off? He looks like he's in as much agony as I am, and when finally he's recovered from whatever helpless feelings have so clearly taken him over, he takes my cheeks in his hands again, and running his thumb over my lower lip he speaks. "I'll be back soon. I will see you. I promise."

He gives up trying to convince me or talk me through my pain and once again kisses me. I finish turning my body to his, crawling up to straddle his hips. Every move I make hurts, but I don't care, and as I close the last inch between us I can feel his body finally against mine. He's aroused, and though I know I can offer him no relief, I don't want to distance myself from him either. He holds me tight against him, and I savor the feel of his erection so firmly against me.

After a long time of clutching one another, he stands, letting me slowly down to the floor and helps me up to Sara's room. He closes the door and crawls quietly in next to me. I want to face him or let him curl himself around my body, but lying on my side is impossible with the pain. It makes cuddling nearly impossible as well, but he pulls himself up to his elbow next to me and does the next best thing.

He kisses soft trails on the skin of my face. He moves down to my neck, studying my bruises before touching and kissing them as well. He unbuttons my top and trails his kisses lower to my breasts. He pulls one nipple gently into his mouth, running his tongue over the hard erect bud. He moves to the rest of my bruises, covering each with kisses. He stops short of crossing my waistline and doesn't allow his touch to become more than what either of us can bear. He finally re-clothes me, and lying next to me he laces his fingers through mine and strokes my hand with his thumb. I fall asleep to his deep breathing.

When I wake, it's early and he's gone. This time, he's left me a note.

Row,

You won't be sad forever. I promise. I'll see you soon.

Logan

But I'm already sad.

CHAPTER FORTY-FOUR

Rowan

By the time my first physical therapy appointment is over, I want to punch the therapist. My body is screaming at me, and I want nothing more than to take it out on her. Mindy. I have a feeling I hate her, and like the poop nurse before her, I have a feeling we're not going to be friends. She's bubbly and optimistic, and she makes me want to burst that stupid bubble she floats around in. It's not her fault. I know she's just doing her job, but I'm upset, I'm sad, I'm in pain, and I just want to hit the rewind button and go back to when Logan was still here. But I can't.

Over the next couple of weeks, I continue meeting with Mindy three times a week. I stretch and work the muscles of my body to keep them loose and strong while I'm recovering. The therapy is less about my injuries and far more about keeping the rest of my body as strong as possible. I do deep breathing exercises to keep my lungs healthy as well. When I started, my entire body ached all the time from the bruising and battery I sustained and general atrophy from lack of movement during the first week of my recovery. My body is used to being used, stretched, and exercised, and the lack of use was quite apparent. It was this atrophy more than anything that was going to be difficult for me to rebound from once my ribs are healed.

Thanks to Mindy—yes, I got over hating her—my range of motion and flexibility stayed intact, and two weeks later she approved my returning to Anthony for flexibility training. I continue to see Mindy twice a week and Anthony twice a week as well, and with every passing day my body continues to return to normal in some small measure. My ribs still hurt, but the ache is dull and not nearly as crippling as it initially was. I can breathe deeply without having to psyche myself up for the soreness, and I'm back to moving through my ballet positions smoothly, gracefully, and staying in balance. I'm not a hundred percent, but I'm getting close. I'm not allowed to do any jumps or strenuous moves until six weeks after surgery, but that's coming up soon enough.

Sara and I will be moving to Ann Arbor in mid-August, just over a month away, and that leaves me with little time to get back up to peak performance. I haven't notified the Performing Arts department of my little injury and have no intention of telling them unless I absolutely have to. I can't afford to lose my scholarship or worry any of the faculty. My hope is no one will be the wiser once my first practice starts in late August. My scholarship is dependent upon my dancing, and I don't want to draw any negative attention to myself so early on.

I haven't heard from Logan for the few weeks he's been gone, and as much as I want to ask when he'll be back, I have no intention of saying anything to his parents about him. I could call him, of course, but I won't. I'm not sure why; I just can't seem to bring myself to cross that line. If I were to call him, it would just restart the countdown clock to when I can get over him and move on with my life, which is ridiculous because soon enough I'll see him again. But calling is like somehow acknowledging I'm not ready to move forward, and I have no choice but to move forward.

I want to say I won't see him when he returns again, or I won't see him alone, or I won't touch him or let him touch me, but I know full well once he's here that won't be a decision I can uphold. In a way, I want it over. I want him here, I want what will happen to happen, and then I want him gone so I can feel the pain and get over it. But I know getting over it will take a long, long time. And I dread it, knowing it will be just like the first month we were apart—every moment a struggle, every day torture.

But Logan continues to keep his distance. Two more weeks pass with no sign of him. Maybe his trip was cancelled. I wouldn't know if it was, and I know he wouldn't call me. The understanding of that fact hurts just as if he wounded me with unkind words. I want him to reach out to me, but I know he can't. He can't for all the same reasons I can't. It hurts too much. It's like an alcoholic taking a sip of wine; the pleasure of the indulgence would be immediate and swift, but the aftermath would be devastating. And with each passing day, I realize, with sadness, he isn't going to be making any trips home soon. What's worse, his family, not understanding my complete obsession with Logan, says nothing of his absence. And I can't very well say anything lest I be ready to admit my utter infatuation with him. I doubt that would go over well.

Before I know it and before I want it, I find I'm only two weeks away from moving with Sara. She already has her boxes packed. She's excited, and I once again envy her carefree optimism and wish I could share it desperately. Logan still hasn't made an appearance, and at this point I've given up thinking he will. I know it's for the best in the long run, but I can't help but long for one more moment with him, one more touch, one more anything—hell, I'd take a fight even! Just some contact so I know he's still there and he still cares.

The only thing I'm even moderately interested in is getting to Ann Arbor and starting dance practices. The schedule is brutal and fast-paced. If anything can steal me from the always-present depression that hangs over my head, it's dance. And the more dance the better. We start performances three weeks after the start of the semester, and learning the new routines on top of my classes will leave no time for anything else, including thinking about Logan. I'm counting on my schedule filling the void that has been left by Logan. I'm desperately counting on it, in fact.

CHAPTER FORTY-FIVE

Rowan

Sara's parents have asked Sara and I to go to the lake house with them for one last summer weekend trip on the coming Friday. I think Ronnie is starting to dread our move, so when she asked me, I went out of my way to find someone to cover for me at the Bistro for Friday and Saturday night. But when Friday rolls around, Sara tells me mid-afternoon there's a change of plans. Instead, Ronnie and Marcus are going to take us out in Grand Rapids for a sort of going away dinner, and we'll leave for the lake house the next morning. They're taking us back to the French restaurant in the historic district of Grand Rapids we celebrated Sara's birthday at.

And when they pick us up, Ronnie is smiling radiantly. She looks happy and vibrant as always as she ushers us out to the car. Sara is dressed like a fashion model in short dress shorts, a sleeveless blouse, and ankle boots, while I'm wearing a simple black dress. Sara picked it out for me to go with my Audrey Hepburn hair, something about it being the perfect little black dress to complete my look. It has capped sleeves and a trim fit that hugs my body to my knees. A simple white satin ribbon at the waist completes the dress. It's beautiful. Sara tried to talk me into heels, but I opted for black flats instead. Thank God she's around to dress me, otherwise I'd probably have left the house in jean shorts. Not that I don't like to look good; she just seems to pull it off a whole lot easier than me.

We hop in the car and make the short drive to Grand Rapids. Marcus pulls up to the valet attendant, and we enter the beautiful old building. We're greeted and escorted to our table quickly. It's a small private room within the restaurant, and there are five chairs around the round table. Odd. We clearly had a reservation, so there's little reason for the extra chair... And this is my first inkling something might be amiss. As we're seated, I look around the table and find all eyes are glued to me. No one says a word to me, but the anxious sets of eyes smiling warmly back at me have my heart suddenly fluttering. I cock my head and wrinkle my brow in confusion as they all continue to appraise me.

My curiosity is overwhelming. "What's going on?"

The slight smile on my lips is simply for lack of anything better to do with my mouth, but it quickly turns to a gaping "O" the second I see Logan round the corner, escorted by the maître d'. As his eyes meet mine, my hand goes to my mouth in shock as he stops mid-stride—his eyes wide and beautiful. He's approaching from behind his parents but facing Sara and me directly. The moment Ronnie sees me cover my mouth she's off her chair, looking over her shoulder for him. And I realize in that moment, my secret has been blown wide open.

Relief and complete joy flood unexpectedly through me as I stare back at Logan. I'm trembling as he approaches the table, unable to move, to speak, to close my gaping mouth. He looks quickly to his parents, giving them an equally quick "Hi" before approaching me as I stand. He pulls me swiftly into his arms, clutching me to him.

He makes no move to separate from me, and it's many long moments before Sara's over-obvious throat clearing catches his attention. "Ahem... Do you think you could put my best friend down now? I picked out that outfit, and you're going to ruin it!"

I look to her quickly to see a very well-played smirk on her face. But she smiles broadly at me and winks. "And who says I can't keep a secret?"

Well, quite frankly, I've said it a million times. I realize my mouth is still hanging open and everyone is still staring at me, waiting for me to breathe. Logan is holding my hand in his, and he makes no move to let me go as we take our chairs next to each other. I turn to him and can do nothing but stare. I hadn't thought I'd see his face before Sara and I moved. I was resolved to this fact, depressed and upset, but resolved. And now here he is, and his entire family is watching our every move.

Logan finally starts to speak. "I might have told them ... some things about us." His face becomes serious and dark, and his brow wrinkles. "You almost died." And as he shakes his head, his lips pursed into a tight line. I see the pain, devastating pain, he has endured because of me. His eyes gloss as he fights his emotion and the inner ache his memories must cause him, and I look up to see Ronnie tearing as well at the sight of her son so emotional. My eyes return to his, wanting to reassure him. I reach up to his face gently, and at my touch he shakes off his memories of that time, and his lips relax into a slight smile. "I just ... can't be apart from you."

With those final words, he leans forward and kisses me gently on the forehead. Our waiter arrives and stands uncomfortably by, waiting for the eyes of our table to leave Logan and me and acknowledge his presence. Eventually, everyone at the table exhales a common breath and returns to the here and now.

We start to order drinks, but when Logan and I can't seem to peel our eyes from each other, Ronnie interrupts the table. "You two don't have to stay for dinner if you don't want. I know you have plans tonight, and it might be better if you got on the road." She's obviously speaking to Logan, considering I have no idea what she's talking about.

I can't shake the feeling I know less about what's going on than everyone else at the table. With that, Logan thanks his mom and pulls me to my feet before throwing a quick "good-night" at his family. Ronnie replies that they'll see us tomorrow for lunch, and again I'm left confused and wondering what I don't know about what's going on. But hey, what do I care? Logan is here with me, and my heart is at ease. For how long, I have no idea. For however long Logan stays in town, I suppose. But I have no intention of thinking about that at the moment.

As we exit the restaurant, he hands the valet his ticket before pulling me into his arms and attacking my mouth with his. He seals his mouth to mine, kissing me deeply and quite inappropriately for a public street. He appears not to care at all that people are passing by as he forces his tongue into my mouth, and my body radiates heat as he continues to consume me.

When the valet soon returns with Logan's Jeep, he reluctantly releases my mouth and opens the door for me. He tips the man and hurries to the driver's door. When he pulls from the curb, he reaches for my hand, holding it tightly in his. I gaze at him as he moves through the traffic.

He occasionally looks over at me with a smile, and when he approaches a red light I start to question him. "Logan, where are we going?"

"Somewhere." He smirks at me with a mischievous grin.

"Somewhere *where*?"

"Just somewhere." And as he glances over at me, he shakes his head slightly with a mild smile on his lips. "God, I can't wait to make love to you."

He returns his eyes to the road, and the light turns green. He's left me with the most provocative words he could have said to me. He wants to make love to me. There was no argument behind what he said, no failed attempts at restraint, no hesitation. And as his Jeep heads out of town, my thoughts wander to what is in store for me. My body is already craving his touch. I'm wet and now eager, and as the minutes tick off the clock and the miles slip away, I start to think I might just lose my mind before we get wherever it is we're going. But Logan keeps heading eastward.

I try on a few occasions to get him to fess up, but he doesn't give an inch. And I'm left to let my mind wander once again. I imagine his first touch, his taste, the sight of his body. It's been so long since I've had any part of him other than his mouth, and I'm a frenzied wreck just thinking about it. I wonder if it will hurt as much this time as it did the last time. I'm sure it will, but I don't care in the least.

The last time was so incredibly bittersweet. Making love to me was so obviously not what he had intended to do that night, but he gave in to my wishes. Why? A parting gift perhaps. Or just complete lack of control more likely. It was sad but incredible. I knew the entire time I was losing him, and making love was like some desperate attempt to hold him as tight as I could before I lost him forever. How is this night any different? I don't know when he's going back to Colorado, but it will, without a doubt, be soon. So how is this night going to be any different?

I'm once again torturing myself with the truth. My internal dialogue is like the bearer of all unwelcome news, and she pops in every time I want to just forget about what is wrong with our situation. Why can I never just be content?

Because, the bitch inside my head reminds me, *this is fleeting. You're practically his Michigan whore.*

My heart drops, and I know my night is doomed to be tormented with thoughts of being parted from him again. I resort to looking out the window at the passing countryside as the sky darkens. We are headed toward Ann Arbor, and after a couple of hours, we approach the exits for my future home. I half expect him to turn off. But he continues by each and every exit ramp.

And soon we've left Ann Arbor in the darkness behind us. Within fifteen minutes, I can see the glow of the Detroit city lights. And as we approach the city I'm reminded that he's probably just in town on business. I get it now. He's taking me to his hotel room for the evening. I really am his Michigan whore. My mood is dropping with every passing second, and he must sense it as he squeezes my hand, appraising my somber face. We travel into the city, circumventing downtown out and along the river. It's dark, and I'm not familiar enough with Detroit to know where exactly we could be going.

I expect him to exit toward downtown, but it seems we're moving on past downtown. Logan starts telling me about the historic old neighborhoods of Detroit that lie to the east of downtown. The Villages, as he calls them, are filled with old homes reminiscent of the Heritage Hills neighborhood of Grand Rapids. I can't imagine why he's telling me all of this now. It's too dark for sightseeing, after all.

My mood has fallen, and as much as I'm eager to be with Logan, I'm confused and frustrated and resentful. I don't want to be the girl he hooks up with when he comes to town on business. I don't want to wish to see him all the time but accept seeing him only once in a blue moon. I'm not built for that, and it makes my heart sink, because while I know I'll give myself freely to him tonight, it will break my heart when I have to give him up again. Will I let myself be tortured like this forever? Will I ever be strong enough to say no to him?

We continue through residential streets lined with the old historic homes, but it's hard to get a good feel for the place. And why should I care? From what I can tell it seems like exactly the type of neighborhood I would love—old, beautiful, huge trees, amazing architecture, but I just don't care.

We eventually turn onto one of many dark and quiet streets, and moments later, Logan is pulling into the driveway of an impressive two-story Arts and Crafts style house with a black iron fence in the front yard. It has a huge porch that runs the length of the front side of the house. One lamp is all that is on in what I assume is the living room. It's quiet and dark otherwise, and it really doesn't appear that anyone is home.

Logan parks and shuts the car off, saying nothing at all. He's still holding my hand, and as I turn to look at him he lifts my hand to his mouth and brushes a kiss along my fingers. I gaze back at him passively and defeated before finding my voice, choked with the emotion that's been building thanks to the nasty voice in my head so intent on ruining my evening.

"Why did you bring me here?"

"Because I wanted to show it to you."

"Show me what? This house? Why?"

"Because it's mine."

CHAPTER FORTY-SIX

Logan

For the second time this evening I've managed to shock her, and were she in better spirits I might be able to enjoy myself more. Her mood has been sinking since we left Grand Rapids, and the moment I saw the shift, all I wanted was to get her here. This home, the culmination of my giving up every last dream I thought I wanted, is now mine. There was never really any chance of my returning to Denver permanently after Rowan almost died. Truth be told, I'm not sure I wouldn't have found a way back to her eventually once I fell in love with her.

The night I watched her sleeping in the hospital, the decision was made. The DA made a few calls to the Detroit DA's office for me the next day, and I had meetings set up almost immediately. Detroit is, fortunately, never short of the need for lawyers in the public sector, and interviewing the following day I had a good feeling about my prospects of being hired as a new assistant DA. I'd be trading a rather ridiculously large salary for a much less impressive one, but Rowan is worth far more to me than the hundred thousand a year I'll be sacrificing. Of course, there will be far more financial sacrifice than just that. Breaking my contract with Brighton came with a pretty damn hefty price tag, but there was simply no choice at that point. She's worth every penny.

I'd enjoyed my time in the Grand Rapids DA's office enough to know I'd fit right in as a criminal prosecutor far more easily than I would ever have fit into private practice, so this was the place for me to be—close to her in a career I could love. But I ended up having to wait for any final job offer for well over two weeks. *Damn bureaucratic red tape.*

But landing a new job in a location that would keep me close to Rowan ended up being the easy part. Breaking the news and coming clean to my parents proved to be one of the most difficult conversations of my life. But they listened, and they accepted what I told them. I really gave them little choice. By the time I made the call to them, I'd already turned in my resignation at Brighton, packed my boxes, and started researching real estate in Detroit.

My father helped me scout out some properties, and a hasty negotiation and closing ensued. I'd only just signed all the paperwork two days prior, after rolling up in the moving truck. I hired movers this time to unload furniture while I settled into my new office. No city skyline views, but I'm thrilled to be here nonetheless. And now I'm sitting in the driveway of my new home, terrified to breathe because the woman whom I love and moved halfway across the country to be with has yet to say a word to me about my decision.

Her eyes are huge, and her mouth is dropped open in shock. Her hand that I still hold in mine is shaking, and she looks like she'll burst into tears at any moment. I finally give up waiting for her to find her voice and step from the car, taking a steadying breath as I go. I help her from the passenger seat and lead her to the front door. I unlock the door and open it for her, and she enters clutching my hand. She stands in the entryway taking in the darkened space, and as she does she starts to cry. I'm desperate to hear her voice and to know what she's thinking. Are they tears of joy, or have I made the greatest mistake of my life thinking she'd want me back after I abandoned her?

"Please say something." My breath is shaky.

And she does. In a whisper hoarse with tears, she tells me the three words I need to hear more than any others—the words that tell me I've made the very best decision for us both—the same three words I've kept from her for far too long. "I love you."

And as I pull her into my arms, I clutch her to me. "Oh God, Row, I love you too."

When I've held her as tight as I can for as long as I can bear, I let her go, lock the door behind us, and lead her upstairs to my room. It's late, and she looks emotionally and physically exhausted, but as she watches me undress and drop my clothes on the chair in the corner of the room, her still wet eyes smolder and burn with desire.

I finish undressing and approach her as she watches me saunter naked across the room. When I reach her, her hands move instantly to my hips and mine reach to her bottom, caressing the round firm cheeks through the skirt of her dress. I slide my hands under the back hem of it and caress the back of her bare thighs, pulling the skirt up as I go. My head is near her neck, and I can hear her panting breaths coming in ragged shudders at my touch.

She turns her mouth toward my ear, and as she reaches for my distended and hard cock she begs. "Please." And I thank God I will never have to deny her again.

At the first touch of her hand on my cock, I lift her legs swiftly up to straddle me and lay her down on the bed underneath me. She's pulling my hips desperately toward her, and I pull away only long enough to pull her underwear off her legs. I push the hem of her dress back up the tops of her thighs and take in the sight of her sex for the first time in what feels like an eternity. She needs no coaxing to spread her legs wide for me, and when she does I can see the slick, pink folds of skin ready for me to take. I want to taste her, smell her scent, plunge my fingers within her, but my cock wants to be buried deep inside her far more.

Her hands are back on my hips pulling me into her, and I let her. I know this is going to hurt her, but I also know it has to. I use the head of my engorged cock to part her lips and nudge against her opening, and with one final look to her eyes for approval I thrust to my hilt inside her tight sheath. She cries out in pain but holds me tight to her body. I can feel her pussy tighten and clench around me.

I ease from her, letting the head of my cock linger teasingly at her entry before plunging into her once again, and as I claim her pussy over and over her moaning and cries intensify. Her tight passage is contracting around me, trying desperately to keep me inside her, and when her body finally explodes in orgasm I let myself come powerfully too. I withdraw from her quickly before making the mistake of losing myself within her again. Instead, my cum spurts out across the bunched up skirt of her dress. She lets her head fall back in repletion as I lay my head on her chest. Our lovemaking was fast, hard, and desperate—everything it needed to be after so long apart.

Once our breathing has slowed, I sit her up and unzip the back of her dress, pulling it over her head and tossing it to the floor; Sara would definitely not approve of my treatment of Rowan's little black dress. I lie next to her on the bed and gaze down at her naked body. The scars from her surgery are still red and knotted but fully healed. The bruises that were so evident and difficult to look at are now gone, and her alabaster skin is once more silken and smooth. She's finally mine again, and I will never let her go.

CHAPTER FORTY-SEVEN

Rowan

I wake to his mouth on the back of my neck as it works its way down to my shoulders. I roll to my back and gaze up at him in the moonlight filtering through the bedroom windows. He's beautiful, and he's mine. I get to keep him, and I will never let him go. He asks how I'm feeling, as if making love is tantamount to being injured. I know he's only concerned, and it melts my heart to see the worry in his eyes, but as I assure him I'm fine and only the slightest bit sore, he relaxes measurably.

With my reassurance given, he makes his way down my chest, stopping to torment my nipples before quickly turning on the bedside lamp and moving between my legs. He pushes my legs open wide and parts the lips of my tender vagina. He studies me for many moments before leaning his mouth to my sex. The touch of his warm, wet tongue soothes the raw, sensitive skin instantly, and he starts to lick every last inch of my flesh.

I watch him, entranced by his attention, and his eyes linger on mine as his tongue searches out my clit, and finding it he pulls it between his lips. I moan loudly, and at my obvious arousal he reaches up with his fingers and slides one long finger deep inside of me. He pulls his mouth away from me, regarding my face as he starts thrusting, coating his finger with my wetness. He pulls his finger from me completely and trails it up to my tight and sensitized nub. There he strokes and massages the most powerful nerve endings in my body with his finger, finally pinching my clit gently between two fingers as electricity shoots through my body.

He returns his mouth to my sex, sucking and pulling my clit back into his mouth. The suction is intense, and I melt at the sound of his wet laving on the most incredibly sensitive part of my body. As I come, loudly, my heels dig into the bed, and Logan grasps the back of my thighs at the junction of my bottom, pinning me in place as he continues to suck deeply and lick intensely through my orgasm. I lie motionless, panting as he crawls back up my body. He kisses my mouth softly—my scent on his lips.

As he reaches up to my chin with his hand, he pulls my bottom lip down and whispers, "Time to open up for me."

Mmmm. I look to his eyes in anticipation as he pulls himself to his knees. He places one foot above my shoulder in much the same position he's had me in before. And with his hand on his penis, he leans forward, guiding himself to my mouth and touching my lips with the head of his cock. And as the head passes over my lips, he sucks in a deep breath. I lean forward, pulling him deep into my mouth, and he starts thrusting with an even and controlled movement.

I reach up to the cheeks of his firm bottom, pulling him to me, and he grasps the headboard to keep himself from falling into me. As he thrusts, I lean in to take more of him, and soon his breath is coming in ragged gasps. When he comes, he shoots his warm salty liquid into my mouth, filling it with his taste. I continue to suck his cock as his thrusting slows and eventually stops. Finally finished with my mouth, he slowly pulls himself from me, letting the head linger on my lips as I lick and suck it clean. His eyes close, and he sighs as I release him completely. He smiles down at me gently before collapsing at my side and pulling me against his body.

What most people consider foreplay was how we made love for the better part of a year, and we do this so well together. I've needed the taste of him on my tongue, and I've needed the touch of his tongue on my most intimate parts. This is how we found intimacy when making love wasn't possible, and complete in one another we drift off to sleep. I'm complete. Not just satiated and relieved of my need; I'm complete. I have everything I need, and the promise of more to come. He belongs to me now.

⌘⌘⌘⌘

When I wake it's morning, and sunlight is filtering in through the windows. I panic for a moment when I realize he's gone, thinking perhaps it was all a dream. But as my eyes take in these new surroundings, I'm comforted by how much Logan's imprint is everywhere. The sheets smell of him, his clothes from the night before are lying over the nearby chair, and his furniture is all here. I can smell coffee brewing somewhere in this strange new house, and it beckons me as only coffee can. As I sit up, I realize my dress is no longer on the floor, and I've been left with nothing to put on. Fortunately, Logan's clothes are already put away in the chest of drawers, and I grab a T-shirt, pulling it over my head.

As I look around at the room, I find it's large with the beautiful, thick, old woodwork of the time period. There is a bank of four windows overlooking the front yard that is shaded by two huge oak trees. The bed sits along the back wall of the room facing the front windows. The headboard is situated between two dormer windows that look out over the back yard, which I now see is also surrounded by the same black iron fence. It's large and well-manicured with a paving stone patio. The walls are a warm tan color and empty at this point of any artwork. There is a connected bathroom that includes a soaker tub, separate shower, and double sink as well. The bathroom has obviously been renovated, but appropriate small hexagonal tiles were used on the floor, and there is a perfect subway tile on the walls of the shower and tub. I appraise myself in the mirror before running a comb through my hair.

As I leave the bedroom, I see two more bedrooms on the other side of the hall across from the open stairwell. There is a bathroom situated between the two rooms. When I hop the last of the stairs that end at the entryway of the house, I'm finally able to explore the downstairs. The house is filled with unpacked boxes and Logan's furniture. Off to one side of the stairs is an office with a desk and more boxes. On the other side of the stairs is a large great room that's open to the kitchen. It has high ceilings with cross beams showing. There is a large picture window looking out over the front yard and porch. The kitchen is open with a large island in the center.

Logan is just pouring himself a cup of coffee, and as he sees me approach he pours me a cup as well, leaning down to kiss me sweetly. He's wearing nothing but a pair of old sweatpants, and as he moves away from me to carry some dirty dishes to the sink, I admire his strong and beautiful back muscles that taper perfectly down to his trim waist. I have to peel myself away from this view to continue exploring his new home.

Off the kitchen, and along the opposite back corner of the house, sits the formal dining room. It has a new mission style table and chairs that seat six, with two additional chairs in the corners. Again, the ceiling is high, and a beautiful stained glass chandelier hangs over the table. The room is spacious with lots of windows and French doors that open to the paving stone patio beyond. There's a small half bath between the kitchen and the dining room in the landing that contains another door to the back yard and the stairs leading to the basement. The paint in the downstairs is as neutral as it is upstairs, and the same thick, old woodwork continues throughout the house.

As I return to the kitchen, Logan regards me with a raised eyebrow. He wants to know what I think, and as I smile excitedly at him he breathes a sigh of relief. He was worried I wouldn't like his new home, and I'm struck by just how vulnerable he can be sometimes. I have so many things I want to say to him. My heart is overrun with joy I had truly given up having in my life, and I want him to know just how much all of this means to me. But I don't know where to begin.

In my usual absurd fashion, I just start rambling. "Logan, I love it. It's perfect ... beautiful. I still can't believe you're here." And as I approach him, he lifts me to the counter, pulling my knees apart and pushing his way between my legs.

"Rowan, I need to say something to you."

Worry hits me swiftly, and I'm sure it shows on my face.

But he clutches my cheeks softly in his hands and hastily continues. "I love you. There is no question in my mind that I want to spend my life with you, but I need you to understand..." He's choosing his words carefully. "I'm still worried you're too young to make that type of decision right now."

My face scrunches up as I start to object, to reassure *him*.

But he stops me before I can say a word. He clearly wants to be heard, and difficult as it is I'm going to have to be patient. "I'm terrified you may think this is what you want right now, but you may not a year or two from now. And that's a fear I'll have to live with until I'm sure you've had plenty of time to decide for certain if you want your life to be with me. But I'll deal with that. You don't owe me forever right now, but God, I hope you'll give it to me willingly someday."

Well, so long as we're giving speeches, I launch in on my own. "I love you too ... and not because I'm some flighty, emotional kid prone to flighty, emotional decisions. I know what I want, and if you don't believe I could want to spend the rest of my life with you, then I'll have to spend every moment we're together convincing you otherwise."

At that, a wicked smile crosses his face.

But I'm not finished. "The past couple of months have been ... agony. Gut-wrenching pain. I'm just not good at being away from you."

"So my family has told me..." The quizzical look that crosses my face is all the question required for him to explain. "Sara's been worried sick—Mom has been too. They knew something was wrong but just didn't quite get it until I filled them in. I assure you, Colorado was filled with my own torture too. I know how impossible it is to be apart." He smiles gently, sharing this understanding.

"Logan, what exactly did you tell your family?"

"I made the decision to move back the second I saw you in the hospital. But I didn't tell anyone until I had a job offer on the table and knew for sure when I'd be moving. I told Mom and Dad on the phone. Mom already suspected something had happened between us, but she had no idea we'd lived together for the better part of the past year. They weren't thrilled we'd been lying for so long, but I think they understood my reasons for having you there—even if they didn't necessarily agree with my decision not to involve them. I didn't tell them every last detail of our relationship, but I'm guessing they don't think we were just holding hands." He says this last part with a sarcastic smile. "My parents told Sara about a week or so ago about my moving back and the reasons. I still can't believe she managed to make it this long without saying anything to you."

"But what about Colorado? You've wanted that for so long, and now you've given it all up?"

"Colorado will be there in four years." He smiles challengingly.

"That's a good point I suppose."

"Yeah? Well, you can thank my mom for it. She's the one who said it... Not that I wasn't completely set on abandoning it already. Do you suppose you'd ever be interested in moving there with me someday?"

"You gave up your entire dream of living there for me. Hell yeah, I'll move there for you."

At that, I pull his mouth to mine and kiss him greedily. But as my lips claim his, he suddenly pulls away and looks at me. "Just so you know, I'm going to be poor for a while." He raises his eyebrows as a small smile creeps across his face. The question in my eyes is all he needs. "Oh, and I might get sued for breach of contract ... but probably not. Hopefully..." The smile remains on his lips, and it's apparent whatever concern he may have about this financial/legal issue he may or may not face is the last thing on his mind at the moment. And then he explains.

Apparently, breaking contracts with law firms is frowned upon in the industry. And while he doubts they'll put any substantial legal force behind it, he will end up paying a year's salary to them for breaking his contract early. And that year's salary is, or should I say *was*, pretty excessive. Given the fact he'll be paid far less, still far more than I can fathom, at his new job in the public sector, he's expecting it to take a few years to settle his contract buy-out. And even after telling me all of this, he's still smiling. I love this man. I'm still in awe of the fact he actually loves me too—loves me enough, in fact, to go broke to get back to me. There will never be a day I don't want to be with him, and I hope he'll realize it sooner rather than later. It's difficult to stomach the idea of him questioning that for the foreseeable future, for no other reason than the fact I'm eighteen and not twenty-five. But convincing him of my feelings for him will absolutely be a most exquisite pastime. And there's no time like the present.

CHAPTER FORTY-EIGHT

Logan

Our kisses turn desperate and passionate in no time, and as swiftly as I moved her to the counter, I lift her back up and carry her through to the dining room, settling myself in one of the armless side chairs. She's straddling me with nothing on but an old T-shirt of mine. I lift my hips swiftly and pull my sweatpants down my legs and past my knees to drop to the floor where I step out of them. I pull her T-shirt over her head and take in her body in the morning sunlight.

The houses are far enough apart, and lots of trees separate the yards, so I don't have to worry about sharing her with my neighbors.

I want her so badly, and my desire from so much time apart hasn't diminished in the least. "Please tell me you're not too sore for this?" I whisper against her ear.

"I'm not." She leans back, studying my eyes with a sweet smile.

"We've been apart entirely too long, and I have a feeling it's going to be a while before I'm done making up for lost time."

She nods as she bites her lower lip.

I lean to her neck again, nuzzling for a moment and then biting into her skin gently. "And don't get me started on how ravenous I can be from going nearly three months without sex or foreplay or any of my other favorite things," I mutter as she laughs. "Now stand up."

She stands, and I turn her around, bending her over the table. I'm left with the most amazing view of her ass and the lips of her pussy at the juncture of her legs. I brush my knuckles over the lips, which sends a shiver through her entire body. I then dust kisses over her bottom and the backs of her thighs.

"Spread your legs." My voice is hoarse and my throat tight.

She doesn't hesitate before stepping her legs out to the side. She's equally obliging when I ask her to spread her lips open for me.

Once finished, I have an incredible view of her wet, pink entry, and I can barely restrain my fingers from invading her body. But I manage to keep my fingers out of her and instead lower my mouth to her hole, plunging my tongue inside. I lick around the entry as she moans quietly, and when I finish with her pussy, my mouth finds its way up to her ass. I press her cheeks open and spit on my finger as I caress the tight puckered skin of her anus. She holds her breath in nervousness. It may not be the first time I've tasted her here, but it still gives her pause when I do.

I put my mouth on her anus and lave the tight hole with my tongue before pushing my tongue past the tight ring of her incredibly private entry. She moans again as she adjusts to my intrusion, and as soon as she relaxes to my mouth I push my finger past the tight rim of her anus and into the smooth, hot passage of her rectum. She tenses again, but as I push and pull slowly and shallowly in and out, she begins to adjust again to my new touch. I add more spit to my finger working the wetness into her hole, wanting to slide easily in and out.

And when I'm done with her bottom, I stand her back up, turn her to face me, and pull her back down to straddle my hips. She looks at me shyly, still wary but accepting of my close attention to her backside. I want her to ride me, and I want to watch as she impales her tight hole on my cock. I reach for her calves, planting her feet on the side rungs of the chair before clutching her hips and raising her bottom off my lap. She reaches back to the table behind her to stabilize herself, and as I use one of my hands to guide my cock to her pussy, she knows what I want.

She slides her entry down the shaft of my cock incredibly slowly as we both admire the beauty of our coupling. She hisses as she reaches her limit and pushes down hard against my body. She lifts her body slowly as I watch my cock withdraw from her passage, and she moves her hand down, spreading the lips of her vagina so we can see every inch of our joined bodies. It's exquisite. She is stretched taut around my shaft, and as the entry of her body meets the head of my penis it pops past the taut skin of her hole. I guide my cock once more to her entry as she pushes down over my erection.

After many more agonizingly slow and incredibly intimate penetrations, our rhythm quickens. But she continues to hold her body angled back from mine so we can watch the penetration together. Her breathing is speeding up, and I know she's close to her threshold. As I approach my own, I pull her body to my chest and tilt my hips upward, sliding my ass down the seat. She rides me now, holding on to the back of the chair and our bodies close, and as she continues to slide up and down my cock I grab the cheeks of her ass and gently, but insistently, force my finger into her still wet anus.

Her body freezes with shock and a gasp passes her lips, but I don't withdraw. I leave my finger buried in her anus, demanding she fuck me. And she starts to move again. I wiggle my finger and thrust with shallow and gentle movements as she fucks my cock, and when she comes she cries out, clutching my shoulders—digging her fingernails into my skin. And as I come I lift her swiftly from my cock, pulling her body tight to mine, releasing streams of cum between us as I clutch her close to me.

She snuggles into my neck, and I hold her tightly in my arms, and she speaks. "I don't suppose you know where my clothes are?"

I chuckle against her neck before responding. "I tossed them in the wash this morning. They're drying. I thought that was better than letting you wear a dress covered in cum when my family shows up in a while."

"Good thinking… Speaking of your family, what is the plan today?"

"They're bringing lunch and will stay to help unpack and organize. Sara's coming too, of course. They'll go home tonight."

"Will I go back tonight with them?"

"Not unless you want to. You can stay as long as you'd like."

"Forever?"

"Forever."

"I don't want to go home yet."

"Good. I'm glad to hear that. When do you need to be back?"

"I have an appointment with Anthony on Tuesday evening."

"Then I'll have you home by Tuesday afternoon. I don't technically start work until next week, so that's perfect really. We can spend a few days together—maybe explore the city or just stay in bed for a few days?" I pull her body from mine, smiling lasciviously at her before I continue. "Come with me."

I lift her from my lap and lead her upstairs, grabbing her dress and underwear from the dryer as we go. I start the master bath, and after I fish the candles from the box on the bedroom floor, I light them and set them on the ledge that surrounds the bathtub. We retreat to our favorite quiet place together, holding one another in the warmth. We have an hour until my family will arrive, and we take every last moment of that time.

As I zip her into her dress, she fixes her hair in the bathroom mirror, and I lean to her ear and speak my most favorite words in the world to her. "I love you, Rowan."

And she tells me the only thing in the world I need to hear from her. "I love you too, Logan."

We rush downstairs to meet my family and start the long hard chore of unpacking my new life—a life that most definitely includes her. Forever.

EPILOGUE
Five Years Later

Logan

As I enter the studio, I see her helping a small girl of nine or ten find her position on the handrail. I know her body more intimately than any other person in the world, and the slight swell of her belly is likely imperceptible to anyone but us. She's now made it past the first trimester and come springtime we'll be meeting our child for the first time.

Rowan immediately told Sara while I listened in on the other line. We swore her to secrecy, knowing it would be a minor miracle if she managed to keep her silence until we were ready to tell my parents. But she managed it, at least as far as Row and I know. Sara is now in medical school in Seattle and is kept busy by her education. She talks to Rowan every week, and we see her as often as her schedule will allow. I'm usually blown off as soon as Sara arrives, and I don't get my hands on my wife until a few days later when Sara leaves again for Seattle. Sara has already started to buy everything baby and shows up with bags full of clothing and bedding and anything else she can get her hands on. It's all fine and good as long as we have a girl, which Sara apparently believes we will, given the overabundance of pink.

We plan to tell my parents when they arrive in a few weeks to spend Christmas with us. Sara will, of course, be there as well, and I might have to tape her mouth shut until we can get the good news out.

When Rowan sees me enter the studio she smiles as she catches me watching her. I love her as much today as the first day I realized it so many years ago, and I know, without any doubt in my mind, she loves me as well. It took a long time for me to trust that she wouldn't change her mind, but she convinced me ... just as she'd promised she would. She chose me, and I understand now there was never any concern she wouldn't.

Her four years of college were a challenge for us both. She was always busy with practice and performances, and I was immersing myself in my new career. It was exhausting at times, but we were always there for each other to share the experience. We married the summer between her freshman and sophomore year, simply unable to stand living apart any longer. Sara was her maid of honor, and as my mother cried her ever eager-to-fall tears, my father beamed at us. They love her as much as I do. She's been a part of this family since the day she showed up, dirty face, tangled mess of hair, and poorly clothed, with Sara one afternoon after school.

With our marriage and her moving in permanently came a considerable commute for her, but she wanted to stay in the house I'd bought to be close to her. She preferred to be in the home that became ours and my bed every night, suffering the long drive every morning.

When she graduated, she suggested it might be time to consider Colorado again. And we settled into a beautiful secluded cabin on a small lake just outside of Evergreen, a small mountain town in the foothills near Denver, a few months later. She gave me back the dream I gave up for her. I stayed in public service in Denver's DA's office, and she opened a very successful little studio in Evergreen.

And now as she ushers the last of the kids from the studio to their waiting parents, I pull her into my arms and kiss her passionately, pushing her body up against the wall of mirrors and the railing that lines the wall. My hand finds the railing, and at its touch I'm taken back to the first time I made love to her here. I now have many memories of this railing, but that first time, only days after we bought the studio, is my favorite.

She was nervous about opening, and I wanted nothing more than to take her mind off her worry. I made love to her, pounding into her from behind with the fabric of her leotard pulled to the side, exposing her vagina to me. Her eyes watched me in the mirror as I took her body vigorously. I had only just left the office, and my suit pants were around my ankles and my jacket tossed on the floor. We came together as her tension melted away. She has given me every last inch and every last entry of her body many times over, and I know I will never and could never tire of her. She is made for me, and I for her as well.

She told me once that when she was with me she felt like the beautiful woman she never thought she'd be. I can't imagine what could ever make her think she wasn't beautiful enough for anyone, least of all me. She's the beautiful one. The most beautiful one in the world to me.

The End

⌘⌘⌘⌘
ABOUT THE AUTHOR

Elizabeth Finn is a multi-published contemporary romance author. Her passion is creating stories packed full of believable conflicts, characters who leave you rooting for them, and romance that might just short-circuit your e-reader. She likes her characters flawed, but they always find the best part of themselves on their journey. And her readers find themselves devoted to her honest and heartfelt voice.

Made in United States
Troutdale, OR
07/30/2023